SPELLFALL

SPELLFALL

Katherine Roberts

The Chicken House
2 PALMER STREET, FROME, SOMERSET BA11 1DS

For my parents.

First published in Great Britain in 2000 by
The Chicken House
2 Palmer St, Frome, Somerset BA11 1DS

Copyright © 2000 Katherine Roberts
Illustrations copyright © 2000 Chris Down

British Library Cataloguing in Publication data available.

ISBN 1 903434 17 3

Cover illustration by Paul Young
Cover design by Mandy Sherliker
Typeset by Dorchester Typesetting Group Ltd
Printed and bound in Great Britain by CPI Group

CONTENTS

1

THE SPELL BANK

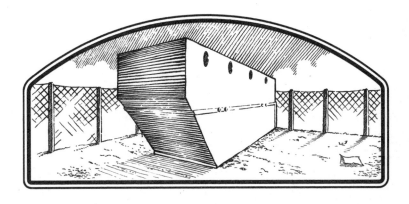

Saturday morning, October 24

Natalie saw the first spell in the supermarket car park. It was floating in a puddle near the recycling bins, glimmering bronze and green in the October drizzle. At first she thought it was a leaf, though as she drew closer it began to look more like a crumpled sweet wrapper – a very interesting sweet wrapper. *Pick me up,* it seemed to say, glittering intriguingly. *Surely I'm worth a closer look?*

She shook her head and hurried past. She was wet and cold and had more things to worry about than picking up someone else's litter. But the trap had been baited by one who knew a lot more about spells than she did. Before she knew what she was doing, she'd put down her chinking carrier bags and gone back for it. As her hand closed about the wrapper, a voice behind her whispered, *"Innocent enough to crawl through the Thrallstone."*

Natalie pushed her glasses up her nose and stared round uneasily. Anyone close enough to have spoken was either hurrying to their car with a loaded shopping trolley or still driving in circles like her stepmother and stepbrother, looking for a space to park.

"Who's there?" she said sharply.

Rain danced on the metal roofs of the bins.

No answer.

Skin prickling, Natalie stared across the river meadows at the wooded slopes beyond. The car park was on the edge of town and the recycling bins were in the corner furthest from the supermarket. This might have seemed bad planning for an eco-friendly development like Millennium Green, except the original plans showed a housing estate was to have been built on the meadows. The official excuse was that the floods would cost too much to divert but everyone at Natalie's school knew the truth. People didn't want to live in the shadow of Unicorn Wood because it was haunted.

"Tim?" she called more sharply. "Is that you? Stop messing around!"

Still no answer.

She shook her head, feeling foolish. It wasn't likely to be her stepbrother, anyway. He'd stayed in the car so he wouldn't get his new jacket wet. He was in a deep sulk because his mother had insisted he help with the shopping, and Tim never liked giving up a moment of his Saturdays to help with anything. It wasn't really Natalie's turn to recycle the bottles. She'd done them last week and the week before that. But when Tim had started on his usual argument – "It's your dad who drunk 'em all, not mine!" – she'd volunteered so as to avoid the inevitable shouting match.

She looked more closely at the wrapper. It had a warm, waxy feel. Raindrops shimmered on its surface. The colours shifted eerily like a hologram. She changed her mind about putting it in the nearest bin and, instead, stuffed it into her anorak pocket which was where she kept things she didn't want other people to see. The pocket was already occupied by her spider Itsy but one of the advantages of having a spider as a pet was they didn't take up much space, even in a matchbox.

She retrieved the carrier bags and hurried to the bottle bank. After a quick look around to check no one was watching, she fed the empty beer bottles into the brown hole as rapidly as possible. She was small for her twelve years so had to stand on tiptoe to reach. Her hood fell down, her ponytail worked its way out in a silvery froth, and drips from the top of the bin went down her neck but she didn't pause to cover herself. The crashes echoing inside made her cringe. As always, she imagined everyone in the car park counting under their breath ...*seventy-six, seventy-seven, seventy-eight...* "Two less than last week, Itsy," she whispered in relief to the spider as the final bottle tinkled to the bottom of the bin.

Her stomach was just beginning to unknot itself when the same voice said, "Couldn't read this notice for me could you, my dear?"

The prickling sensation returned, twice as strongly. This time a figure was lurking in the shadow of one of the bins, watching her.

An old man, she decided. He leant on a curious stick with its handle carved into the head of a bird. Rain dripped off the brim of a battered trilby hat and darkened the scarf that hid most of his face. Then he took a step towards her and *shimmered* – there was no other word for it. For a moment, the old man grew erect and tall with a hooked nose, flowing black hair, and piercing yellow eyes. While Natalie stared, suspecting the raindrops on her glasses of distorting what she saw, he gave her a long, disconcerting stare in return. Then he was old again, shuffling forwards, the hat pulled down to hide those strange eyes. "Can't see as well as I used to," he explained.

Natalie relaxed slightly. No doubt he'd been there all along, camouflaged by the bad light and the dark colour of the bin. His hands trembled and she couldn't help feeling sorry for someone whose eyes were worse than hers. Then she remembered that he must have watched her putting her dad's bottles in the recycling bank and heard her talking to Itsy. Her cheeks burned with embarrassment.

Quickly, she examined the bin he'd been hiding behind. She didn't remember seeing it last week but the Council were always adding new ones. First it had been bottles, then cans, then paper, then plastic, then clothes. She looked curiously at the new one. At first, there didn't seem to be any notice on it, but after a moment she spotted some curly silver letters at the very bottom. As she crouched to see better, they shimmered into focus:

SPELL BANK

Just that. No instructions, explanations, or lists of what should or shouldn't be put into the bin.

Natalie frowned. *Spell* bank? A shiver ran down her spine before she remembered that they sold silver spray-paint at the garage on the corner.

She turned back to the old man. "I can't see a notice; must've come off. Vandals... I'm sorry." She waved vaguely at the graffiti, then wondered why she was apologizing.

The stick whipped out and its handle encircled her elbow. "You can't hide it, you know," hissed the man.

Natalie's stomach fluttered. His voice wasn't quavery any more. It was strong – menacing almost. Maybe he was an undercover security guard? They had them inside, watching for shoplifters. Why not in the car park, watching for car thieves and vandals?

"It wasn't me," she said quickly.

The man chuckled. "What are you afraid of? That I'll tell on you? You and I are of the same blood, the ancient blood that sees what men do not. That's why I asked you to read the notice for me. It was a test – which you passed, by the way. Most people can't see the spell bank at all."

Natalie blinked. Obviously, he was quite loopy.

"Excuse me," she said firmly, extracting her arm from his stick. "Julie— I mean, my stepmother is waiting for me over there." She pointed to the supermarket doors, which suddenly seemed very far away, and stepped between two cars.

The stick swung round so fast she barely saw it move. "Careful," said the man, hooking her back by the other elbow. "You'll get yourself run over. I'd hate anything to happen to one who shows such promise."

"Let go of me!" Natalie's heart pounded. "I'll scream."

"Just looking out for you. All those windscreens steamed up like they are, people won't see you until it's too late. And you wouldn't want your little familiar to get hurt, would you? What did you call him? Itsy? Can I see him?"

"No!" Which was being rude, she knew. But the way she saw it, the old man had been rude to her first. She made another try for the traffic, only to be tugged back again.

"Tut tut. In such a hurry, and you haven't even asked me about the spell yet. Aren't you curious to know what it can do?" He gave her a little smile that chilled her more than anything he'd said or done so far.

With more difficulty than last time, Natalie disentangled herself. The bird's head handle had a curved beak that dug into her elbow and its horrible little eyes were bright yellow like its owner's. "Leave me *alone!*" she said. "I haven't a clue what you're talking about."

"Is that so? I saw you pick it up." His tone hardened. "Let's stop pretending, shall we? I want you to join my spellclave. You know exactly what I mean or you wouldn't have been able to see the spell in the first place. I left it for you as part of the test. And now I want it back." He opened his hand and waggled his fingers.

He means the wrapper, Natalie realized with relief. She felt in her pocket and almost let him have the thing. But something stopped her. Suddenly, she was angry with the whole wet, miserable world – with Tim for pretending it was her turn to do the bottles; with Julie for letting him get away with it; with Dad for drinking so much beer; with the rain for ruining the half-term holiday. She was especially angry with the crazy old man for scaring her so much.

She set her jaw. "You shouldn't drop litter," she said. "It's your own fault you've lost it, whatever it is. And if you touch me again, I'll tell the police."

He glared at her from under his dripping hat and said in a hard voice, "You'll be sorry you didn't join us willingly. Now give me back my spell!" His stick slammed into the side of the bin, trapping Natalie's ponytail. The clang vibrated through her entire body, almost stopping her heart.

Before the echoes had died away, she'd dived into the traffic. There wasn't time to look one way, let alone both. Brakes squealed. Drivers blared their horns. Cars swerved. There was a loud CRUNCH behind, followed by the tinkle of breaking glass. "Stupid kid!" someone yelled. "Are you trying to get yourself killed?"

Natalie ran faster, one hand in her pocket to stop Itsy's box from bouncing out. *Don't look back,* she told herself firmly. *Whatever happens, don't look back.*

Behind her, the old man grew erect and tall, loosened his scarf and tapped his stick against the kerb. Narrow yellow eyes watched his prey flee into the supermarket, while all around him the drivers involved in the accident argued.

"You drove straight into me!" sobbed a woman. "Look at my car! My husband's going to kill me."... "My windows were steamed up," said another. "I didn't see you."... "At least no one's hurt," said a third. "Which is a miracle, if you ask me."... Eventually someone thought to ask, "Where's the old man? There was an old man and a girl..." and people started to peer through the rain but by this time the recycling bins were deserted. No one could say which way the man had gone.

*

In the passenger seat of a battered white van parked behind the recycling bins, a red-headed boy hugged his bony knees to his chest. Unlike the people involved in the accident, Merlin hadn't taken his eyes off his father since he'd jumped out into the rain more than three hours earlier, ordering Merlin to stay put. It was cold with the engine turned off and every time someone passed with a laden shopping trolley his stomach growled. But he hadn't dared move, not even to get one of the filthy blankets from the back. Now, he watched in a mixture of relief and panic as the man everyone called Hawk strode through the traffic towards the van, waving his stick at any car that refused to stop for him. It was probably too much to hope for that they'd just go home.

The driver's door squeaked open and rain gusted in. The barrage started immediately. "Take your feet off the seat, boy!" The stick cracked across Merlin's knees before he could move them, stinging through the holes in his jeans. "What are you shivering for?"

Seeing the pretty blonde girl in the anorak stand up to his father made Merlin bold. He muttered, "I wouldn't be shivering if you'd let me have a spell."

This earned him a sharp look. "A spell? And what good would that have done?"

"I could've made spellfire."

"Ha! You'd never raise a spark. Either that, or you'd have burnt the van down round your grubby ears."

"I could've tried..." Merlin could hear his own voice growing fainter.

"Meaning you don't usually try?" His father's tone was dangerous. But Merlin was spared a second whack from the stick, as Hawk's yellow gaze had fixed itself back on the supermarket doors, obviously a lot more interested in the girl than he was in his son. "You know very well we need every live spell we've got for the Opening next weekend," he went on, still not looking at Merlin. "That's two wasted this morning already, and nothing to show for it." He reached under his scarf, pulled out something that looked like a dead leaf and flung it into Merlin's lap.

Merlin cringed but caught the spell by reflex. It was cold as only a dying spell can be. His father must have used up most of it, making himself look old and frail. "Er... she wasn't one of us, then?" He surreptitiously shifted the spell from hand to hand.

"She's one of us, all right," his father said very softly. "Even saw through the illusion I cast. It's a long time since anyone's done that to me."

Merlin blew on his left hand, shifted the spell again. "Then she's going to join us?"

"Oh yes. She just doesn't know it yet."

"Good!"

He must have sounded too eager. His father's eyes nar-rowed. "Don't think I'm finished with you yet, boy! You might be the most useless Spellmage ever to carry the ancient blood in your veins – if anyone deserves to be called a Caster, it's you! – but you're still my son. I'll not allow you to make a laughing stock of me. I'll be keeping Redeye a little longer."

Merlin's heart sank. He'd been hoping his father might let him have Redeye back once the spellclave was complete. Sometimes, the thought of his poor defenceless mouse locked in that cellar made him physically sick. He quickly thought of something else before the link he shared with his familiar could drag him into the dark again.

"She isn't going to be as easy as the others," his father con-tinued, his gaze back on the supermarket doors. "She's got a family, so we're going to have to be careful. And she's a smart little thing. Powerful, too, though she doesn't seem to know it yet. I'm looking forward to teaching her but if we're going to catch this year's Opening, we'll have to move fast. No time for the soft touch." Again, those eyes blazed gold.

Merlin crouched in his seat, trying to make himself as small as possible. He felt a flicker of sympathy for the girl; but rather her than him.

Unexpectedly, Hawk reached across and opened the passen-ger door. "Make yourself useful for a change," he said. "Get out there and go make friends with that girl. I don't care how you do it but get hold of her familiar. She keeps it in her anorak pocket – some sort of insect I think. Then come back here fast." He pushed Merlin into the rain and added darkly, "Don't come back without it or you know what'll happen to Redeye."

Merlin's legs turned weak. He clung on to the door. "B-but what if she won't give it to me?"

"Use your brain! She looks about your age. It shouldn't be too hard, even for you. Get my spell back too if you can. Oh, and I suppose you'd better recycle this one on your way, or we won't be getting any more visits from the Thralls. Not that we'll need them after the weekend but no sense alerting them to our plans before we're ready." He chuckled.

Merlin had dropped the icy spell on the floor of the van, hoping his father wouldn't notice. Now it was thrust back into his hand and his fingers cruelly crushed around it.

"It's in your own interest to help me," Hawk said, still crushing his hand. "When she joins us, I'll no longer need you and Redeye."

Merlin had thought of little else since he'd seen his father bait the first trap all those years ago. He bit his lip and nodded. The rain was going down his neck, water was seeping through the holes in his old gym shoes, and the dying spell was slowly turning his arm numb. But he knew better than to let his discomfort show. The more fuss he made, the longer the torture would continue.

At last, his father released him. "Hurry up then," he said with a cold little smile. "Before she goes home."

*

Natalie didn't stop running until she'd skidded through the supermarket doors, where the warmth and brightness calmed her. Panting, she pushed back her hood and shook out her ponytail, took off her glasses and wiped them on her sweatshirt with trembling hands.

In all her life she'd never done anything so stupid as diving into traffic without looking. Her heart was pounding and her legs felt weak but at the same time she wanted to laugh. Among the familiar trolleys and bickering families doing their food shopping, her fear seemed silly. She almost expected the weird wrapper the old man had insisted upon calling a *spell* to have gone. But when she checked, it was still in her pocket on top of Itsy's box. She pulled it out, stared for a moment at the shifting colours, then put it back again. Jo was coming round later. Maybe she'd know what it was.

Natalie made her way slowly through the crowded aisles until she found her stepmother scratching her head over a long shopping list. "Julie," she said. "I was just outside, and—"

"Natalie love! What happened? You've been ages. I sent Timothy out to look for you." Her stepmother's face assumed that look of concern adults tended to give Natalie from time to time. "You look awfully pale, love. I do hope you're not coming down with something for half-term."

The story of the old man and his "spell" was on Natalie's lips but the whole thing seemed so pathetic now. It wasn't as if she were five years old any more. "I'm just cold," she mumbled.

"And no wonder! You're soaked through. Are you sure you're feeling all right? I don't want you catching pneumonia." Julie's hand found her forehead.

People were starting to stare. She pulled away, embarrassed. "I'm fine," she said, then bit her lip. "Uh, Julie?"

"Mmm?"

"Did you notice the new recycling bin?"

But her stepmother was frowning at her list again, pushing a wisp of hair behind her ear. "What was that, love?" she said distractedly. "A new bin, did you say? That's good. We have to be sharpish now or your father will be wondering where we've got to. Can you be a darling and find me some salt? Big packet, you know, the one with the blue stripes?"

Normally, Natalie enjoyed the challenge of finding awkward items, especially when the supermarket changed the shelves around as they had this week. But today, her thoughts kept drifting to the crazy old man and his spell bank. She found herself wandering along aisles she didn't recognize, bumping into bad-tempered people in dripping raincoats. They scowled at her as if the rotten weather and the fact they couldn't find anything were her fault. To make matters worse, a grubby boy with red hair and holes in his jeans seemed to be following her, stopping to look hard at something on the shelf every time she turned to scowl at him.

The hairs on the back of Natalie's neck rose. She kept her hand firmly in her pocket with Itsy and the wrapper. The redhead looked like just the sort of boy who would sneak up behind you and try to steal something. Whenever she turned fast enough to catch him looking at her, his eyes made her shudder. They seemed so *desperate*.

She was so busy keeping one eye out for the boy and the other for salt, she didn't see Tim until he grabbed her arm. "What you got in your pocket then, *Sis?*" he hissed in her ear, nearly bringing on her second heart attack of the day.

Tim only ever called her "Sis" when he wanted to be cruel. His blond curls were plastered to the collar of his birthday jacket like wet straw, and raindrops shimmered on the shiny black leather. The jacket looked a lot more waterproof than her own tatty anorak but Tim obviously didn't see it that way.

"Suppose you thought that was funny, did you?" he went on. "Lettin' me search the whole car park for you, when all along you were hiding in here in the dry? C'mon, Sis, show me."

Natalie caught the red-headed boy staring again and made a face at him. "It's nothing," she said.

"Funny nothing." Tim scowled. He must have thought she'd been making the face at him. His nails dug painfully into her wrist as he dragged her hand out of her pocket. "It's that stupid spider of yours, ain't it?" he said with a smirk. "Fancy bringing it shopping! Aren't you worried it might escape and get *trodden* on?" One by one, he forced her fingers open.

Natalie squirmed. But her stepbrother was more than a year older than her and quite a bit stronger. Shoppers frowned at them but pushed their trolleys past and pretended not to see. She began to wish she'd left Itsy at home and risked her dad finding him and stamping on him just as he'd stamped on her last spider. "That hurts, Tim," she said, fighting tears. "Stop it! If you let him out in here, there'll be a panic."

"And whose fault will that be?" Tim bent back her last finger.

Natalie blinked in surprise. She'd been certain it was Itsy's box in her hand, but it was the old man's "spell". Beneath the fluorescent tubes the colours glimmered brighter than ever. A strange heat crept up her arm and tingled into her toes. Vaguely, she became aware of the red-headed boy creeping closer, his desperate eyes fixed on her hand. The shelves blurred and shifted... everyone seemed to be moving in slow motion as if they were underwater.

"Huh!" Tim dropped her wrist in disgust. The supermarket snapped back into focus, the wrapper fluttered to the floor and the red-headed boy dived after it.

Natalie's blood rose. With the same strange determination that had come over her in the car park, she flung herself on top of the boy and wrestled with him among all the feet and trolley wheels. They both made a grab for the wrapper at the same time and, for a second, their eyes met over the glimmering, shifting colours. "Please," whispered the boy. "If you don't let me have it, he'll—" The rest of his words were lost in a blinding purple flash.

Someone screamed, "Firework!" Natalie's stomach clenched. But the boy let go. Quickly, she pushed the wrapper back into her pocket. In the resulting purple smoke, a foot knocked her glasses askew. Stars exploded in her head, tins rattled and rolled, and a sickly smell of burnt sugar forced her to cover her nose. By the time she'd climbed to her feet, rescued her glasses, and sorted herself out, Tim was fidgeting over by the checkouts where Julie had just reached the front of the queue. The red-headed boy had vanished, leaving Natalie to face the aisle full of furious shoppers looking for someone to blame for their overturned trolleys and spilt food. "Sorry," she said, backing out of the mêlée. "I must've tripped. Sorry..."

An employee came hurrying along to disperse the crowd who, in the absence of physical evidence, had begun to argue about what they'd seen. Natalie seized the opportunity to slip away. Her legs trembled as she joined Julie and Tim at the checkout but inside she was fuming. Fancy setting off a firework in the middle of a busy supermarket on a Saturday morning. That red-head must be a prize idiot.

They were halfway home before she discovered that, in all the confusion, Itsy had escaped.

2

SECRETS

Saturday afternoon, October 24

To Merlin's relief, they returned home the slow way, the van rattling along muddy lanes that soon deteriorated into woodland tracks as they took a detour to avoid the Thrallstone. Every pothole jolted Merlin out of his seat, almost making him glad of his empty stomach. By the time they reached the Lodge, he felt as if he'd been trampled by a herd of wild unicorns. But he kept his mouth shut because no matter how many bruises he ended up with, it was better than being transported by a spell.

As soon as they pulled up, his father called Claudia-the-Fish. The two Casters who liked to call themselves Spellmages then disappeared into the cellar with the girl's spider. Merlin sighed. He had no idea what they did down there, but whenever Claudia went down they were gone for hours. It looked as if he'd have to get his own lunch again.

He crept past the shed where his father's goshawk lived and made himself a large pile of marmalade sandwiches which he took into his room. Shivering, he pulled on an extra jumper.

Then he crossed his fingers and turned on his computer.

The Lodge was a terrible place to live. Five miles from civilization, it had no TV, no telephone, and no heating except smoky open fires when someone bothered to light them. Water had to be drawn from an ancient well in the overgrown garden. There was a cesspit which ponged in hot weather and was probably the reason none of the spellclave ever did much gardening. Electricity came from a generator in the cellar, its output strictly controlled by Hawk. Sometimes there was power for Merlin's computer, more often not. If he did something that annoyed his father the power could be off for days and he'd be reduced to reading his computer magazines by candlelight.

Today, though, there was a comforting whirr and coloured light from the monitor flickered across the tightly-shuttered windows, old dark furniture and bare floorboards. Merlin's eye fell on the stack of glossy magazines on his bed and for the first time that day he grinned. On top of the magazines was a new game. Eagerly, he ripped off the wrapping and loaded it up. None of the monsters were half as terrifying as his father in a bad mood but it was so long since he'd had anything new to play he forgot the time and was soon lost on a quest in which he was the hero, strong and brave...

A chill draught across the back of his neck snatched him back to reality. Quickly, he grabbed the computer mouse and exited.

Hawk stood in the doorway, scowling at the screen. Merlin made the computer beep a few times, hoping it might make his father go away. Apart from Claudia, who used to be some kind of scientist before his father found her and brought her to the Lodge, all the spellclave were wary of his computer – technology was supposed to interfere with Spellmage powers. Merlin didn't care. What he really wanted was to get on the Internet and the faster it drained his power, the better, because then his father would have no excuse to hurt Redeye.

The silence was getting to him. He made the computer beep

again and the hawk-headed stick rested on his shoulder. A gentle threat.

"Stop that."

Merlin gripped the mouse harder and swallowed.

"New game?" His father's question was deceptively mild.

"Er... yes."

"Who gave it to you?"

"I don't know."

A chuckle. "Do you and Claudia really think I don't know what goes on behind my back in my own spellclave?"

"No! I mean, yes, she... I mean..." Merlin swallowed again. The last thing he wanted was to get Claudia into trouble and lose his supply of magazines and games. None of the others would dare defy Hawk so openly.

"You don't know what you mean, do you? Stop trembling, boy! I'm not angry with you."

"You're not?" Merlin waited for the stick to leave his shoulder but it stroked his ear, making him cringe.

"You did quite well today."

Praise? Merlin tensed. His father wouldn't come in here just for that. Something more was coming.

"Now we've got her familiar, we'll soon have the girl. I've sent Claudia to watch her house. The little madam should be more cooperative now, but we'll get her here one way or the other. When she arrives I want you to talk to her, find out how much she knows. Show her Redeye."

"You'll let me have Redeye back?"

It was as if the sun had risen in his room. Merlin twisted in his chair and searched his father's face. But there was no kindness there. The yellow eyes regarded him in amusement as their owner caressed the head of his beloved stick.

"If you get results, I might let you visit him in the cellar."

Merlin's heart sank again. The cellar. Dark, airless, where no one could hear you scream... "I'll do my best," he whispered.

Hawk smiled. "Of course you will, because you know what'll happen to Redeye if you don't. Now then. Why don't you tell me what went wrong in the supermarket? That spellflash must have been visible from the other side of Earthaven! No point worrying about getting it back now, a dead spell's no use to anyone." His boots echoed on the bare boards as he began to pace the room.

"Earthaven Spellmages bring dead spells back to life," Merlin mouthed but didn't quite have the guts to say it aloud. Every time his father passed behind his chair, the back of his neck prickled.

"Well? I'm waiting. What's your excuse this time?"

"I— er—" He considered lying, then changed his mind. Raising his chin slightly, he said, "I used it to transport her spider out of her pocket."

Hawk stopped pacing and laughed out loud. "Don't be silly! You couldn't transport a flea if it hopped half the distance itself! If you're going to lie to me, at least make it halfway believable. You need two spells to transport – one at each end. I must have told you that a thousand times."

Merlin bit his lip. "I kept the old one, the one you told me to recycle," he admitted. "It wasn't quite dead, and I... ah... thought it might be useful." In truth, he'd forgotten the spell, he'd been so anxious to get the girl's familiar. But his father didn't need to know that. "I didn't have time to think," he rushed on. "So I dunno how it happened. But you're always telling me to stop analysing magic and just *do* it, so maybe that's why it worked?"

Silence behind. He twisted in his chair and saw Hawk frowning, stroking his stick. "This changes things," his father said slowly. "So she cast it herself, did she? Was she trying to get rid of you? I wouldn't blame her but I thought she didn't know who we were. If she suspects the truth about her mother's death it could make things complicated. Tell me exactly what happened. Did she know what she was doing?"

So the girl had lost her mother too? Merlin thrust away the memories of his own mother's death and thought of the surge of power he'd felt when he'd touched the spell. It *must* have been the power of a casting. "I cast it," he said, less sure now.

Hawk's lips pressed tight. "I thought I told you not to lie to me. You can't even cast illusions, let alone transport."

"Then maybe it was both of us? Like we combined our power, or something?"

For a second, doubt flickered in the yellow eyes. Then his father laughed again. "You're such an idiot! Only a Spell Lord can transfer power like that, and that's one thing you'll never be, my boy! Neither will that girl, not with a spider for a familiar. Even in Earthaven, becoming a Spell Lord is a lifetime's work. Out here, it's an honour achieved only by those of us willing to risk all." He chuckled nastily. "When my spellclave's complete, maybe I'll show you what a power transference *really* feels like."

Merlin shuddered.

"For now, though," Hawk went on, no longer laughing, "I don't like being lied to. You never learn, do you?"

The door slammed. After a moment, Merlin's computer turned itself off with a sigh like a dying animal and shadows rushed at him from the cobwebby corners of the room. He clenched his fists, part in frustration, part in fear.

"I wasn't lying," he whispered to the dark screen. "I did cast that spell. I *did*."

*

At that very moment, the spell in question was spread on Natalie's bed in the Marlins' warm, energy-efficient house back in Millennium Green. Natalie had taken off her glasses to see if the colours would come back. Jo, who had perfectly good eyesight, was turning her head from side to side and squinting.

"It's no good, I can't see it," her friend said finally, flicking an unruly chestnut fringe from her eyes. "Looks like a dirty old crisp packet to me."

Because of the weather, they were confined to Natalie's bedroom, which was small for two people, especially when one of those people was Jo. As the tallest, strongest girl in their school, Jo was always picked first for all the sports teams. She could have had any friend she liked. But when the school bully Gaz (whose real name was Gerald, only no one dared call him that) had snatched Natalie's glasses off her nose and run around the playground waving them in the air, Jo had knocked him out cold, brought the glasses back to Natalie and linked arms with her. No one tormented Natalie after that. Even Tim went quiet when Jo was around.

Natalie picked at a loose thread in her skirt. She wished she hadn't told her friend about the old man now. People thought she was weird enough, keeping a spider as a pet. They didn't know she only kept Itsy because her dad forbade animals in the house. If Jo was to abandon her, she'd have no one.

Rain lashed the window so hard, it sounded as if someone were throwing buckets of water against the glass. She scowled at the wrapper. Why on earth had she picked it up in the first place? It had brought nothing but trouble. Suddenly angry, she crumpled the thing into a ball and threw it at the wall.

Jo grinned and rolled on to her stomach, kicking her bare feet in the air. "You're having me on, Nat, aren't you? That's the best yet. Witches in Millennium Green!" She giggled.

Natalie blew on her fingers which had gone unaccountably numb. "I know what I saw. And it looked different earlier. Had a sort of a hologram thing on it." She scowled at the wrapper which had fallen under her homework desk. "Oh, forget it! I expect it was just some Hallowe'en prank."

"Bit early," Jo pointed out, still giggling. "Hallowe'en isn't till next weekend. Bet you anything it'll still be raining, though! I hate this weather. I'm so bored I could climb the walls. C'mon Nat, where's that new CD of yours?"

Natalie hardly heard the music. Her gaze kept straying to the crumpled wrapper. She still half expected it to start glowing as it had in the supermarket but it remained stubbornly dull.

"I lost Itsy," she said in the pause after the first song had finished.

"Itsy?" Jo frowned. "You mean your little spider?"

Natalie nodded. "He must've escaped when the firework went off."

"Oh Nat, I'm so sorry. Why didn't you say so before?" Jo's arms went around her. The magazine she'd been reading slipped to the floor.

Natalie shrugged her off, embarrassed. "It's no big deal. It was only a spider and at least he didn't get stamped on this time. I can easily get another one."

"If I lost Bilbo, I'd kill myself."

"No you wouldn't. Anyway, spiders don't matter as much as dogs."

"Yes they do! Itsy was a pet and pets are important no matter how small they are."

"I lost my mother when I was three," Natalie said through gritted teeth. "I'm not about to start crying over a stupid spider, am I?"

Her gaze strayed to her parents' wedding photograph which lived in pride of place on her bedside table. Her mother held her father's arm, dark glasses staring sightlessly at the camera. Dad looked young and proud in a smart grey suit. No beard in those days. At her mother's feet a large white mongrel sat patiently staring out of the picture with eyes of liquid amber. Eyes that saw the world for his mistress, except on that terrible morning when she had fallen in the river and drowned. She knew Dad blamed the dog. That was why he wouldn't let her have a proper pet but it seemed so unfair. Despite what she'd said to Jo, her eyes filled. She snatched off her glasses and angrily dashed the tears away.

Jo regarded her steadily for a moment, then opened the window and stuck her head out. "Hey, do you think it's stopping?" she said brightly. "We could cycle down to the supermarket and see if your new bin's still there. Find out what's really in it."

Rain gusted in, soaking Natalie's desk and fluttering the pages of her school books. Glad of the distraction, she jumped off the bed and shut the window. "It's not stopping, silly, it's getting worse! Anyway, Julie would never let me out in this, not after me getting so wet this morning."

"All right," Jo said. "Then why don't we go down there when

it's dark? If that old man really is a witch or a wizard or whatever, he's more likely to come out at night. You can easily climb out your window on to the shed roof and slide down the drainpipe."

"Don't be stupid, Jo."

"Tomorrow morning then. Six o'clock sharp. With any luck, the rain will have stopped by then. I'll meet you on the corner and I'll bring my skates. I want to show you a new trick I taught Bilbo. I know! I'll bring my sister's skates too. She never uses them and her feet are about the same size as yours. The car park will be deserted at that hour, lots of space. It'll be fun." Bored, Jo was dangerous.

"You know I can't skate," Natalie said in alarm.

"Time you learnt, then. Don't worry, it's easy. You'll love it."

"Why can't we just walk?"

Jo frowned. "What's up? You scared, or something? That's not like you."

Not of the skating, Natalie wanted to say. But it was too complicated to explain. She wasn't even sure she knew herself.

"Nobody gets up at that time on a Sunday," she mumbled instead.

Wrong thing to say. Jo's eyes lit up with that gleam she knew all too well. "That's why we're going so early, silly! So there won't be anyone around to see us when we climb into your bin." She swung her jacket over one shoulder, giving Natalie a sly look from under her fringe. "You will come, won't you? I'll let you hold Bilbo's lead."

Jo knew very well Natalie would never miss a chance to walk a dog, not even a fat soppy one like the Carter family's Labrador. But Natalie supposed the supermarket car park was tame compared to Unicorn Wood where, last summer, they'd lost Bilbo down a badger hole and had to get Mr Carter up there with a spade to dig him out.

"All right," she agreed reluctantly.

Jo grinned and glanced at the wrapper, still crumpled under the desk. "Why don't you ask your dad about that thing, Nat?

He used to sell weird stuff, didn't he? He might know where it came from."

"I don't think so..." Natalie began, but her friend was already letting herself out and didn't hear. Thoughtfully, she retrieved the wrapper and smoothed it on her knee. It was a long time since she'd had a decent excuse to talk to Dad.

*

Natalie slipped the spell into her skirt pocket, hoping to catch her father at teatime, but he was in one of his moods and didn't come to the table. Julie had to take his egg and chips out to the garage on a tray. Tim picked at his food, not even pulling his accustomed faces behind his mother's back. Natalie assumed he was still in a sulk because of this morning and ignored him in return. She ate as fast as she could get away with, and as soon as she'd cleared her plate, she jumped up and took it to the kitchen. "I'll go and get the tray off Dad," she called.

"It's your turn to help with the washing up!" Tim shouted after her, miraculously coming out of his sulk. But Julie said, "Leave her alone, Timothy. I'll manage – unless *you're* volunteering, that is?"

Tim grunted. "I gotta get ready. I'm goin' out." A chair scraped and after a moment his heavy footsteps could be heard clumping upstairs.

Natalie went through the utility room and stopped at the door to the garage. She took a deep breath and knocked. "Dad?" she called, letting herself in.

It was dark inside with the up-and-over door shut. A blast of chill air brought garage smells – oil, polish, paint. Taking up most of the space, Mr Marlins' car crouched like a caged animal. As far as Natalie could remember, this car hadn't left the garage since the day her mother died, although Dad spent hours out here polishing it. Above its gleaming black roof, loops of cable hung like giant cobwebs. As her eyes adjusted, shelves took shape in the gloom supporting the usual garage junk of sagging cardboard boxes, rusty tins, jars of old nails.

"Dad?" Her voice squeaked slightly. "Are you there? I've come for the tray." She stood on tiptoe to reach the dangling light cord. Electric light flooded the garage, making her squint.

As if she'd woken it up, the car gave an angry lurch. The driver's door opened and a rumpled figure with egg yolk in his beard lurched out. He frowned when he saw Natalie. "I thought I told you kids to stay out of here. Where's Julie?"

"Washing up."

He grunted and clutched at the car. Inside, empty bottles rolled on the passenger seat. Natalie counted them. Six. Mr Marlins' gaze followed hers and for a moment he looked sheepish. Then his expression tightened. "Go back in the house, there's a good girl. I'm busy."

"I... need to ask you something."

He blinked at her, as if surprised she might think he had anything useful to give. "Is it trouble with homework? Ask Julie, she'll help you."

Natalie gritted her teeth. "She can't help me with this. I need to know about something I found today – something weird."

The frown came back.

Feeling slightly foolish, Natalie brought out the wrapper.

She didn't know what she'd been expecting. Sarcasm, maybe. Or indulgent laughter as if she were five. Her father provided neither. Before she could move, he lurched around the car, kicked the door shut, and snatched the wrapper from her hand. His beer-breath made her feel sick as he thrust her against the wall. Natalie's heart hammered. The garage was insulated from the rest of the house. Would Julie hear if she screamed?

Her father made as if to rip the wrapper in two, then seemed to change his mind and grabbed her upper arm, fingers digging in painfully. "Where did you get this?" he demanded. "Who gave it to you? What lies did they tell you? Answer me, girl!" He shook her until the elastic holding her ponytail snapped. Green beads rolled across the floor.

Tears sprang to her eyes. "It wasn't my fault—"

"Who gave it to you?"

"No one. At least, not really. An old man dropped it in the car park at the supermarket this morning."

"Dropped it?"

"Yes! By the recycling bins. He was throwing it away." Not quite a lie.

The bloodshot eyes narrowed. "You're never to touch one of these things again, d'you hear? Never!"

He let go of her arm so suddenly she stumbled and bruised her knees. While she stared, heart pounding, he snatched a tin off the nearest shelf, tipped out the screws it contained, and folded the wrapper until it would fit inside. Then he put the tin on the floor and stamped on the lid several times. Natalie put her hands over her ears. Finally, Mr Marlins unlocked the boot of his car and threw the rather mangled tin inside. There were other things in the boot. Small, sealed boxes. But before Natalie could read their labels, the boot slammed shut and her father turned the key.

Still trembling from the unexpectedness of his reaction, she picked herself up. "What *was* that thing?" she whispered. "Is it something to do with what you used to sell?"

"What do you know about that?" He rounded on her, scarlet-faced.

Natalie cringed, and a strange look passed through her father's eyes. He sagged across the roof of his car. "Never you mind," he said more gently. "Run along inside now. It was dead, so no harm done. But if anyone else tries to give you one of those things, you come straight to me and tell me so, understand?"

She ventured closer and touched the patched elbow of his jacket. "Dad—" He flinched, but didn't push her off. "Dad, you know something, don't you? The old man, he… uh… told me some weird things."

A grunt.

Encouraged, she took a deep breath. "Dad, there's no such thing as spells, are there? Real ones, I mean, not kids' stuff?"

He stiffened. Without looking at her, he said, "Grow up, Nat. You're not a baby anymore." He put the tray into her hands and gave her a firm push towards the utility room door.

Natalie went, her thoughts spinning. Then she remembered something else the old man had said. Before she left the garage, she turned and whispered, "What does *'innocent enough to crawl through the Thrallstone'* mean?"

Her father had started to open another beer. He paused, knuckles white on the bottle, and for a horrible moment she thought he was going to throw it at her. Then he made a sound in his throat which she eventually identified as a chuckle. "Don't ask me – apparently I don't qualify any more."

Was it supposed to be a joke? Her father certainly seemed to think so. When she left him, he was collapsed over the roof of his car, thumping it with one fist, chuckling helplessly. Natalie closed the door and hurried through to the kitchen. She hated it when he was drunk like that.

"Everything OK, love?" Julie gave her a quizzical look as she took the tray.

"Fine," Natalie mumbled. Stupid to think she'd get any sense out of Dad, and yet he'd acted so strangely when he saw the wrapper. Was it the beer talking, or something else?

Angrily, she pushed her loose hair behind her ears, snatched up a tea-towel and started drying the dishes. She and Jo had better find some answers tomorrow, because this whole spell-thing was getting weirder and weirder.

3

KIDNAP!

Sunday morning, October 25

During the night, it stopped raining and the wind dropped, allowing thick fog to collect in the river valley. By the time Natalie's alarm went off at 5.30 a.m. she could barely see the streetlight outside the house. The world seemed muffled by the weather, even as the pillow had muffled her alarm. She shivered and dressed as quickly as she could, added an extra sweatshirt, then crept downstairs in her socks. Quietly, she let herself out, shut the front door and sat on the step to put on her shoes.

She was just congratulating herself on getting out of the house without waking anyone when a voice hissed from the fog, "And just what do you think you're doing?"

Natalie's breath stopped in her throat. A stranger stood over her, silhouetted against the eerie orange glow of the street-lights. His head was shaved, a miniature metal skull dangled from one ear, and the cold scent of the night was on him.

For a horrible moment, she couldn't move. Then she recognized the leather jacket and boots. She giggled in relief. "Tim! You gave me a scare! What have you done to your *hair?* Dad'll have a fit!"

"Doubt he'll even notice," her stepbrother said with a twist of his lips. "He's such a piss-head."

"Don't call him that." She glanced back at the house and lowered her voice. "Where have you been, anyway? I thought you were in bed." The chain hadn't been on the door, but Tim often forgot to lock up when he came in late.

"Likewise." With some amusement, he eyed the two sweatshirts sticking out beneath Natalie's anorak. "Going somewhere?"

"None of your business." She glanced at her wrist, and realized she'd forgotten her watch. "Does Dad know you've been out all night?"

Tim's eyes narrowed. His hand shot out and seized her shoulder. "No, he don't. And don't you go whining to him about it or you'll live to regret it."

Natalie stiffened. "Let go! Anyway, I thought you didn't care what he thought?"

"Don't wind me up, you half-blind little runt. Keep your mouth shut, d'you hear?"

"I'll keep mine shut if you do."

Tim stared at her. For a moment she thought she'd gone too far, and her heart hammered. Then his lips twitched and he released her. "So. My little Sis has got secrets of her own, has she?" He watched, smiling, as Natalie hopped down the path still trying to tie her lace. "Where you off to, then?"

"Nowhere."

"Maybe I'll follow you and see."

That was the last thing she needed. "I'm going to walk Bilbo with Jo, if you must know," she told him, raising her chin.

Tim shook his head and slid his key into the lock. "At this time in the morning? You're quite crazy, the pair of you – it isn't even light yet. I'm off to bed. Mind you don't fall in the river like your mother did."

Natalie's heart twisted. But before she could think of a suitable reply, the door closed and she heard the chain rattle as

Tim locked up. She clenched her fists, tears in her eyes. Sometimes she hated him so much she wanted to scream.

As she hurried to the corner, worried Jo would think she wasn't coming, an engine spluttered to life further up the street. Milkman, she thought vaguely, forgetting he didn't deliver on Sundays.

*

Ringed by the silver cones of the perimeter lights and filled with drifting mist, the supermarket car park was spooky. Shivering, the two friends broke into a run. Jo carried both pairs of skates round her neck, swinging from their laces, while Bilbo bounded ahead, yellow ears flopping and tongue hanging out. Without vehicles to fill it, the car park seemed a lot larger than it had yesterday and Natalie began to wonder if they'd missed the recycling area completely. By the time the metal bins suddenly loomed ahead, dark and dripping with moisture, she was tense enough to scream.

"Steady on, Nat! It's only your spell bank." But Jo's breath was coming faster too. "Which one is it, then? This one?" She gave the side of the bottle bin a thump which caused a resounding clang that must have echoed halfway across town. Bilbo began to bark.

Natalie glanced nervously over her shoulder. "Shh!" She blinked at the collection of bins, trying to remember. They looked different in the fog. She crouched by the one next to the bottle bank, wiped the moisture from its side and looked for the silver graffiti. Gone. A battered Council sign said PAPER AND CARDBOARD ONLY. She sighed, feeling stupid. "I thought it was this one. But it was smaller with a higher opening and it definitely didn't say paper."

"Well, it isn't here now. Or maybe I just can't see it?" Jo squinted at the empty space between the bottle bin and the one Natalie had just examined.

Her stomach twisted. People had been teasing her all her life about her bad eyesight, but Jo never had before. "Stop it," she whispered. "That's not funny."

Jo's grin faded. "Oh, Nat... I didn't mean it like that, silly. I believe you. I expect they took it away last night to empty it."

"On a Saturday?"

"Maybe it was full. We can come back and look for it tomorrow." She perched on the kerb and began to change into her skates. "Here, put yours on."

Natalie glanced round again. If anything, the fog was getting thicker. The car park was eerily quiet. No traffic on the ring road, not even an owl hooting from the river meadows. No sign of dawn.

"I'm not sure this is such a good idea," she said with a shiver. "Maybe we should go home now? I didn't tell Julie I was going out, she'll be worried if I'm not back for breakfast—"

"Oh come *on,* Nat! Don't go getting cold feet on me now. This is the best time to learn. No one around to laugh when you fall over, is there?" She gave her a sly look. "Anyway, bet it doesn't take you half as long to learn as it took me. You've a lower centre of gravity, haven't you? Not so far to fall."

With an effort, Natalie shook off her nerves and let Jo strap on the skates. Once they were skating, she felt better. Balancing on the thin lines of wheels wasn't as difficult as it looked. She soon felt confident enough to let go of her friend's arm and totter about on her own. The next thing she knew, she was enjoying herself. Spell banks and weird old men faded to the back of her mind as she mastered the rhythm. Her breath came faster and she laughed as the cold air made her cheeks glow. Jo gave her the thumbs up, then called Bilbo so she could demonstrate her trick. This consisted of whistling at the dog until he streaked off across the car park, dragging Jo at the end of his lead like a water-skier behind a furry yellow four-legged speed boat. They looked so funny, Natalie got a fit of giggles and had to grab the bottle bank to stay upright. Her friend waved her cap in the air and hollered as she vanished into the fog.

They were gone a long time. While she was waiting, Natalie took off her glasses and wiped them. She'd got her breath back now but the eerie feeling was back as well, twice as strong as before because now she was alone.

"Jo?" she called nervously.

Silence.

This was silly. Bilbo had probably stopped to do his business. He wasn't a young dog, so it always took him ages and then Jo would have to scoop it up and dispose of it properly. She put her glasses back on and skated carefully round the bins to where they'd left their shoes – then grabbed the bottle bank again, her heart in her throat.

A tall figure stood beneath one of the lights, fog dripping from the ends of his black hair, her shoes in one hand and an all-too-familiar bird-headed stick in the other. He gave her a cold smile. "Looking for these? Or maybe you're looking for your little spider? Care to come with me and find out what I've done to him?"

Natalie shook her head. "Go away," she whispered. "Leave me alone."

The man smiled again. "Not this time, my little spider-girl. This time you're coming with me."

He made a lunge for her, and the air rushed back into her lungs. She screamed.

"Jo-o-o!"

That was all she had time for before strong hands caught her anorak and dragged her backwards away from the bins. On the skates, she was helpless to fight him. She had a vague impression of a blonde woman picking up her shoes which her captor had dropped when he lunged at her. Then she was slammed against the side of a white van, the stick pressing across her chest.

"Hurry up," her captor hissed. "Before that hound comes back."

"I thought you said you could deal with it?" The woman's voice contained a challenge.

Twisting her head, Natalie caught a glimpse of blue eyes so empty of emotion, they made her shiver.

"Only if I have to. I want to leave as few clues as possible. The last thing we need so close to the Opening is the human authorities on our backs."

The woman gave a peculiar little smile and, just for an instant, a spark lit those empty eyes. "Surely you don't doubt your power, Hawk?" she said very softly.

They seemed to have forgotten Natalie. She began to sidle along the van, ready to make a break for freedom as soon as they relaxed their guard. But her captor grabbed her arm and pulled her back. "Enough!" he hissed. "Get your things. We're obviously going to have to do this the hard way."

He twisted Natalie's arm behind her, pressing her cheek against the metal, and clamped his other hand over her mouth. It tasted foul, as if he'd been handling paint. She struggled as hard as she could but only succeeded in hurting her shoulder.

The woman went round to the passenger side of the van. When she returned, her eyes were cold and empty again. In her gloved hands she carried a little box, from which she extracted something that glittered in the silver light.

Needle.

Natalie heaved against her captor in fresh panic, kicking backwards with the skates. One connected with his shin and he grunted, his hand slipping from her mouth. She screamed as loudly as she could, and a yellow streak came flying out of the fog, barking madly, lead trailing. "Bilbo!" she shouted in relief.

The woman jumped aside, her eyes on the dog, and knocked into the man she'd called Hawk. The lead caught around his ankle and he stumbled, cursing loudly. "Don't be so stupid!" he shouted to the woman. "It's not a magehound, is it?" Bilbo leapt on top of Hawk, snarling and growling, uncharacteristically savage. The bird-headed stick went rattling beneath the van. Suddenly, Natalie was free.

She took off across the car park as fast as she could make the skates go. "Help!" she yelled as she went. "Jo! Anyone! Help!"

Behind her, Bilbo's barks cut off with a sudden yelp. She heard the pounding of running feet. Natalie skated faster, her breath rasping in her throat, and let out a sob of relief as a small figure materialized in the fog ahead. It was the red-headed boy she'd seen in the supermarket yesterday, but she instantly forgave him everything. Right then, she'd have been glad to see Gaz and his entire gang. She changed direction and raced towards the boy, hoping he was with his parents or someone who could help.

The boy's eyes went wide as Natalie realized she didn't know how to stop. She managed to swerve at the last minute but the boy made a wild grab for her anorak and they went down together in a tangled heap of arms, legs, and skates.

"Go!" Natalie gasped, pushing him off. "Get help! Some lunatics are trying to kidnap me, and—"

The boy disentangled himself and backed away, rubbing his elbow. Behind him, two breathless figures ran out of the fog. They pushed the boy out of the way and came at her. He just stood there, staring dumbly.

Natalie's heart sank. She tried to get to her feet but one of the skates had broken in the fall. Her ankle hurt. Her ribs hurt. Everything hurt. The man knelt beside her, gripped the back of her neck and held her ponytail aside. The woman with the empty eyes crouched next to him and squirted a dribble of yellowish liquid into the fog.

"*Sorry*," the boy mouthed.

"Hold still," advised the woman, not unkindly. "It'll be easier."

"Just get on with it!" hissed Hawk.

Natalie closed her eyes. She thought she heard Jo calling, faint and far away, but fear had stolen her voice and she couldn't call back. She felt the prick of a needle beneath her ear. Someone whimpered... and the world slid softly away.

4

QUESTIONS

Sunday afternoon, October 25

When the police car drew up outside the Marlins' house on Sunday afternoon Tim was still in his boxer shorts. He'd just woken from a nightmare in which Gaz's entire gang were chasing him to shave off his hair. At first he thought the car was part of this. Then he caught sight of his reflection in the mirror and his knees turned weak. None of it was a dream. He was now a full member of the Death Heads and last night he'd broken the law for the first time in his life. How had the police found out so fast?

He thought madly back over his actions of the night before. After the ritual head shaving at midnight, Gaz had stuck a needle through Tim's ear so he could wear the gang's skull emblem. It had hurt like hell. Then they'd all cycled down town, where Tim's first gang dare had been to add his name to the graffiti round the back of the public toilets. His heart had hammered the whole time. The five minutes it took to spray those three letters had been the longest minutes of his life, but he'd done it. Gaz, Dave and Mike had slapped him on the back and told him what he suspected were greatly exaggerated stories of their own dares. Then Pizzaface (who'd run out of his emergency supply of crisps) and Little Paulie (who was only tolerated in the gang because he happened to be Dave's brother) had complained they were hungry. So they'd all gone home.

He tweaked the curtain aside to see better. A policewoman got out of the car and walked slowly up the path, looking at the house. The doorbell rang and after a moment she was let in. No one stormed upstairs. No one kicked down Tim's door.

His heart slowed. He dragged on his jeans and T-shirt and waited, chewing his nails, but still no one came. Unable to bear the suspense any longer, he quietly opened his bedroom door. Muffled voices came from the lounge, then the sound of his mother crying. Tim frowned. As far as he knew, she hadn't seen his hair yet, so that couldn't be it. Barefoot, he crept downstairs and put an ear to the wall. On the other side, someone was pacing up and down.

"...and I'm telling you my daughter wouldn't be so stupid!"

Mr Marlins.

"Even if she'd done something wrong, which I assure you she hasn't, she wouldn't run away from trouble. Besides, I've told her never to go off on her own. She knows the dangers. She wouldn't have left her friend."

Nat!

Tim felt a pang of guilt as he remembered how he'd locked her out this morning. But surely the little idiot had enough sense to ring the bell?

He listened carefully. There was a pause, as if the policewoman didn't quite believe Mr Marlins. Tim imagined stale beer-breath wafting her way every time his stepfather marched past and he could understand her scepticism. "You say Natalie went to bed early last night because she wasn't feeling well?" the policewoman asked.

A sniff from Julie. "That's what she told me. She'd got wet in the morning and she was very quiet after tea. I thought she was coming down with a cold."

"And what time was that, exactly?"

"About half-past eight, I suppose."

"And neither of you saw her after that?"

"No."

"And what about your son, Mrs Marlins? Ah, Timothy Lockley, isn't it?"

Tim froze. He eyed the open door of his bedroom, then the hall. Did he have time to sneak out the back way?

"I don't think he'll be able to tell you anything. He'd gone out by then."

"Where's your son now?"

"Still asleep, I think. He lies in late when he hasn't got to get up for school."

"You think?" The policewoman sounded surprised.

"Well, he's at that age – you know, doesn't like to be disturbed."

"Nevertheless, I'm afraid I have to ask you to disturb him, Mrs Marlins. I need to talk to him as well. It'll only take a few minutes."

Tim beat a quick retreat to his room. He missed what was said next but as he closed his door and put his back against it, he could hear raised voices below. Hesitant feet came up the stairs. His mother's gentle knock made him jump, even though he'd been expecting it.

"Timothy? You in there, love?" There was a catch in her voice. "The police are here. They want to ask you a few questions."

Tim steeled himself and opened the door.

His mother's eyes were red. She talked fast, as she always did when she was upset and trying to hide it. "Apparently Natalie went out early with Joanne this morning to walk the Carters' dog, and something happened. Joanne came back in a right state, going on about it all being her fault. From what I can gather, they went skating in the supermarket car park. It was foggy, the dog got loose and Joanne lost them both. I expect Natalie's off playing with Bilbo and she's forgotten the time. You know how scatterbrained she gets when she sees a dog,

but we can't be too careful these days and the police—
Timothy!" Her hands flew to her mouth as her mind registered
what she was seeing. "What have you done to your hair?"

"Just shaved it," Tim mumbled. It wasn't having quite the
effect he'd planned. He'd never intended to upset his mother –
just get Mr Marlins to notice him for once.

"And your *ear!* Who did it? Oh no! Let me see. I hope you
didn't use a dirty needle, it looks infected to me."

"It's fine." He jerked away. Actually his ear was throbbing
like a bass guitar but he wasn't about to admit it. Gaz had
rinsed the needle in a puddle first – did that count as clean?
"Why do the police want to see me?" he asked, focusing on his
more immediate problem.

His mother's hands were still over her mouth. For a second,
she looked as if she might cry. Then she took a deep breath
and took her hands away. "I expect they want to ask you about
Nat. Your father'll have a fit," she added quietly.

"He's *not* my *father*," Tim said through gritted teeth. "It's not
up to him what I do."

"Timothy! Not that again, not today. Please."

Immediately, Tim felt bad. He rummaged under his bed and
found an old pair of gym shoes he used for slopping around
the house, then ran his hands over his smooth skull. "At least
you won't have to nag me to comb it now," he said. This
attempt to lighten the atmosphere didn't work. His mother's
face twisted as she shepherded him downstairs, making Tim
glad of the distraction the police were providing. Now he knew
it was Nat they were interested in and not him, he felt a bit
more confident.

Mrs Marlins had shut the lounge door when she'd come to
get him. Tim opened it without thinking to knock and walked
into the middle of an argument.

"Are you suggesting I don't know my own daughter?" Mr
Marlins was shouting as he paced by the French windows. His
clothes were crumpled, his hair and beard a mess. He'd slept in
his car again.

"I'm suggesting you're acting very strangely for someone whose twelve-year-old daughter has just gone missing," the policewoman said, calmer. She was young and slim with light blonde hair. Her back was turned to Tim but he could tell she'd be pretty. Mr Marlins always got upset when confronted with a pretty woman who had hair that colour.

Don't underestimate her, Tim thought. According to Gaz, women police constables were the worst. He reckoned WPCs are really nice to you, then suddenly, when you're least expecting it, they spring a trap.

"Was Natalie having any problems at home?" she asked.

"What sort of problems?"

"Why don't you tell me?"

The two stared at each other.

"Look, I've had just about enough of this!" Mr Marlins clenched his fists and took a step towards the policewoman. With a peculiar sort of thrill, Tim wondered if he was going to hit her. But at that moment Mr Marlins noticed his wife and stepson hovering by the door.

He stared at Tim's head for a full thirty seconds. His face flushed crimson as he shoved past the policewoman. Tim braced himself. But Mr Marlins didn't touch him. One hand on the door handle, he turned and growled, "Just do your job and find my daughter!" On his way out he hissed at Tim, "I'll deal with you later, my boy." He shook his head at Julie and slammed the door.

The policewoman considered Tim with her pretty blue eyes. He could almost see her categorizing him. He straightened his shoulders and faced her defiantly. If she asked where he'd been last night, he'd deny all knowledge of the public toilets. The others wouldn't tell. Death Heads never told the police anything.

She didn't ask. She made him and his mother sit down on the sofa, took the armchair for herself and chatted to them as if they were friends. Tim relaxed a bit. "No," he said innocently when she asked if he'd seen Nat go out. "I was in bed. Sleep like the dead, me. I didn't hear no one creeping about the house."

This earned him a sharp glance from Julie. She didn't say anything even though she must have known he'd been out later than usual last night. He felt a bit bad about lying. But it couldn't be important, could it? After all, Jo had been with Nat since he'd seen her leave the house.

"I see." The policewoman double-checked the time he claimed he'd gone to bed, wrote "half-past midnight" in her notebook, then asked him how he got on with his new family and how he liked living in Millennium Green after the big city.

"Mr Marlins don't like me much," Tim said finally, to shut her up. "Which is fine by me, 'cause I don't like him much neither."

His mother told him off for being cheeky and apologized to the policewoman, who looked at Tim's head and gave her a sympathetic glance. Tim set his jaw. Then the policewoman's radio crackled and she excused herself while she held a quiet one-sided conversation over by the French window.

Tim stole a look at his mother. She was curling the ends of her hair round and round her fingers. She's really worried, he thought with a jolt.

After a few minutes the policewoman came back, a peculiar look on her face. Julie jumped up. "What?" she demanded. "What is it?"

The two women stared at each other. Julie went deathly pale. Uneasy prickles worked their way up and down Tim's spine.

"They've found the dog," the policewoman said gently. "In the river. I'm afraid it was dead."

Tim turned cold. "What about Nat?" he said but no one answered.

His mother flopped back on to the sofa with a little moan. The policewoman sat beside her and held her hand, saying soothing things.

Forgotten, Tim fiddled with his earring. "Nat can swim," he said stubbornly. "Don't worry, she'll be OK. I bet she'll be back in time for tea."

*

In her dream, Natalie was drowning. She'd been skating with Jo but she'd fallen into the river in the fog. The water was freezing and stole her breath away so she couldn't even scream. Dad, Julie and Tim were on the bank but they didn't see her as the river carried her further and further downstream. She tried to swim against the current but the skates were too heavy. They were dragging her under. It grew darker as the river plunged into a haunted wood where huge trees reached for her with gnarled fingers and whispered strange secrets into her ear—

She woke with a gasp, drenched in sweat, to find herself tucked up in bed and the room in darkness. She rolled over with a sigh of relief and reached for her bedside lamp. Just a nightmare, that was all.

The lamp wasn't there.

In a cold rush, it all came back. The supermarket car park, the fog, the needle in her neck. She jerked up and stared around in terror.

Her captors had taken her glasses – the room was blurred. But she made out bars across the moonlit window, their shadows falling across unfamiliar furniture, sloping attic ceilings, and a chair in which a small figure slumped, his head resting against the wall.

Natalie clutched the blankets to her chin and stared at the boy. Even without her glasses, there was no mistaking that unruly hair, those awful clothes. Without stopping to think, she fought off the blankets and clambered out of bed. "You little slime-bag!" she yelled, thumping him. "You deliberately tripped me!"

The boy jerked awake and jumped off the chair, arms over his head. "No, don't get up! He took your—"

Natalie's fury died in a flood of embarrassment, confusion and fear. Sometime while she'd slept, her jeans and anorak had been replaced by a thin cotton shift that barely came to her knees. She grabbed the blanket she'd just discarded and wrapped it tightly around herself.

"—clothes," the boy finished, staring fixedly at his feet. "It wasn't my fault. Don't hurt me, please."

Did he really think she was going to hurt him? Like this?

Movement had revived all the bruises she'd suffered in the car park when she fell. Her legs were wobbly, her ankle stiff, her mouth felt like sandpaper. She was standing on bare boards, freezing air whispering up the backs of her legs. There was no sign of a radiator. She shivered and looked round more carefully: ancient chests of dark wood, a couple of cupboards, no rug, just the one chair. The door had been cut at an angle to fit the sloping ceiling and was firmly closed. "Where am I?" she whispered. "Who are you? Why have you brought me here?"

She pulled the blanket closer, tiptoed to the window and squinted through the bars. Everything outside seemed blurred by rippling silver, like trying to see through frosted glass, but she made out a crumbling wall smothered in ivy, a garden choked with brambles, high iron gates, black trees losing their leaves... "The wood," she whispered, remembering her dream. "We're in Unicorn Wood, aren't we?"

Electric light suddenly flooded the room, making Natalie jump. Somehow, she'd expected candles. The light brought her fully awake. She sprang past the boy and made a dash for the door. It was locked. She rattled the handle, tears in her eyes, then took a deep breath and turned back to the boy. "Let me out?" she said. "Please."

The boy stood awkwardly by the wall, his hair brushing the low ceiling, watching her. "Can't," he said simply. "It's bolted on the outside. And I'm not supposed to tell you where you are."

Was he a prisoner too, then? Her arms were a rash of goosebumps. She couldn't think straight. She returned to the bed and tucked the covers around her cold feet. "Don't you ever wash?" she said, uncomfortable with the way he was looking at her. "Those clothes look like they've come out of a bin."

The boy rubbed his elbow and said nothing.

Natalie sighed. At least he *had* clothes. She tried again. "Look, I'm thirsty and my head hurts. I don't understand any of this. Can't you just tell me what you want? If you've kidnapped me, you've got the wrong person. My dad hasn't got any money. He hasn't even got a job, not any more, and all Julie's money goes to buy food." She squinted at the boy. "What's your name? What school do you go to?"

The boy chewed his lip. "Promise you won't laugh."

The last thing Natalie felt like doing was laughing, but she said, "Promise."

"My name's Merlin, and I don't go to school. I've got my computer instead. *Encarta*, and lots of other stuff. Father gives me lessons in spell casting. Least, he used to before he started all this Earthaven business."

In spite of everything, Natalie spluttered. "Merlin? As in the great wizard, you mean?"

He coloured. "You said you wouldn't laugh! It's a joke of my father's, 'cause I'm so useless. We're sort of like wizards, you see, even if we don't have the power of the Earthaven Spellmages. But we still keep familiars and most of us use their names like in the old days. When I was little, Father got me a real merlin and made me take it out into the forest so we could bond." He gave her a hesitant look. "It's a kind of hawk."

"I know what a merlin is. I'm not stupid."

"Sorry. Then you know a merlin's much smaller than a goshawk, which is what Father has for his familiar, but its claws are just as sharp. I was scared and let it go, so he bonded me with a mouse instead. I think that was supposed to be a joke too, 'cause I play with my computer so much. It's got a plastic mouse, see?" Catching her expression, he rushed on. "Of course, I expect you know lots about computers if you go to school. But I don't care. I'd much rather have a mouse than a silly bird, anyway. He's called Redeye." The boy's face softened but his smile soon disappeared. "I'm supposed to show him to you, only Father's still got him locked in the cellar."

Natalie shifted uneasily on the bed and a spring *poinged*.

Merlin was obviously as crazy as the rest of his family. The blonde woman who'd stuck the needle in her neck must be his mother. With parents like that, she'd be pretty loopy too. And yet, her own father had reacted strangely when he'd seen that wrapper.

"Your father gave me something he called a spell," she said slowly.

Merlin nodded. "Right! To test you. We can use spells, see, but we can't recycle them. The Spell Lords have to do that for us in Earthaven. Father hates having to buy spells from them but he's got no choice." He licked his lips and ventured out from the corner. "Uh— I don't suppose you remember what happened in the supermarket?"

Memory momentarily banished her fear. "That firework, you mean? You were so stupid! Don't you know it's dangerous to let them off indoors? You're lucky no one was injured."

Merlin frowned at her. "It wasn't a firework, it was the spell-flash. So you didn't cast it, then?" His voice had a strange edge.

She stared at him. "Oh, stop it! I've had enough. There's no such thing as spells, everyone knows that. This isn't funny any more, Merlin. I want my clothes back and I want to go home."

It had never been funny. Waking up in a strange house after being drugged and kidnapped wasn't funny at all. But maybe if she kept thinking of all this as an elaborate Hallowe'en prank, the fear would stay away.

Merlin sighed. "I'm glad I don't go to school. You don't seem to learn much there."

"At least I don't think I'm some sort of wizard!"

He coloured. "Don't call us that – it's rude. We're Spellmages, least that's our proper name. In Earthaven they call us Casters but that's rude too. You're one of us. Father tested you and he's never wrong."

"Well, he is this time," Natalie said firmly. "So you might as well tell him to let me go."

The boy chewed his lip. Then he asked in a small voice, "Aren't you worried about your spider?"

She frowned. "So you *did* steal him! I thought you were after something, you little rat."

Merlin cringed. "Mouse," he whispered. "My familiar's a mouse, not a rat. And please don't shout. Father's got your spider in the cellar with Redeye. He's down there now. He'll hear us."

"I don't care. You can keep Itsy if you want him that badly. Just let me go."

Merlin blinked. "Without your familiar? But don't you *feel* it?"

"Feel what?"

"The things—" He swallowed and glanced at the door. "The things Father does to your spider to control you."

His words reminded Natalie of the needle in the car park. She shivered and clutched the blanket closer. "I don't know what you're talking about," she said. "I'm cold. Where are my clothes?"

"I'm not allowed to tell."

They watched each other warily.

"Can I have my glasses back, at least?" Natalie asked. "I can hardly see you."

Merlin chewed his lip, glanced at the door again and shook his head. "Father thinks you might try to run away."

Her blood rose. "I can run away without them just as well! I'm not *blind*, you know."

This earned her a very strange look. "I know. But you'd need your shoes. You won't get far in the woods barefoot."

True enough. And getting worked up obviously wasn't going to help get them back. She took a deep breath. "How long have I been asleep?" she asked.

"All day."

No wonder she was so thirsty! She shivered again.

"Look," she said as reasonably as she could. "I know none of this is your fault. From what I've seen of your father, I don't blame you for doing what he says. But surely he doesn't watch you all the time? You said you had a computer?"

He nodded.

"E-mail?"

"No."

Natalie sighed. It had been too much to hope for. "Telephone?"

Merlin shook his head.

"There must be *some* way you can get a message out. If you help me contact my folks, I'll tell the police you had nothing to do with all this."

Merlin shook his head wildly, rolling his eyes at the door. "I can't! Father'll find out, then he'll hurt Redeye."

She twisted the blanket in frustration. Then she had an idea. "I know! You can slip something into the ransom note."

"There won't be a note."

Ice crawled down her spine. She hardly dared ask. "Then why am I here?"

Merlin stared at his feet. "You're going to be the thirteenth member of Father's spellclave," he mumbled. "Then he'll be a Spell Lord and have enough power to invade Earthaven." He glanced up and gave her a little grin. "It's not as bad as it sounds. If Father hadn't found you in time he'd have used me instead, only I'm so hopeless the spellclave thought I'd be a liability. He probably wants to steal some spells, that's all. Don't worry, you won't have to use the Thrallstone. Next Saturday between midnight and dawn, the Boundary opens. It passes right by our gate; that's why Father bought this place. After he's got his spells I expect he'll leave you alone. We can play games together on my computer. It'll be fun."

Quite crazy. But something clicked. "You mean Hallowe'en, don't you?"

"That's what some people call the Opening, yes. But it's been happening for ages, ever since the Boundary was first created. It's had lots of names. But surely your parents told you all this? They're Spellmages, aren't they? At least one of them must be or you wouldn't have the ancient blood." His grin faded, as if he'd remembered something. He crept closer and suddenly clutched her hand. "I'm supposed to find out how much you know about us," he whispered with another glance at the door. "If you tell me, I'll see if I can send a message to your family. I'm not promising anything, but I *might* be able to use a spell to transport it—"

Natalie snatched her hand free. "Of course my parents aren't Spellmages!" she screamed. "Or Casters or wizards or anything else like that! My dad's a salesman, or used to be before he lost his job, and Mother's— Never mind. I can't stay here a whole week, Julie and Dad will be worried sick."

"Shh!" Merlin backed to the door. "Anyway, you'll have to stay longer than a week. Don't you understand? When you join a spellclave, it's for ever."

She stared at him, ice once more creeping down her spine. *"For ever?"*

"I'm sorry," he whispered. "I can't stop him, but maybe—"

He broke off as rapid footsteps approached the door and the bolts scraped back. Natalie's stomach clenched. But the door opened only a crack so the bird-headed stick could hook Merlin out, then slammed shut behind him. Hearing the bolts shoot home, she scrambled off the bed and thumped the door. "Come back!" she yelled. "I'm thirsty! I'm cold! You can't keep me here like this! Oh, please come back—"

Two sets of footsteps walked away, and the single bulb dimmed. She held her breath until it came bright again, then slumped to the floor. All the tears she'd been holding back since she'd woken suddenly flooded out. "I'm not a stupid Spellmage," she sobbed. "I'm normal, normal, *normal!* And I want to go home."

5

CAPTIVE

Monday, Tuesday, Wednesday,
October 26, 27, 28

Natalie wasn't back for Sunday tea, nor for tea the next day, nor the next. No one was pretending any more and the holiday was ruined. Julie spent half her time at the Carter house consoling Jo's mother, and Mrs Carter spent the rest of her time at the Marlins' house consoling Julie. Meals arrived on the table at unpredictable hours, either overcooked or almost raw. Jo's little sister, who until now Tim hadn't realized existed, trailed after Mrs Carter like a freckle-faced ghost making idiotic suggestions such as, "Maybe she skated into a ditch and broke her leg," or, "Maybe she knocked herself out and lost her memory." Then she remembered whose skates Nat had been using when she disappeared and whined, "I will get my rollerblades back, won't I?" Tim could have strangled her. But Mrs Carter merely said, "Hush, Sarah. Don't be so selfish. People are more important than skates." Which set both mothers off again.

With all the fuss, Tim found himself ignored even more than usual. Mr Marlins had disappeared back into his garage and had yet to carry out his threat to deal with him later. The only reaction Tim got to his earring and haircut was from Sarah who giggled and told him he looked like a sissy. She was hiding behind her mother's skirts at the time, so Tim had to content himself with glowering at her.

He saw Jo just once, when she came over with her mother and sister on Monday morning to say she was sorry for taking Natalie out in the fog. He'd never seen her so pale and quiet. She stared through him as if he weren't there and after she'd apologized she fled straight out of the door, tears streaming down her cheeks. It was an ideal opportunity for the Death Heads to wreak their revenge on Jo for making their leader look stupid in front of the whole school. But when Gaz and Mike cornered him in town later that day, Tim kept his mouth shut.

"Heard your kid sister ran off," Gaz said. He rested one foot on the crossbar of his mountain bike and casually balanced against the wall, swinging his other leg. "Give us some tips, then. I'd like to get rid of mine."

Tim wondered if it was supposed to be a joke. Gaz's smirk said not. Before he thought what he was doing, he'd kicked Gaz's bike out from under him. It fell with a clatter and Gaz sprawled on top, yelling. Mike rushed forward to help him up but only succeeded in knocking the bike down again. Before either Head could recover, Tim fled.

It was typical. Now he had nothing to go out for. No one seemed to care whether or not he turned up for meals or how late he came in. After a frustrating ten minutes kicking his heels in his room, Tim grabbed his jacket and left to make a thorough search of Millennium Green for traces of Nat. Apparently, Jo had told the police about an old man who'd scared Nat on Saturday near the recycling bins. The latest theory was that this man had kidnapped her. But so far no ransom note had arrived and the police had found no clues as to where she might have gone or been taken. "It's as if she vanished into thin air," Julie told Tim tearfully when they crossed paths in the kitchen on Tuesday.

And now the police were dredging the river. No one had told Tim why, but he wasn't stupid. He hated having to be nice to Nat all the time, hated the way his mother fussed over her as if she were his real sister. But no matter how infuriating she was sometimes, she didn't deserve to be dead.

She *couldn't* be dead.

If she died, it would be his fault.

*

Without a ransom note, her family would think she was dead and eventually stop looking for her. This terrifying thought came to Natalie as she struggled to wakefulness on what must have been her second or third day in the attic. She had to escape. The only question was – how?

She still didn't know where her clothes were. She didn't know the time, nor even the day, since there was no clock in the room and she slept such a lot between meals. They never let her out, not even to go to the bathroom – there was a chemical toilet and a basin of water crammed into one of the cupboards. It stank whenever she opened the door but she didn't have a lot of choice. Her tiredness probably had something to do with the drug they'd given her in the car park but she had to shake it off. No matter what, she had to get out of here before Hallowe'en. Who knew what crazy things the man called Hawk and the empty-eyed woman had planned for her then?

"Next time the door opens," she promised herself, hugging her knees for courage.

She knew the routine by now. When they brought her meals, two sets of footsteps would approach the door. One person would stay outside while Merlin slipped in with her tray. Although she'd tried talking to him several times, he just shook his head like an idiot and backed out again. If she hurt him it would be his own fault.

The warning creak of the stairs wasn't long coming. She tensed as the double set of footsteps approached along the passage and stopped outside her door. Very quietly, she eased

herself out of bed and put her back to the wall. The bolts
scraped and the door opened its usual crack to let Merlin slip
inside. Before he was completely through, Natalie sprang into
action. She seized her supper from his surprised hands,
elbowed him out of the way and jammed the tray into the
closing gap.

A curse came from the passage and the bird-headed stick
crashed into the tray, loosening Natalie's grip. At the same
time, the door was pulled shut. The tray went rattling into
the corridor and the door slammed on Natalie's fingers.
She snatched her hand back with a scream – half pain, half
frustration.

"I hate you!" she yelled, sucking her sore knuckles. "When I
get out of here, you'll be sorry! I saw your face in the car park!
I'll identify you to the police and then they'll lock *you* up. For
ever and ever!"

"No, Spider!" Merlin cried, breaking his rule of silence and
catching her arm. "Don't make him angry, or he'll hurt Itsy!"
He had spaghetti bolognese all down the front of his jumper.
She shrugged him off in disgust.

A nasty chuckle came from behind the closed door. "Maybe
a small demonstration wouldn't go amiss. But soon her little
familiar will be meeting my goshawk – after that she won't be
identifying me to anyone unless I say so. In fact, I think we'll
bond her tomorrow. She'll be less trouble then."

Merlin paled. "No, Father, please. Claudia says she's not
ready yet. She'll be good – won't you, Spider?"

The door slammed back on its hinges. Natalie stood her
ground, though her heart hammered so loudly she thought it
would burst. Hawk strode in, his black hair flowing, eyes fierce
yellow in the harsh shadows cast by the bare bulb. He carried
his stick like a sword. His gaze swept the room, taking in the
cowering Merlin, the broken plate, the spaghetti on the floor,
finally coming to rest on Natalie in her crumpled bolognese-
stained shift, her hair tangled across her face.

As she glared back, his lips twisted. "She looks ready enough to me. I'm aware of what you and Claudia are up to, boy, but you won't find anyone else with her sort of power in three days. What do you think I've been doing all these years? Watching spell banks for fun? Besides, my little Spider's special." He chuckled. His stick prodded Natalie's chin, pinning her against the wall. She clenched her fists, determined not to cry.

"Have to clean you up a bit before the ceremony," Hawk went on. "Can't have my spellclave looking as if they've just crawled through the Thrallstone when I invade Earthaven, can I? A Spell Lord has certain standards to keep up."

"You're crazy," Natalie whispered. "All of you."

This made him laugh. "You're much sweeter asleep, I must admit, but after tonight you won't need sleeping pills when I want you sweet. Come out of there, boy. Leave her to think about it. Won't do her any harm not to have any supper tonight, she's not going anywhere." The stick left her chin and hooked Merlin's elbow, tugging him out of the room. The door slammed. The bolts scraped home.

Natalie sank on to the bed, trembling. "Stupid, stupid, stupid!" she hissed into the pillow. All she'd achieved was the loss of her supper. Plus that chilling revelation.

"You put sleeping pills in my food," she whispered, rubbing her throat where the stick had bruised it. Of all the things they'd done to her so far, that seemed the worst. And yet... "If you were real wizards, you wouldn't need drugs and locks to keep me here."

She sat up and stared at the door, an idea taking root in her brain. If their powers weren't real, it would do no harm to play along, would it? Then, when her kidnappers trusted her enough to give her back her clothes, she'd run. As fast and as far as she could.

6

CHE CHRALLSTONE

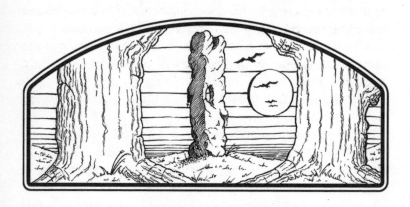

Wednesday night, October 28

On Wednesday evening, at about the time Natalie was making her escape bid, Tim came to a decision. He locked himself in the bathroom and hunched before the mirror to examine his ear. The miniature Death Head skull grinned back at him. Nothing had gone right since he'd started to wear it, almost as if the skull contained the evil powers Gaz claimed it did. He clenched his teeth and slowly eased the earring out.

It came free in a spurt of yellow pus. He wiped it clean and dropped it into one of the many pockets in his birthday jacket. Then he hurried downstairs where his mother was just getting into her coat.

"I'm going round to Mrs Carter's," she said without looking at him. "There's a pizza in the freezer for supper if you get hungry."

He took a deep breath. "I have to tell you something. It's about Nat."

She froze, one arm half in the coat sleeve.

Tim rushed on. "I lied to that policewoman. I… uh… didn't

get back till early Sunday morning and I saw Nat go out. I thought it was weird, her going out in the dark and all that fog. I know I should've stopped her but I thought she'd be OK with Jo and the dog. I'm real sorry I let her go off like that. I've looked everywhere I can think of round town. Do you want me to help you search the woods or anything?"

"Oh Timothy." Her hand touched his smooth scalp – the weirdest sensation, sending shivers through him. "I already know you lied."

He blinked. "You know? Then… you're not angry with me?"

His mother sighed. "I'm not pleased you lied to the police, no. That was stupid. But I was stupid, too. I heard the door go that morning and assumed it was you coming in. If I'd checked, I might have stopped Natalie myself." Her voice broke and she sniffed before continuing. "Thanks for the offer of help, love, but the police have already got people searching the woods, and it's been on the news. I'm sure they'll find something soon." She gave him a brave smile. "Be good for your father, now. You might take him something to eat if you remember."

"But—" Tim scowled at the closing door. If he went into the garage he'd only get his head bitten off.

But his stepfather must have been listening. No sooner had his mother's car pulled away, than Mr Marlins came into the kitchen. He gave Tim a speculative look. "So you want to make up for your stupidity, do you? That makes a change."

Tim frowned at his stepfather. Something was different but it took him a moment to work out what.

Mr Marlins had shaved off his beard.

Tim fiddled with his jacket zips. "Julie says we're to get our own supper," he mumbled. "D'you want me to put a pizza on?"

"How about we go out for a takeaway?"

Tim stared at him in disbelief. "She's taken the car."

A comradely hand rested on his shoulder. "We'll take my car.

You haven't had a ride in it yet, have you?"

"No..." He blinked a few times, trying to understand what had brought on this change. Not only had Mr Marlins shaved but, for the first time Tim could remember, his stepfather's breath didn't smell of beer.

"Come on then if you're coming."

Still bemused, Tim followed Mr Marlins into the garage. He'd never seen his stepfather's car close-up. It looked sporty and he'd have liked more time to examine its sleek black curves. But Mr Marlins had already opened the garage door and was in the driver's seat, turning on the ignition. Tim hurried round to the passenger side. The seats were real leather and creaked against his jacket. The engine spluttered, then roared into life. Despite the circumstances, he couldn't help being excited by the deep, powerful throb. This was a *real* car.

He reclined the passenger seat, feigning casualness. He considered himself rather good at this, having hung out with the Death Heads so long. But Mr Marlins saw through it at once.

"Put that seat back straight," he snapped. "Strap yourself in. And don't touch anything else unless I tell you."

"Sorry, Mr Marlins." He quickly returned the seat to its original position and eyed the fog. It was already dark outside. Street lamps cast misty orange cones, reminding him of the morning Nat had vanished. He shivered.

Mr Marlins revved the engine, more like a joyrider than a middle-aged dad. Tim felt uneasy. He shifted in his seat and glanced at the door handle. But before he could change his mind and get out, the car leapt forward, wheels spinning sickeningly for a moment before they screeched out of the drive. Tim was thrown against the door as Mr Marlins took a hard right. He fumbled desperately for his seatbelt.

"Warned you, didn't I?" Mr Marlins said. By this time, they were hurtling through town, weaving in and out of traffic and swerving dangerously around corners. Somehow, Tim got the seatbelt fastened. He swallowed his stomach.

"All right?" Mr Marlins asked.

"Fine," he managed in a croaky voice. "But where are we going? The pizza place is back that way."

"I know."

"Are we going to eat somewhere else, then?" Tim's unease was growing by the second. They'd left Millennium Green and were speeding along an unlit country road, black tree trunks looming out of the fog on each side and vanishing behind them. Every time the car squealed round a bend he thought they were going to die.

"You hungry?" Mr Marlins said, after a few minutes of pure terror.

"Not really."

"Good, because I've a better idea. Why don't we go rescue Nat?"

Tim sat very still. He eyed his stepfather's profile.

"You think I'm still drunk, don't you?" Mr Marlins said.

"No."

"Yes you do. You're thinking I wouldn't be driving like this unless I'd had a few." They roared into a right-hand bend and Tim's side of the car glanced off the crash barrier. He shut his eyes as sparks hissed against the passenger window. Mr Marlins smiled grimly. "If I'd been drinking, we'd have been upside-down in that ditch by now. Relax. Enjoy the ride. You told your mother you wanted to help search the woods, didn't you? Well, now's your chance."

Tim swallowed his stomach once more and considered his stepfather. "Does that mean you know where Nat is?"

"Let's say I've a very good idea."

Anger rose. "Why didn't you tell Mum? She's been going frantic!"

"I have my reasons."

Finally, it dawned on Tim what must have happened. "Oh, I get it! Nat's been kidnapped, hasn't she? You've had a ransom note that warned you not to say anything to the police! That's why they told us they hadn't found anything."

His fear vanished, replaced by a shivery thrill. At last someone was *doing* something. Mr Marlins really did seem to know what he was doing with the car. Obviously he wouldn't have told Julie. This sort of thing was man's work. Tim felt a glow of pride that his stepfather thought he was grown-up enough to help, and another glow at the news that Nat was still alive. When all this was over, he'd have something really exciting to tell Gaz and the gang, much better than spraying their names on toilet walls. Then he remembered what he'd done to Gaz last time they'd met and his excitement subsided slightly.

Mr Marlins gave him a sharp look. "Maybe," he said. "Sit still and do what you're told."

Tim cupped his hands to the cold glass and watched the trees race past. At the speed they were going, in the dark and with all the fog, it was difficult to read the signposts. At some point they left the main road and wove their way along deserted lanes with no white lines or catseyes to guide them. Mr Marlins drove with intense concentration, both hands gripping the steering wheel. Tim stayed silent for as long as he could but when they turned off the lane and headed down an unmade track into the woods, he couldn't keep quiet a moment longer.

"Where does this lead?"

"To where I used to work."

Tim took his eyes off the trees to glance at his watch, then shook it in frustration. The stupid thing had stopped. "Aren't offices usually shut at this time of night?" he said, frowning because he was sure his watch had been working earlier.

"The people I work for don't have offices."

"But what about Nat? I thought we were going to get her back?"

"We are."

Mr Marlins spun the wheel and an impressive spray of mud splattered the windscreen. The fog was thicker under the trees. Tim thought he saw a pair of amber eyes caught in the headlights but before he could open his mouth to yell a warning, the eyes had gone.

"Are we nearly there?" he ventured.

Mr Marlins grunted. "Don't distract me. I'm trying to remember the way."

Tim turned up his jacket collar. For all its looks, it was cold in the car. He thrust his hands into his pockets and hunched lower in his seat. He was beginning to see the disadvantages of having a shaved head. Hair had been a lot warmer.

He was still trying to work out what Mr Marlins' old employers could possibly have to do with Nat, when without warning his stepfather jammed on the brakes.

The car skidded to a stop and Tim sat up. They were in a clearing surrounded by dense, drifting fog. An articulated truck, no less, was parked in the middle, being unloaded by ghostly figures in long cloaks. Silver dogs the size of Alsatians padded around as if on guard. One came to investigate the car, put its nose to the passenger window and stared at Tim with bright amber eyes. He shuddered.

"Scared?" Mr Marlins said.

"Not me!"

"Perhaps you should be."

Tim peered at the truck, trying to see what they were taking out of it. Sacks? The harder he looked, the less he could make out. The cloaked people kept walking into the fog at one side of the clearing and vanishing. So did the dogs. He wiped his window and squinted after them. Was that a standing stone over there? He pulled his jacket closer.

"Something wrong with your eyes, is there?" Mr Marlins said.

Tim scowled. "It's dark," he said, fed up with all the mystery. "No one can see in the dark."

There was a tense silence.

"All right," his stepfather said at last. "I owe you an explanation. This is how it is. We're at one of the gateways in the Boundary between worlds. Over there, on the other side of that stone, is a place called Earthaven, which is where I think they've taken Nat. My employers control the gate and those hounds you can see guard it. It's not open all the time, of course, only when they need to make a transfer. Took me a few days to find out when they'd be here, but I still have my contacts."

"Who are your employers?" Tim asked, not sure he wanted to know.

"We call them Spell Lords. Nat's mother came from Earthaven and that's why they're so interested in her. They think she's inherited her mother's power, which is nonsense of course."

Tim shifted uncomfortably in his seat. "What power? I thought Nat's mother was blind."

"Only in our world. In Earthaven, she could see better than you can now."

Which wouldn't be difficult, Tim thought, squinting at the ghostly shapes around the truck. If it hadn't been for Nat's disappearance, he'd have thought Mr Marlins was playing a huge joke on him. Except, Mr Marlins and jokes didn't go together. "What does that make you, then?" he mumbled, wondering if he could hitch a ride home in the truck.

His stepfather gave him a dark smile. "I'm a Thrall."

The very word made Tim shiver all over. He stared at Mr Marlins, uncomfortable yet unwilling to ask.

"You don't know what that is, do you?"

Tim shook his head.

"If you'd read your history books, you'd know."

Tim kept quiet. He never read *any* book unless he had to. Piles of them were sitting upstairs in his school bag right now, waiting for him to get around to his half-term homework.

"Technically, it means slave," Mr Marlins went on calmly. "Though these days, travelling salesman would be more appropriate for what I do. Some of us work on the recycling side, as you can see." He indicated the truck.

Tim wet his lips. "Does Nat know you're a... one of these Trawls?"

"*Thralls.*" Mr Marlins' face darkened. "No, she doesn't. And don't you go telling her, my boy."

Another shiver passed down Tim's spine. "I won't tell her," he promised quickly. "But I don't understand. Is she here, then?" None of the cloaked figures looked small enough. "What's in the truck? What do you sell?" Visions of illegal contraband flashed before Tim's eyes.

Mr Marlins smiled mysteriously and got out of the car. The silver dog that had been circling outside sniffed at him but didn't attack. "Wait here," he said, then slammed the door and walked away.

Tim twisted in his seat in alarm. Now the engine had stopped, the car was freezing. He began to feel quite panicky. He slid across the seat and felt for the keys but Mr Marlins had thought of that. The dog put its huge paws on the bonnet and stared at him through the windscreen. He scowled at it but didn't dare get out.

Over by the truck, Mr Marlins was exchanging angry words with the people doing the unloading. Then a tall man dressed in shades of green like shifting leaf shadows shimmered out of the fog and strode across. Tim stared. The man's white hair reached down almost to his knees and was full of twigs and thorns as if he'd just crawled out of a thicket. Mr Marlins subsided at once, bowed his head to the newcomer and pointed to the car.

Tim caught Nat's name and wound down the window a fraction so he could hear, but the men had lowered their voices and he only caught fragments.

"...don't know what Lady Atanaqui was thinking of..."

"...Casters must have her..."

"...neglecting your duties..."

Mr Marlins called the man "Lord". This made Tim smile. But his smile soon died when the Spell Lord raised his head and stared at the car with eyes full of pale green light. A chill rippled through Tim as the Spell Lord came striding across the clearing, Mr Marlins hurrying behind. Before Tim thought to lock it, his door was wrenched open.

"No!" he yelled in terror as the dog closed its jaws on his arm.

"Get out," said the Spell Lord.

Tim got out, trying to see if the animal's teeth had ripped his sleeve. Relieved they hadn't, he turned on its owner. "Call your dog off!" he demanded. "This jacket's brand new."

The Spell Lord smiled coldly. "I can see why you brought him here," he said to Mr Marlins. "The question is what do we do now? We can't just let him go home."

"But if you haven't got my daughter..."

"Even if we did have her, do you think we'd trade her for this surly specimen?" The Spell Lord's lip curled.

"Hey!" Tim said, realizing with a sudden chill what Mr Marlins must have meant when he'd said Tim could make up for his stupidity. His stepfather meant to swap him for Nat! Forget the jacket – he could save up for another one. He braced himself and tugged as hard as he could, kicking the dog. Its snarl turned ugly, and the Spell Lord's eyes blazed emerald fire.

"Stop that!" he snapped.

Tim subsided as Mr Marlins caught his employer's sleeve. "Let him go. Please. We ought to be looking for Nat."

In any other circumstances, Tim wouldn't have dreamt of sticking up for his stepfather, but this was different. Gritting his teeth, he said. "That's right! I'm helping search the woods."

The Spell Lord gave him an amused glance. "Easily fooled, aren't you?" He turned back to Mr Marlins and his tone hardened. "You were supposed to bring your daughter to us on her twelfth birthday so she could bond with her mother's hound and decide for herself. Now she's not only in enemy hands but I assume she knows nothing at all about us. If the Casters harm her, you've only yourself to blame."

"There was no point telling her! She's a normal, happy little girl. She's got friends, she goes to school. If you need proof, she can see in our world! She'll hate Earthaven. I only wanted her to have a normal life."

Mr Marlins seemed close to tears. If he hadn't been so scared himself, Tim would have been embarrassed. He forced himself to stay calm and listen.

"What sort of life do you think she'll have after the Casters have finished with her?" the Spell Lord was saying. "I agree it's unusual she can see so well among you but that's probably because she was born in your world. The important thing now is to get her out of the Casters' hands before they do some irreparable damage. We'll send K'tanaqui to find her. Meanwhile, you can distribute those spells you've been hoarding in your car before they die of old age. Better wait till after the Opening before you come up here again. We're expecting trouble this year. As for your stepson... I'm sorry, but he's seen too much."

Tim's blood chilled. It had been a struggle to follow the exchange, but he understood this last part only too well. He glared at Mr Marlins. "Do something!" he hissed.

His stepfather's eyes slid away. He bowed to the Spell Lord, got into his car and drove away.

Tim stared after the vanishing tail lights in disbelief. "Coward!" he yelled.

*

After Mr Marlins had gone, the dog let go of Tim's sleeve. But before he could make a run for it, two of the cloaked men detached themselves from the group around the truck and came to stand one each side of him. Tim glimpsed long knives glittering in their belts and changed his mind about running. He also changed his mind about hitching a ride. When the Spell Lord pointed to a fallen log and told him to sit, he had little choice but to obey.

While he waited, he turned his attention to the standing stone. It was about twice his height and twisted like the trunk of an ancient tree. With the fog drifting around its moss-clothed coils, it looked as if it had grown out of the earth itself. Shadows cast by the truck's headlamps writhed around it. Just below eye level, a hole the size of a human head appeared to go right through the stone. The cloaked people were putting their sacks into this hole, yet strangely they didn't come out the other side. Each time a sack disappeared, there was a green flare and a strange chill seeped out of the stone, penetrating Tim's bones.

There had to be some kind of hidden mechanism, Tim decided, triggered by a lever inside the hole. Maybe the stone was hollow and the sacks were being stored inside it for collection later? What he really needed was a closer look. But every time he started to rise from the log, the dog growled and his two guards stiffened, causing the Spell Lord to glance his way. Tim sat down again and fiddled with the zips of his jacket.

"What's in the sacks?" he asked his guards. "Why are you putting them in the stone?"

The two glanced at each other but didn't answer.

"Are you Casters?" Tim asked curiously.

This got a reaction. One of his guards spat on the ground. "No we're not! Casters aren't allowed to live in Earthaven. They spend their whole lives squabbling over spells and casting silly little illusions at each other. Half of 'em can't even do that properly. There's a spellclave in some old lodge not half a mile from here but they never come near the Thrallstone, they're too frightened of the Boundary spells. Pah!"

"Spells?" Tim said, starting to get interested. "That's what Mr Marlins sells, isn't it? What do they look like?"

"The live ones glitter—"

"Shh!" said the other guard with a nervous glance at the Spell Lord. "He's not a Thrall candidate."

"So what? Won't matter after, will it?"

But they shut up and wouldn't say a word more. Tim went back to fiddling with his zips and watched the sacks more carefully, hoping someone would get careless and drop one. No one did.

It seemed to take forever for the truck to be emptied. But, finally, a driver climbed into the cab and the engine spluttered to life. Moving cautiously through the mud, the huge vehicle left. The Spell Lord approached Tim's log, beckoned him to his feet and led the way to the Thrallstone. The rest of his people fell in behind and stood silently around the stone, waiting for something. By this time, Tim's eyes had adjusted and he realized the sky wasn't as dark as it had been. He must have been sitting on the log all night! No wonder he was so cold.

"How long have I been here?" he demanded. "My mother will go spare if I'm not back for breakfast." His watch had definitely stopped but he made a show of peering at it anyway.

The Spell Lord frowned at him. "It's no good looking at your timepiece. We've powerful anti-technology spells all around the Boundary. I regret you had to wait so long, but I'm sure you understand we couldn't risk someone stumbling on us unloading that lot. Don't worry, you'll be home soon enough if you cooperate."

"Why can't I go home now?" Tim said, glancing uneasily at his guards.

A sigh. "You're hardly Thrall material, so we're going to cleanse your memories of us. Think of it as having a bad tooth extracted. It's for your own good as well as ours. If you relax and let Oq do her work, it'll be quicker."

"Who's Oq?" Tim whispered, shuddering. Cleanse his memories? Like those films where they turned people into vegetables? Not if he could help it.

In answer, the Spell Lord walked up to the stone and thrust his hands into the hole. Green light flared around his wrists and rippled up his arms, staining his hair. Tim stared in disbelief. The stone was *melting*. As the Spell Lord raised his arms, so the hole stretched and grew, revealing more trees and a drift of white flowers, ghostly in the dawn mist. The dog leapt through and vanished just as the sacks had done.

"All right," the Spell Lord added to the cloaked men. "I can handle the boy now. You take those spells and bury them. We don't want them lying around when the Boundary opens. When you're done, keep clear of the Thrallstone so Oq can do her work."

Mouth dry, Tim began to edge towards the trees. To distract the Spell Lord, he talked fast. "You don't have to cleanse me, I never remember nothing. You ask my teachers! I'm always bottom in all the exams..." Another step.

The Spell Lord laughed. "Is that so? Then maybe they don't teach you the right things. In my experience when people are interested enough, they learn just fine."

Another step. "I'm not interested in Earthaven."

"Really? For someone who isn't interested, you ask an awful lot of questions. Stand still! Oq's trying to reach you."

The cloaked people had been hurrying through the hole in the stone and vanishing into the green light, but at this the ones who remained turned, hands on their knives. Tim frantically searched his pockets for something he could use as a weapon. His fingers touched his earring.

The Spell Lord whispered a soft word. There was a rustle on the other side of the stone. Then a golden tentacle as thick as Tim's arm quested through the hole and wound itself tightly about his waist.

His blood turned to ice. Out came the Death Head earring. With a yell, he jabbed the hook as hard as he could into the thing. It recoiled with a sharp crackle and a whiff of burnt sugar. Tim took off towards the trees. Before he'd gone three strides, the Spell Lord shouted something. Willing hands grabbed Tim's arms from behind. He struggled as hard as he could but the cloaked men dragged him back to the stone.

"Take him through," the Spell Lord said coldly.

Tim shut his eyes as that green light surrounded him and black lightning began to flash inside his head.

My name is Timothy Lockley, he repeated desperately, over and over. *Mr Marlins is a Thrall. He sells spells. I'm in a place called Earthaven, and my stepsister Nat is in the hands of the Casters... in the hands of the Casters... in the hands of the Casters...*

7

LORD HAWK

Thursday morning, October 29

Natalie spent an uneasy, sleepless night listening to the creaks and groans of the old house. It seemed morning would never come. But finally the shimmer outside her window took on colours – a shifting blur of bronzes, reds and golds. She made herself sit on the bed and wait. This might be her last chance. She mustn't bungle it this time.

When she heard the footsteps in the corridor, she sat up straight, folded her hands in her lap and pasted a smile to her face. "All right," she called meekly. "I'll help you get your spells. What do you want me to do?"

Hawk was first through the door. Surprise flickered in the yellow eyes, quickly replaced by satisfaction. "See?" he said to the empty-eyed woman who had followed him in. "She only needed a little persuasion in the right place. You're too soft, my Fish, that's your trouble."

He turned back to Natalie. "Good, I'm glad you've decided to be sensible, it'll make this so much easier. First, I want you to clean yourself up. Then you'll come with us."

The woman laid a white dress on the bed, no more substantial than the shift Natalie was wearing. On top of the dress was a hairbrush.

Natalie glanced at them, then at the woman. "I'm not getting changed with *him* in here," she said firmly.

Hawk chuckled. "You won't be so shy after today, my little Spider." But he left the attic and went downstairs while the woman helped her into the dress and rinsed her hair with water from the basin in the tiny bathroom. When Natalie's damp silver curls had been brushed around her shoulders, the woman stood back to survey the result, then unexpectedly pressed a hand to Natalie's cheek and stared at her in a most peculiar way.

Natalie shivered and glanced at the half open door. "What's he going to do to me?" she whispered. "He's crazy, isn't he? If you help me escape, I'll tell everyone you were kind to me—"

Immediately, the hand retreated and the blue eyes emptied again. "We have to go now," the woman said. "Come on."

They descended a shadowy staircase, its banisters decorated with huge wooden acorns. There was no carpet and Natalie could feel the roughness of the treads beneath her bare feet. Cobwebs floated in every corner, reminding her uncomfortably of Hawk's threat of the night before. *Soon your little familiar will be meeting my goshawk and after that you won't be identifying me to anyone.* Why had she said that about seeing his face? So stupid!

She tried to see into the rooms as they went but most of the doors were shut. In the ones she could see into, the light was bad. Those windows that weren't boarded up were covered in thick dust through which the sunlight leaked the colour of syrup. She kept stubbing her toes in the gloom and bit her lip, determined not to cry. When they reached the first floor, a door opened a crack and frightened eyes peered out. She caught a glimpse of unruly red hair before the door shut again. The woman must have seen, but she said nothing, simply took Natalie's hand and hurried her past.

The stairs ended in a long, narrow hallway where they found

Hawk poking his stick into dark corners and behind heavy items of furniture. At the end of the hall was a heavy front door, bolted top and bottom. It had a large keyhole, but no visible key. Natalie twisted her head, getting her bearings. Yes, that door must lead to the gate she'd glimpsed from the attic window. If she could just—

The woman gave her elbow a warning squeeze and she abandoned the idea. Anyway, Merlin was right. Even if she could undo the bolts before someone caught her, she wouldn't get very far in the woods without shoes.

She waited with the woman at the bottom of the staircase while Hawk's explorations took him to the front door. He rattled the end of his stick in the keyhole, then bent and extracted something. He swung round, frowning, his eyes glittering dangerously in the shadows.

"Someone's been messing with the illusion spells," he said. "I put a new one in here just this morning and now it's dead. Even the recycled rubbish the Thralls are bringing us these days lasts longer than that!"

Natalie squinted at the thing in his hand. Another of those stupid wrappers. He caught her looking, strode up and gripped her arm. He waved the spell before her nose. "Know something about this, do you?" Natalie quickly shook her head.

"How can she?" the woman said softly. "She's been sleeping in the attic for four days. More likely someone's tampered with it from the outside, maybe her family. I warned you they wouldn't just sit back and do nothing."

The yellow eyes narrowed. Hawk looked hard at Natalie, then grunted and dragged her to another heavy door, this one hidden in the shadows behind the stairs. "The Thralls can't stop us now," he muttered, taking a key from his belt and unlocking the door. "Come on, Spider. Let's get you bonded, then it won't matter if they do break in."

The door opened on darkness. From below came a deep throbbing, like a giant's heartbeat. Natalie eyed the steps going down and balked.

The grip tightened on her elbow and Hawk chuckled. "See how she resists me, my Fish? Remind you of anyone? Better get her glasses now. I don't want her to miss anything."

The woman's blue gaze slid to Natalie, then quickly away again. She hurried back up the hall. Natalie tried to see where she went but Hawk clicked on a light and tugged her down the steps.

The throbbing grew louder as they descended. It was a large cellar with brick arches, whitewashed and quite brightly lit but a chill oozed out of the walls and breathed down the back of Natalie's neck, raising goosebumps on her bare arms and legs. The air had a musty smell, reminding her of the pet shop where she and Jo went to buy Bilbo's dog chews. There were whiffs of a sharper odour too, maybe urine. She wrinkled her nose.

Hawk positioned a stool under one of the arches and told her to sit. Then he pulled a handful of spells out of his pocket and set them carefully on the floor around her feet, forming a circle. As he laid each one down, he smoothed it with his hand and chanted a soft word in a language she didn't recognize. The spells began to glimmer, exactly like the one she'd found in the puddle in the car park. Natalie drew her bare toes under the stool and pressed her knees together. She started to wonder if playing along was such a good idea.

To her relief, the woman returned then with her glasses, stepped carefully through the ring of spells, and pushed them on to Natalie's nose. She blinked as the cellar snapped into focus. It was larger than she'd thought. What she'd assumed to be shadows at the back turned out to be a tunnel leading into the wall. The throbbing was coming from some large machines at one side, and under one of the arches she made out a long bench with a collection of cages and glass tanks. Most of them seemed to be empty, though the overpowering smell suggested they hadn't always been. She hugged herself, cold and sweating at the same time.

Hawk regarded her in amusement. "Not so confident now,

are you Spider? Sit still and don't touch the spells. I'm going to collect Hunter, then we can start. Fetch her familiar, Claudia, and watch her."

He took the cellar steps three at a time, while the woman – *Claudia, remember that* – disappeared into the shadows.

Natalie eyed the steps and the open door at the top, then transferred her attention to the spells. Eleven of them, evenly spaced, with gaps the length of her arm between each. Easy enough to avoid, except she was supposed to be playing along. Before she could decide, Claudia returned carefully carrying a small glass tank with a lid. She stepped between the spells, gave Natalie a hesitant smile, and placed the tank next to the stool.

At first, Natalie thought the tank was empty. Then a large spider scurried across the glass floor. "Itsy?" she whispered. It certainly looked like a house spider but that didn't mean it was the same one she'd lost. One of its legs was missing. She frowned.

Claudia was watching her, the sympathy back in her eyes. "I couldn't stop him," she said. "He was furious when you tried that trick with the tray and wanted to teach you a lesson. Don't worry, that sort of thing won't be necessary once you're one of us. After a while it doesn't hurt so much." Her eyes misted and she stared at the tank as if she were seeing something other than a spider inside.

Of course. *My Fish.*

"Where's your fish?" Natalie asked.

At once, the blue eyes emptied. "You'll find out soon enough," she said. She retreated under one of the arches and stared at the cellar door.

Natalie followed her gaze and her breath stopped. Merlin's father was coming down the steps, one arm held horizontally before him, a leather glove on his fist. Perched on this glove, a huge grey and brown hawk fluttered its wings for balance. Natalie gripped the stool. She'd never been so close to such a large, fierce bird without wire netting between them. Its tail and breast were barred black, its legs bright yellow, its beak curved and very sharp. She shrank back instinctively as the hawk regarded her from one shining gold eye. Excited by her movement, it opened its cruel beak and screeched.

Caaa-caaa-caaa!

The cry echoed around the cellar, drowning out the throbbing of the generators and making a small animal in one of the cages scuttle in alarm. Natalie slammed her hands over her ears. Under her arch, Claudia cringed.

Hawk smiled fondly at the bird and smoothed its feathers until it settled again. "This is Hunter," he said. "He's a pure bred goshawk. Isn't he a beauty? He's hungry because I haven't flown him today." He looked meaningfully at Natalie.

She wet her lips and glanced at the glimmering spells. "Maybe you should fly him, then?"

Two pairs of yellow eyes blazed at her. "Give it up, Spider. You know very well why he's here and you told me you'd cooperate. This can be easy or it can be hard. Spiders have eight legs, remember."

Natalie eyed the cellar steps and wondered if it might, after all, be a better idea to risk the woods barefoot.

Play along, she told herself firmly. It's only a bird.

She took a deep breath. "I'm sorry, but I don't know what to do. You see, I've never taken part in a ceremony like this before."

The anger died as suddenly as it had come. "I was forgetting your education has been gravely neglected. After you've recovered, I'll give you a few lessons in the basics. You'll have to wait until after the Opening for the rest. Claudia, my darling Fish, explain will you?"

Claudia cleared her throat. "The girl's very young," she said. "Are you sure this is such a good idea, Hawk? Her disappearance will have caused a fuss. It's not like taking an adult no one cares about. You were so careful with me and the others. Why risk discovery now?"

Hawk hissed, and his bird beat the air with its huge wings. Although these were a long way from her head, Natalie ducked. Her stomach clenched as the goshawk's shadow leapt around the cellar.

"How many more times do I have to explain it to you?" Hawk said. "The Boundary opens on Saturday night. Everything's set. Going in with our spellclave incomplete would be suicide, you know that, and if we're going to take on the Council of Oq, we need to make ourselves as powerful as possible. You can't deny Spider will be a lot more useful than Merlin. Either she joins us or we wait another year with all the increased risk of discovery by the authorities while I find another who possesses her sort of power. Fancy that, do you my Fish? Being locked up for the rest of your life? They'd destroy Hunter, you know. What would your imprisonment be like then, do you think?"

Claudia paled. "It'll be quick," she said to Natalie. "Over before you know it. You don't need to do anything. Just sit still and try to relax. Whatever happens, don't touch your spider."

Natalie's heart thumped uneasily. She eyed the steps again. The door at the top was shut now, but not locked. Quietly, she began to shift her weight to the edge of the stool.

Hawk walked around her, touching the spells with his stick and chanting under his breath. The air in the cellar gave a peculiar crackle. Hawk stepped back, and the shadows around the stool *shimmered*.

Natalie froze.

Claudia raised an arm to shield her eyes, which should have warned her. Before Natalie thought to do the same, blinding purple light flooded the cellar, followed by the smell of burnt sugar she remembered from the supermarket and clouds of drifting purple smoke. A little scream escaped her, which the goshawk upstaged with another of its wild cries.

When the smoke cleared, the cellar was full of people.

*

Natalie gripped the edge of the stool and blinked round the ring of faces, still trying to calm her heart. Surely they hadn't stepped out of thin air? She began to tremble, then shook herself. No, they must have crept along the tunnel under cover of the smoke while she'd been blinded by that explosion. She'd seen a magician do something similar on television once. She started to feel a bit calmer. Hawk hadn't even got the number of spells right. Only ten people had "appeared" in the cellar – seven men and three women of various ages, quite ordinary looking except for their eyes, which regarded her with fierce interest.

As if I'm their prey, she thought with a shiver.

"This is our little Spider," said Hawk, gentling his bird. "Some of you have already seen her asleep in the attic. Today, I'm pleased to announce she's very much awake and willing to complete our spellclave. Today, our power increases thirteenfold. Today, I become a Spell Lord!"

Excited whispers rippled round the cellar, but quietened as Hawk raised his stick. "Silence," he said. "Stand still." Immediately, everyone was silent and still.

Hawk counted them, peered into the shadows at the back of the cellar, then prodded one of the spells, which unlike its neighbours was still glimmering. He scowled. "Where's that boy got to now? I *told* him to be ready for transportation. I want him to witness this. Damn him, he never learns..." He carried his goshawk across to the cage from which the sound of a small animal's panic had come earlier. Natalie watched uneasily as Hunter beat his wings in excitement. Inside the cage, a white mouse vanished into its bedding.

There was a short pause.

Then Merlin came racing down the cellar steps at dangerous speed, pushed through all the people and snatched the cage into his arms. "No!" he screamed, shielding the mouse with his body. "Leave him alone, please leave him alone!"

His father's lip twisted. "Put that down, boy, don't be such a baby. Now we're all here at last, perhaps we can start. We'll use spellfire, I think, since this is such a special moment. Ferret! Turn that thing off, it's driving me crazy."

A black-bearded man crossed to the generator. After a

moment, the throbbing stopped and the electric lights died. Darkness rushed from the walls, leaving only the faint bronze glimmer of the single unused spell by Natalie's feet. Everyone's breathing grew louder. Over by the bench, Merlin whimpered. Natalie started to feel sick.

Hawk touched the glimmering spell with his stick and it burst into flame. Haloed in purple fire, the goshawk twisted its head and eyed her upside-down. Shadows whispered chill threats across her neck. If the cellar had been spooky before, it was a hundred times worse now. She hugged herself tightly, tears coming.

"Don't hurt me, please don't," she whispered, knowing she sounded like Merlin but unable to help herself. "If you let me go, I promise I won't tell the police anything. I'll say you kept me blindfolded. I'll say anything you want—" Her voice cracked on a sob.

"Get on with it," Claudia said. "Stop torturing the child."

In two swift strides, Hawk crossed to the stool. Natalie made herself as small as possible and shut her eyes tightly. But he didn't touch her and after a moment she heard a scrape near her feet. She risked a peep. She'd quite forgotten Itsy – if it really was Itsy. Hawk had removed the lid of the tank. As she watched, hardly daring to breathe, Hunter hopped down, stretched his neck into the tank and delicately swallowed the spider.

For three heartbeats, no one and nothing moved. Then the goshawk shrieked, Merlin's father raised both arms to the roof, and everyone except Merlin went down on their knees and shouted, "Lord Hawk! Lord Hawk! Lord Hawk!"

It was all too much. The tension ran out of Natalie as if someone had punctured her. Her legs, that had been clenched together since the lights went out, seemed to become liquid. She slipped off the stool and crumpled in a little heap at Hawk's feet. The others crowded forward, a strange mixture of eagerness and pity in their eyes, tiny purple flame-reflections dancing in their pupils.

Hawk patted her head. But instead of helping her up, he pushed her further down. "Good girl. Now kiss my feet, then I'll let you rest."

Natalie's blood stirred. Kiss his feet? His boots were caked in mud. She started to tell him so, then stopped herself. *Play along.* Meekly, she crawled forward and touched her lips to the cleanest boot. A sigh rippled around the cellar.

She waited a decent moment, then raised her head and said as sweetly as she could, "Please Lord Hawk, I'm cold and my feet hurt. Could I have my clothes and shoes back now, do you think?"

She held her breath. Had she overdone it?

Hawk smiled and fingered a lock of her still damp hair. "Of course you can, my little Spider. No need to keep them from you now, is there? Merlin! Stop that pathetic whimpering. Go fetch Spider's clothes and take them up to her room. Fish, you can help her upstairs and put her to bed. The rest of you, get down to the archery range and start practising! This is the year we show the Council of Oq who has the real power. I want everyone capable of shooting a unicorn at twenty paces when we cross that Boundary!"

8

ESCAPE

Thursday morning, October 29

Merlin took his time fetching Spider's clothes. With the girl recovering in the attic and his father and the rest of the spell-clave practising down at the archery range, no one would know what he was about to attempt. If it didn't work, he wouldn't get into trouble. And if it did, he'd be free. He felt a bit guilty as he remembered the price of that freedom. But he didn't see what he could have done to help Spider and it was all over now. Not even his father could turn back the clock.

He thrust the girl to the back of his mind and waited in his room, listening to doors slam and feet crunch down the path until everything was quiet. Then he crept to the window and peered through a crack in the shutters.

His room looked out on the shed where the goshawk lived, the idea being that Hunter should keep an eye on Merlin. But it worked both ways. He watched his father shut the bird in, then take a short cut across the garden, swinging his stick at the undergrowth. He'd put a braid in his hair and fastened it with a black-barred feather. As he passed beneath Merlin's window, he looked up and smiled. Merlin ducked, heart banging. But footsteps crunched away along the gravel path and when he dared look again his father had gone.

He let out the breath he'd been holding and hurried down to the hall. Faint bronze glimmers behind the coat hooks betrayed the locations of dying spells, but Merlin ignored these and went for the big one. As he'd hoped, Hawk had replaced the dead spell in the keyhole with a fresh live one. Shining in the gloom like an emerald star, its illusion reached all the way to the gates, making the Lodge appear uninhabited to human eyes. A little shiver ran down Merlin's back. Very carefully, he began to ease the spell free.

"What are you doing?" demanded a voice behind him.

The spell dropped to the mat. Merlin whirled, desperately trying to think of an excuse. As always on these occasions, his mind was a complete blank. "I—" He broke off, staring. He couldn't help it.

In her white dress, her silver hair shining in the shadows, Spider stood on the landing at the top of the first flight of stairs. She was wearing her glasses and looking at him in a very peculiar manner. Merlin's heart gave a little jump.

"I thought you were supposed to be getting my clothes?" she said, frowning at the mat.

Merlin came to with a start, retrieved the spell and hurriedly stuffed it under his jumper. His cheeks burned. "I... er... was just getting them," he said. "I thought you were still asleep." She *should* have been asleep. Even Claudia had slept for nearly two days after Hunter ate her familiar.

"I've had quite enough sleep, thank you very much! I'm cold and I want my clothes back. Your father said I could have them."

He noticed she was shivering. As she spoke, some of the haughtiness seemed to run out of her. She came down the rest of the stairs, still frowning. "What were you doing with that spell?"

Merlin almost told her. But she was part of the spellclave

now. One of the enemy. "Nothing," he mumbled, sidling past her. "Father put your clothes in the spare room. I'll get them. You should be resting, Spider."

To his surprise, she giggled, though it sounded a bit strained. "My name's not Spider, stupid. It's Natalie, Nat for short. And I'm getting out of here before those crazy parents of yours come back. If you had any sense in your skull, you'd come with me."

"Getting out?" Merlin repeated. "But, you can't! You're bonded to the spellclave for life. Anyway, Claudia's not my mother," he added, realizing what she must have thought. Prickles of memory threatened. He thrust them away before they brought tears.

Natalie sighed. "I'm not bonded to anything, silly. That spider wasn't my familiar."

"Wasn't your familiar? But Father said—"

"Your father told you it was, so you believed him? Grow up, Merlin! There's no such thing as real magic, everyone knows that. Nothing happened to me in the cellar, doesn't that prove it? I think your father's horrible, letting his goshawk eat people's pets. But that's what hawks do, they're meat eaters so it's natural for them. The hawk doesn't know any better."

Merlin stared at her in disbelief. He'd never forgive Hunter if he ate Redeye. Did that prove her spider hadn't been a familiar? Or that the bonding had worked so well she wasn't even aware of it?

"You fell off the stool," he pointed out. "Are you sure nothing happened? Don't you feel sick or dizzy or anything?"

"I was only pretending," she said, but she sounded less sure than before. Then she shook herself and her voice became firmer. "Where are my clothes? I'll get them myself if you're afraid of getting into trouble."

Merlin led the way, occasionally glancing back at the girl. She might sound scornful but she didn't look at all well. She was very pale and her hands trembled. She had to use the banister to pull herself up the stairs.

"Are you *sure* you're not bonded?" he asked suspiciously, opening the door of one of the second-floor bedrooms.

She sighed. "Of course I'm sure. Even if there was such a thing as real magic, I'd know something like that, wouldn't I? Turn around and don't peek."

Merlin turned his back and chewed his lip. "Not necessarily. Not until you defied Father and he wanted to punish you, you wouldn't."

Natalie dressed so quickly that before he knew it, she'd pushed past him, stumbled downstairs and was wrestling with the front door. Since the spellclave were all outside it was unbolted but still it didn't budge. "Father locked it before he replaced the illusion spell," he explained. He often wondered why Hawk bothered with keys, since the spells were designed to keep curious strangers from seeing the truth, but now he was glad of the delay. "You're serious about running away, aren't you?"

She turned, closed her eyes for a few seconds then opened them again. "Where's the key?"

Merlin hesitated. She certainly wasn't acting as if she were bonded but she could be testing him. "Father's got it." He considered her carefully. "I know where there's a spare, though. I'll unlock the door and show you the quickest way out of the wood, if you'll help me get Redeye out of the cellar." He held his breath.

Natalie stared at him. He couldn't read her expression but several different emotions crossed her face. Finally, she said, "All right," and looked at him expectantly.

He fingered the spell and licked his lips. "The cellar's locked too," he admitted. "But if there's another key anywhere, Father keeps it well hidden. He probably used an illusion spell on it."

"I haven't time to help you look for it, if that's what you mean. We'll just have to leave your mouse and come back for him later when we bring the police up here. He'll be safe enough. I doubt your father will do anything to him if you're not around to see."

Merlin turned queasy at the very thought. "No! You don't understand! I can't go without Redeye."

"Merlin!" She grabbed his jumper and shook hard, showing the same fierce strength as when she'd snatched the tray. He cringed, but she took a deep breath and continued more reasonably. "Look, I know you're fond of your mouse. I was fond enough of Itsy and he was just some spider I found in the bath. But you have to get things into perspective. If we don't get out of here soon, your father's going to come back and catch us both. Then we *will* be in trouble. Accept it, there's no way you're going to get a mouse out through a locked door."

Merlin shrivelled inside. "Don't. That's not fair. I know I'm hopeless at spell casting, but I thought you might help."

She let him go, scowling. "Not that again! I *told* you, I'm not a witch."

"And I told *you* we're not witches, we're—"

"Spellmages! So you keep saying."

They stared at each other, both of them trembling.

"Call us Casters," Merlin said with a sigh. "Everyone else does."

She didn't laugh but she looked less angry. Hesitantly, he brought out the spell he'd taken from the keyhole. Her gaze flickered to his hand. She said nothing.

"At least let me try?" he said. "I think I managed to transport your spider when you were touching the spell in the supermarket. While you were being... er... bonded, I managed to smuggle a spell into Redeye's bedding. That's how you do a transport, see? You put a spell at each end. I thought if there was one inside Redeye's cage and I got a powerful one this side of the door, then it might work – especially if you help me, like you did before. Father says it's not possible to transfer power like that unless you're a Spell Lord but I've been thinking about it and I'm sure something happened when we fell down together in the supermarket—"

"Just get on with it. What do I have to do?"

"Nothing. Er... that is... touch the spell, that's all."

Natalie grasped the spell firmly and raised her chin. Her eye held a challenge. "Go on then. But this time I'm watching you, great wizard Merlin. Don't try that firework trick again, all right?"

Merlin closed his eyes.

Draw the power up your arm. Feel it flow through your veins, feel its heat fill you...

In the early days, one of his father's favourite lessons had been to lock him in his room and make him practise transporting food. He used to say when Merlin was hungry enough he'd stop being so useless. Merlin had stayed hungry but he knew the theory off by heart.

Hearing Natalie's sharp intake of breath he opened his eyes and looked round eagerly. If wanting was enough he'd have transported the entire contents of the cellar into the passage: .generator, bench, stools, empty tanks, the lot. Not only did he want Redeye safe but almost as badly he wanted to show Natalie he *could* do it.

But there was no spellflash. The spell cooled and dimmed, and Natalie let go. She frowned at her fingers a moment, then shook her head.

"Satisfied now?" she said.

Merlin clutched the spell tighter, a chill breathing down his neck as he realized what must have happened. That dark smile. "He knew," he whispered. "Father must've seen the spell in Redeye's cage and taken it out. Oh, he's going to murder me!"

"All the more reason to get out of here then, isn't there? If you won't tell me where the key is, I'll climb out of a window." With a determined look on her pale face, Natalie opened the door to one of the downstairs rooms.

Merlin ran after her and caught hold of the back of her sweatshirt. She scowled at his hand. "The key's under the mat," he said, hopelessness closing about him like a cloud. "Take it and go. Turn right when you get over the gate, otherwise you'll end up at the archery range and someone will see you. I'll put Father off the scent for as long as I can. But I'm warning you now, if he tries to pull off one of Redeye's legs like he did to your spider, I'll tell him everything right away."

Natalie was already scrabbling under the mat. She found the key and flung the door wide. Sunlight lanced into the hall, bringing cold air and damp woodland smells. She raised her face to the sky and inhaled as if she were taking her first-ever breath. Then she turned and gave him a hesitant look. "Are you going to be all right?"

Tears filled Merlin's eyes. "Not really. Hunter will eat Redeye now."

He didn't think she'd heard. She was already running down the path. But after three strides she stopped, kicked at the gravel and came back. "What would make your father open the cellar door?"

Merlin tried to think. "I dunno. There's the generators. If they went wrong, he'd have to go down and fix 'em, I suppose. And there's the spells, of course. I think Father and Claudia are doing experiments on them, they've got 'em down that tunnel you saw."

"How about a fire?"

He blinked again. "Set fire to the Lodge, you mean?" It was a dreadful, wild idea. "But what if the spells catch? Spellfire's dangerous, you can't put it out till the spells die, and there's whole sacks of 'em down there. They'd burn the whole wood down!"

"We only need a small fire, just to make some smoke. Then when your father opens the cellar to rescue his spells, we sneak in, grab your mouse and run."

Merlin's heart did peculiar things. "Redeye might burn too."

"We'll get him out before then."

He cast a doubtful look upstairs. What if the fire spread to his room? Then he shook himself. He'd have to leave his computer behind anyway, and computers could be replaced. Unlike familiars. He shivered – half excitement, half terror. "I s'pose we could soak some of my old clothes in diesel oil," he said slowly. "There's a tank of it outside for the generators."

A strange gleam came to Natalie's eye. For a full minute she stood and stared at the cellar door, ripples shivering down her silver hair. When she finally spoke, her voice had a hard edge to it that hadn't been there before.

"Let's do it."

*

The fire took hold a lot faster than Natalie had anticipated. As the diesel-soaked rags smouldered, choking black smoke filled the passage. One hand over her nose, she retreated to the back of the understairs cupboard where she and Merlin had taken refuge. Smoke forced its way through the cracks around the door, making her eyes sting. She couldn't take a breath without coughing. The longer they waited, the more stupid the whole idea seemed.

She still didn't know what had made her turn back. She could be in the wood by now, running in the sunlight. Free. Instead, she was crouched in a tiny cupboard with a boy who thought he was a wizard, both of them in danger of being roasted alive. And all to rescue one small mouse.

Or maybe more than a mouse.

Either way, she hated to think what might happen if Merlin's father didn't see the smoke in time.

Merlin must have been thinking along the same lines, for he suddenly flung himself at the door and rattled the latch. "Redeye!" he spluttered. "He's burning!"

Natalie caught his jumper. "Wait," she whispered, though she wanted nothing more than to rush out herself. What was taking them so long?

Then the front door crashed open. The passage filled with yelling Casters falling over one another in their haste to reach the cellar. Still holding tightly to Merlin's jumper, Natalie put her eye to a crack in the door and peered through the smoke. Some of the spellclave had brought their bows, impressive modern ones, which they used to fling the burning rags out of the way. Ferret rushed in with a bucket of water and threw it at the cellar door. There was a loud hiss as it created yet more smoke.

Then Hawk – *Lord* Hawk – pushed his way through, his scarf wrapped around his mouth and nose, swinging his bird-headed stick. "Back, you fools!" he thundered. "Get back!"

Using the stick, he flicked aside a flaming pair of jeans as if they were an irritating fly. "Get the fire extinguishers!" he ordered as he unlocked the cellar. "Get blankets from the beds! The Raven's down there and so are our spells! Quickly!" Without waiting to see if they obeyed, he took a running leap through the smoke at the cellar door and disappeared. The spellclave scattered, some pounding upstairs, others heading for the kitchen.

"Now!" Natalie hissed. She kicked open the cupboard door and tugged Merlin out. The cellar steps were clogged with smoke. Flames licked at the light cord but with the generators off it wouldn't be much use anyway. Thick black silence lurked below. She listened carefully... Lord Hawk must have gone into the tunnel. "Quick," she whispered. "Get your mouse before someone comes back."

Merlin crouched on the top step, trembling. "I can't. It's dark."

Natalie resisted an urge to thump him. Was this what Jo felt like when *she* refused to go along with her harebrained schemes? "Of course it's dark!" she said. "Even your father's not crazy enough to use the generators in a fire. You know where Redeye is, don't you?" But she could have kicked herself. She should have thought to ask Merlin if he had a torch.

The boy hugged himself. "Please Natalie," he said in a tiny voice. "Get him for me?"

The sensible thing would be to leave him and run while the coast was still clear. But he looked so pathetic and scared. Before she knew it, she'd pulled her outer sweatshirt up over her mouth and was groping her way down the steps. It wasn't as dark as she'd thought. Flickers of gold from the fire in the passage picked out the ghostly shapes of the nearest arches, and an eerie purple glow leaked from the tunnel at the back. Eyes smarting, Natalie paused to get her bearings. This was

where she'd sat on the stool... That was where Claudia had
gone to fetch Itsy... The spellclave had appeared just here, a lot
further from the tunnel than she'd thought – so how had they
done it? The mouse's terrified squeaks reminded her what
she'd come for. She made her way towards the sound, grabbed
the cage and fled back up the steps.

Not a moment too soon. A scrape came from the tunnel
behind her and a sudden draught blew her hair across her face.
"Who's there?" came a furious shout. "Is that you, boy? Just
wait till I get my hands on you!"

The purple light brightened, casting Natalie's shadow before
her and reflecting in the mouse's frightened eyes. She took the
steps two at a time, her heart in her mouth. Redeye squeaked
as he tumbled from side to side in his cage.

Merlin was still crouched at the top, peering into the smoke.
When Natalie appeared, he jumped back with a little scream,
then rushed forward again, arms joyfully outstretched.
"Redeye—" He froze. All the colour drained from his face as he
stared at something behind her.

Natalie's heart missed a beat as Lord Hawk's stick encircled
her ankle. She kicked frantically but, with her hands full,
couldn't keep her balance. Desperate, she threw the cage at
Merlin. "Run!" she shouted, dropping to all fours.

He caught the cage but didn't seem to know what to do
next. For a full ten seconds he just stood there, fumbling under
his awful jumper.

"Get out of here, you little idiot!" Natalie hissed.

Merlin dropped a glimmering green star near her hand.
"Cast it," he mouthed. Then, at last, he turned and ran.

There was no time to think. She couldn't get free of the stick
and Lord Hawk's hand was tightening on her other ankle,
pulling her back. She seized the spell and threw it blindly over
her shoulder. As she did so, she yelled the first word that came
to mind. "Abracadabra!"

Her captor let go.

Natalie didn't wait around to see if anything had happened.

She scrambled up the rest of the steps, squirmed her way through the people fighting the fire and ducked out of the open door before they had time to react. Merlin was already halfway across the garden, Redeye's cage clasped tightly to his chest.

"Stop them, you fools!" roared Lord Hawk, crashing out of the cellar. He was dusting himself off as if something had fallen on him.

His spellclave, hampered by fire extinguishers and half blinded by smoke, rushed to the door in a mass, tripping one another up in their desperation to obey. By the time they sorted themselves out and gave chase, Natalie and Merlin had reached the gates.

Breath rasping, Natalie looked back. The fire seemed to be under control now, having chewed the wooden panels of the passage but not a lot more. Foam from the extinguishers frothed out of the door and around the ankles of Lord Hawk who stood tall on the step, his eyes brighter than the autumn sun. He halted the pursuers with a raised hand and pointed his stick at Natalie. His voice crept over her skin like ice. "By the ancient bond of the spellclave, I command you, Spider. Stop, or be turned to stone!"

Natalie's stomach did a peculiar dance. With an effort, she tore her gaze from the Lodge. She'd forgotten her own rule. *Don't look back. Whatever happens, don't look back.*

The gates were chained shut but the ornate ironwork provided plenty of footholds and Merlin had already started to climb. He was having trouble with Redeye's cage, though. As he let go of the gate to get a firmer grip on it, his foot slipped and he fell flat on his back at Natalie's feet.

"Are you stupid or something?" she yelled at him. "Let Redeye out. He'll be safe, plenty of places for a mouse to hide out here."

Merlin looked doubtful but fumbled with the cage fastening. To Natalie's surprise, the mouse shot straight under the gate and streaked into the trees. The boy went up and over much

faster than before. Natalie scrambled after him, her feet slipping on the wet iron. At the top, she paused to catch her breath
and risked another glance back.

None of the spellclave were giving chase. Lord Hawk
remained standing on the step, the fire-draught fluttering the
feather in his hair, staring at her and shaking his head.
"Impossible," he said, his voice faint in the distance. "I bonded
you."

Claudia joined him, her blonde hair in disarray, a smudge of
soot on one pale cheek. As she watched the escape, her lips
curved into the faintest of smiles.

9

K'TANAQUI

Thursday morning, October 29

During those first desperate minutes of their flight from the Lodge there wasn't time to think, let alone worry about which way they were going. Natalie ran faster than she'd ever run in her life, stumbling over tree roots and into muddy ditches, convinced that at any moment Lord Hawk's horrible stick would encircle her neck. Wet leaves slapped her face, twigs caught at her hair, dappled sunlight flashed overhead, leaves spiralled down, the damp fungus smells made her want to sneeze. But there were no crashing footsteps behind, no furious shouts, and no way anyone would be able to drive a vehicle between these closely growing tree trunks.

She stopped to catch her breath and pressed a hand to the stitch in her side. Merlin, who she'd soon passed and left behind, caught up and stopped too. His face was as red as his hair and he was gasping for breath.

"Why aren't they chasing us?" Natalie panted.

The boy looked nervously over his shoulder. "Dunno, but—"

Even as he spoke, the birds stopped singing and an eerie hush fell. The back of Natalie's neck prickled as the silence was broken by a series of rapid flaps. She twisted round, suddenly realizing why the spellclave didn't need to give chase on foot. Heading straight for them, huge wings spread in a deadly glide, came the goshawk, Hunter.

"Run!" Merlin screamed, and shot into the trees. Natalie plunged after him, caught her foot in a bramble and sprawled face-first in fallen leaves. There was a rushing sound as the hawk passed overhead so close she felt the wind of its feathers. She caught a glimpse of its pale belly, of its black-barred wings blotting out the sun. Then it was gone after Merlin, wing tips clipping the close-growing tree trunks.

Still shaking, Natalie scrambled to her feet and brushed herself off. Her heart was pounding, her palms clammy. Hawks didn't hunt people, did they? At least, normal hawks didn't.

What if it were all true? In the wake of the goshawk's flight, an ominous silence reigned. No birds sang, nothing moved in the undergrowth. Even the breeze had stilled. Uneasiness whispered over Natalie's skin. What kind of revenge would a wizard take on someone who'd set fire to his house? She broke into a jog, worried about Merlin, then ducked in alarm as the huge bird flapped out of the branches overhead and glided back the way it had come, making her heart start thumping all over again.

Merlin stood motionless under the oak Hunter had just vacated, staring into the bronze-dark shadows beyond. The hawk must have missed him, she thought in relief.

"What's wrong?" She couldn't see what he was looking at. She gave her glasses a quick wipe, then had a horrible thought and jammed them back on. "Redeye?"

"Shh!" Merlin whispered. "Stand very still. It might go away."

"It's already gone. Didn't you see? It was in that tree—"

"Not the hawk. The *hound*."

As he spoke, a huge silver dog glimmered out of the shadows and padded towards them. Its coat seemed to catch every scrap of light. Natalie's breath caught in her throat. She'd never seen such a beautiful animal in all her life, except— She frowned. Where *had* she seen a dog like this before? Almost a wolf. A white wolf.

Only when the dog came closer did she see that its long curly fur was rather moth-eaten and yellowed at the ends. One ear hung like a torn handkerchief across bright amber eyes. Merlin made a choked sound and ducked behind the nearest tree. The dog bared its chipped canines at the boy, flipped its ear out of its eyes and growled softly.

"Don't make any sudden moves," Merlin whispered. "That's a magehound. Only Spell Lords who serve on a soultree Council are allowed to have them." He shivered and added, "Even Father's scared of magehounds. I wonder what it's doing out of Earthaven?"

Natalie had a sudden flashback of Bilbo attacking her kidnappers in the car park, Claudia ducking in fear... She shook the memory away before it reached the needle part and took a step forward, one hand lowered so the hound could catch her scent. "My mother used to have a dog like this," she said, captivated by its amber eyes that seemed to stare right into her soul. "I don't really remember him but I've got a photo on my bedside table. Here, boy, come to Natalie."

"What are you *doing*?" Merlin squeaked, clutching at her sweatshirt. "Didn't you hear me? That's a Spell Lord's familiar. And believe me, you don't want to annoy him. Or her."

She let the words wash over her. She couldn't seem to stop Merlin talking about spells but she didn't have to listen. The hound sniffed at her hand, gave her another disturbing amber stare, then flipped its ear again and padded off into the trees, bushy tail waving like a silver flag. Natalie's heart gave a peculiar tug. She grabbed Merlin's hand. "C'mon! Quickly!"

The boy dug in his heels. "Where are you going?"

"He wants us to follow him, isn't it obvious?"

"No!" Merlin's eyes widened. "Follow a magehound? Are you mad?"

Natalie had to laugh. Meeting the dog had banished what remained of her fear. She was out of the Lodge, the goshawk had gone, and it was a glorious autumn day. The hound wasn't wearing a collar but he was obviously tame. All they had to do was find his owner and she could be sleeping in her own bed tonight.

She let go of the boy and gave him a tolerant smile. "You're the one who's mad, going on about spell-this and spell-that all the time. You can stop now. You're not with your father any more and, unless that thing wriggling under your jumper is a very big flea, you've got your mouse safe. So you don't have to keep trying to scare me, all right? I was scared enough as it was, back there in the cellar."

"I'm not trying to scare you," Merlin said quietly, still eyeing the dog as if it might eat him at any moment. "I'm telling you the truth. It belongs to a Spell Lord of Earthaven."

She frowned at him. "You're afraid of dogs, is that it? Well, you don't have to be afraid of this one. He's friendly. He didn't bite me, did he?"

It was Merlin's turn to frown. "No... though I don't know why not. Magehounds hate Casters."

"Maybe this proves I'm not one of you, then." She couldn't resist the gibe.

Merlin went into a sulk. "Go on, then," he muttered. "Follow it. You'll find out soon enough. I'm staying here."

Though her stomach churned uneasily, Natalie set her jaw. "Don't be so stupid! Do you *want* your father to catch you?"

"Better than being caught by a member of a soultree Council."

The hound had returned when they didn't immediately follow. Now it growled, gently took Natalie's sleeve between its teeth and pulled. The meaning was obvious – *leave him*. It was very tempting. She couldn't help remembering how Merlin had tripped her up in the car park and let her eat all those sleeping pills without saying a word. Then she thought of Lord Hawk's stick crashing across those small shoulders and sighed.

"I'm not going without you," she said firmly. "If you won't come with me, we'll wait here until your father finds us. Shouldn't be too long if that hawk really is his familiar. Then we'll see if Hunter can swallow a mouse as easily as a spider."

Cruel, maybe, but it worked. With a fearful glance at the hound, Merlin came.

*

The silver hound led them deeper into the wood, occasionally looking over its shoulder to check they were following. Merlin grew more and more quiet as they walked. Natalie opened her mouth a couple of times to reassure him but couldn't think of anything to say. What *did* you say to someone who'd just run away from home? Even during the worst times when her dad was sobbing in the garage and Tim was being deliberately nasty, she'd never considered leaving.

"You can have my room when we get back," she said in an attempt to cheer him up. "I'll sleep on the sofa. It's quite comfortable."

Merlin gave her a startled look. But before he could say anything, the hound's head shot up. It sniffed the air, then cleared a holly bush in a single bound and started barking joyfully.

"C'mon!" Natalie said, breaking into a run. "We'll be home for lunch."

Tail waving, tongue lolling, the hound waited for them in a clearing where a carpet of red-gold leaves reflected the sun like a burnished pool. The dog looked pleased with itself. But there was no sign of a human being, only a huge, twisted mossy stone with shadows writhing around it. The air was strangely still.

Natalie stopped dead, uneasy prickles working their way all over her skin. "What's *that*?"

"The Thrallstone," Merlin whispered, hugging himself under the trees. "I knew it'd bring us here."

Natalie ventured closer. She noticed the leaves had been churned up by large wheels. Mud glistened in the tracks, and in the mud were footprints. Hundreds of them. She frowned.

Then she remembered. *"Innocent enough to crawl through the Thrallstone,"* she murmured, and turned cold all over.

Merlin came out of his paralysis and stared at her. "Where did you hear that?"

"It was something your father said to me in the car park. I didn't understand what he meant. But no one's going to be crawling through that in a hurry!" Forcing herself through the strangeness, she walked up to the stone and giggled. It did have a hole in it but only a tiny one about the size of her little finger. She patted the hound who was watching her again with those amber eyes. Then she stood on tiptoe and set her eye to the hole.

"No!" Merlin squeaked. "Don't!"

The stone was surprisingly cold. As Natalie touched it, her hands sank into the moss. She snatched them back with a cry of surprise. Then she forgot the strange feel of the stone, Merlin's insistence that there were such things as real spells, and even her own unease that there might be. For, lying motionless in the grass on the other side of the Thrallstone was a boy in a leather jacket, his head freshly shaven.

"Tim! It's my stepbrother," she said, relief tumbling through her. "He must've come to find me. Looks like he fell asleep!" She sprang eagerly around the stone – and stopped in confusion. She wiped her glasses and took a more careful look.

Leaves, mud, trees, dappled sunlight. No Tim!

She stepped back and peered through the hole again. Tim, lying on the ground with his head wrapped in green shadows.

She stared again at the trees on the far side, then turned to Merlin. "Is this another of your silly tricks?" she whispered. "Because if it is, it's not funny."

Merlin crept closer, one hand cupping his mouse, nervously eyeing the Thrallstone. "I kept tryin' to tell you but you wouldn't listen. It's a gateway. That's Earthaven you can see through the hole." He tried to peer through from where he was standing. "I've never seen it before, though when I was little Father kept threatening to bring me here to make me crawl through it. That's what it means, see? *Innocent enough.* Small children and animals are supposed to fit."

Natalie giggled, though part of her felt like screaming, or weeping hysterically, or running as far from this place as possible. "Even your mouse wouldn't fit through there!" she said, sticking a finger into the hole to demonstrate.

Merlin sucked in his breath. Everything up to Natalie's wrists went ice-cold as the stone *shimmered,* suddenly no more solid than air. She lost her balance and stumbled forwards. There was a blinding green light, and her ears popped. She shook her head, blinked to clear her vision, and found herself staring at a tall man with the longest white hair she'd ever seen. He had his back turned and was talking to a group of men in cloaks, knives glittering in their belts. At her feet, Tim twisted and moaned as if he were having a nightmare. What she'd thought were shadows, she now saw to be a net of green and gold creepers twisting out of the ground to wrap themselves tightly around his head.

She couldn't think where the men had come from but they obviously had something to do with whatever was hurting Tim. She hurried up to the white-haired one and grabbed his sleeve. "What are you doing to my stepbrother?" she demanded, trying to sound braver than she felt. "Let him go!"

The white-haired man whirled and stared at her in pure astonishment. Natalie had an impression of eyes full of green light set in a stern face framed by thorns. More vines and creepers curled out of a glittering haze far above and stroked his shoulders. The cloaked men were pointing to the Thrallstone, whispering excitedly, but the man she'd challenged grabbed her wrist and snapped, "How did you get through the gate? I don't recall leaving it open."

His nails dug into her skin, bringing tears which she blinked away. "Let me go," she whispered. "Or I'll—"

She'd been going to say scream, until she realized the uselessness of it. She was in a different world. Through the gate. Merlin had been telling the truth, after all. Her knees turned weak. She closed her eyes in terror.

A sudden snarl made her open them again in time to see the old hound leap through the hole in the stone and fling itself at a second dog she hadn't noticed amidst all the shadows. Silver fur flew as the two animals engaged in a furious battle.

The white-haired man's eyes widened. "You!" he whispered, hastily dropping her wrist. "For Oq's sake!" he shouted to the dogs. "K'veriyan! K'tanaqui! Stop that at once!"

They carried on fighting.

He glared at Natalie. "Call him off, you crazy girl! Don't you know who I am? I'm Lord Pveriyan, First Member of the Council of Oq. I was the one who sent K'tanaqui to look for you, though I have to admit I didn't anticipate quite such a fierce meeting. Still, I suppose I should have expected it of Atanaqui's daughter."

As soon as Natalie was free, the two hounds separated and eyed each other, growling softly. She focused on the only thing that made any sense.

"What's wrong with Tim?" She knelt beside her stepbrother's prone body and tried to clear the creepers away but they seemed to have penetrated Tim's hairless scalp and wriggled beneath it. Her stomach turned queasy. She stopped pulling, suddenly glad he was unconscious.

Lord Pveriyan sighed. "Don't meddle. His memories of us must be wiped clean, otherwise we'll have no choice but to seek him outside Earthaven when the Boundary opens, which will be painful for him and a waste of Oq's power when we need it most."

Natalie frowned. His words were strange, yet it was almost as if she knew what he was talking about, as if she'd learnt all this once but had forgotten it. She stared hard at the trees. They were similar to the ones in Unicorn Wood, yet subtly different as if they'd all been washed or someone had painted them with brighter colours. Beyond the curling vines, invisible in the distant haze, she sensed something huge and ancient and powerful. As she gazed around, a squirrel cracked a nut somewhere above them – or maybe it wasn't a squirrel? She looked up uneasily just as one of the hanging creepers descended with a soft rustle and began to explore Tim's scalp.

Suddenly, it was all too much. Something snapped inside her. "Let him *go,* you stupid tree!" she yelled, grabbing the thing and pulling as hard as she could.

There was a crackle, a whiff of sugar, and all the creepers retreated, the one in her hand slipping through her fingers and recoiling into the haze, the others disappearing into the earth. She rocked back on her heels in surprise and relief. Tim still showed no sign of coming round but his breathing steadied.

"Now you've done it," Lord Pveriyan said. "Hardly in Earthaven two seconds and already you've challenged a member of the Council and overridden my order. Now I suppose I've got to reconnect him. This is so tiresome. Stand back."

Natalie stiffened. But before Lord Pveriyan could once more entwine Tim's head in creepers, there was a green flare from the Thrallstone. With a little shriek, Merlin came stumbling through the hole, fell to his hands and knees and began patting at the grass.

"Redeye!" he called, a desperate edge to his voice. "Redeye! Come back here."

Lord Pveriyan's head whipped round. He crossed the distance to the stone in two swift strides, gripped Merlin's shoulder and hissed, "*Caster.*"

Merlin scrambled to his feet. "No I'm not, Lord! I'm hopeless at casting, really I am. We haven't come to steal your spells, I promise. We were running away from Father's hawk and we took a wrong turn, that's all. We'll go back now—"

"I think not," said the Spell Lord. "In fact, I think you'd both better come with me to see the Council. We've been waiting to meet Atanaqui's daughter for quite a while now. As for you, young Caster, you can come and explain how it is you happen to be here with her. The last we heard, she'd been kidnapped."

Merlin made a break for the stone but Lord Pveriyan was faster. He motioned to the cloaked men and one of them gripped Merlin's elbow. The Spell Lord fired questions at the boy, which Merlin replied to in whispers. Natalie wanted to help him but a fit of shivers had come over her.

With a trembling hand, she touched the bloody hole in Tim's ear. He'd lost his little skull earring. "Tim," she whispered. "Wake up. Please wake up!"

"But I don't know anything!" Merlin protested over by the Thrallstone, where he was being shaken vigorously by the cloaked man. "Father never trusted me."

"I think we both know that's a lie."

"I don't want to go with you!"

"I'm not giving you a choice. Where's your familiar?"

Merlin paled. "Think I'd tell you?" he whispered, but his eyes slid sideways.

The Spell Lord smiled and dived into a pile of leaves between two tree roots. He emerged with the struggling mouse. Merlin moaned.

"I'll ask you again," snapped Lord Pveriyan. "What's your father planning to do when he gets across the Boundary?"

"I don't know!" Merlin said. "Really I don't! All I know is they've got bows and arrows and a sack of live spells. Maybe he's going to use 'em to transport?"

Lord Pveriyan drew a sharp breath and his hound growled. "He *transports*?"

"Yes, I thought you knew—"

"This is more serious than we thought! A transport spell could get them to the Heart of Oq and back again before the Boundary closes. We have to call the Council! Here, someone take care of this mouse. Put the human boy through the gate and leave him in the clearing. I can't waste any more time on him. The rest of you, take Atanaqui's daughter and the Caster to the Root System. Quickly! I'll be along as soon as I've closed up here."

"But what if he's not fully cleansed, Lord?" one of the men ventured. "I thought Oq was having trouble?"

In answer, Lord Pveriyan's hound snarled at the men until

they hurried to obey. Natalie tried to protest as they lifted Tim but a great wave of strangeness was rushing towards her and she couldn't even get off her knees.

It's all true, she thought. I should be screaming, or weeping hysterically, or—

Before the wave could break, the old hound padded up, thrust his muzzle into her hand and flipped his tattered ear. She put her arms around his neck and clung to him gratefully but he wouldn't let her bury her face into his sweet-smelling fur. As he gazed at her with those beautiful amber eyes, a barrier shattered inside her head and words formed clear as crystals.

Of courrrse it's trrrue. Pup listen to K'tanaqui now. Pup got a LOT to learrrn.

10
SOULTREE

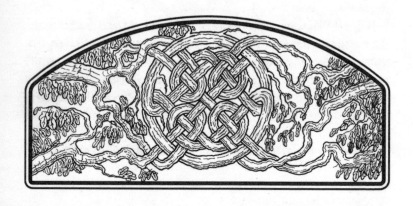

Thursday afternoon, October 29

The cloaked men took Merlin and Natalie underground into a system of bewildering tunnels where their feet made no sound on the mossy floor. A faint green glow came from the walls, adding to the eeriness of the place. No one spoke. Staring straight ahead, Natalie walked with one hand twisted in the old magehound's ruff. She looked pale and frightened. Merlin supposed Earthaven must be quite a shock to her after her haughty dismissal of spells. In other circumstances he might have enjoyed watching her squirm as she was forced to admit everything he'd been telling her was true. But he was having problems of his own.

He'd never really believed his father's scare stories – that if you lived too long outside the Boundary you lost the ability to see in Earthaven, except through the eyes of your familiar. But now, whenever someone closed their hand about Redeye, Merlin's view of Earthaven was reduced to shadowy silhouettes and he halted, shivering, until the men realized their mistake and let his mouse peep out again. Even this wasn't perfect.

The picture he received through his familiar's eyes was like a badly flickering monitor stuck on the colour green, and walking ten paces behind his "eyes" made him feel queasy. Added to this, being able to understand his mouse wasn't quite as wonderful as he'd imagined it would be.

Well, what do you expect? Redeye said, picking up his thought. *Some rescue this is! First you put a live spell in my bed just where I'd blister my tail on it. After that you half suffocate me with smoke, bruise me in places I'd rather not talk about, dangle me like some kind of sacrifice under the talons of that arrogant hawk, then for good measure drop me head first through a gateway into enemy territory. And, as if that wasn't enough, you manage to get us both arrested as spies. I think I preferred it in the cellar. At least my cage didn't jerk about down there. Spellclaves! Can't you tell this bully to slow down? If he doesn't stop swinging me around soon, I'm going to throw up all over his fine cloak.*

"No!" Merlin squeaked. "Don't do that! He'll kill us."

One of the men had plaited some vines to make a little carry-cage for Redeye, which he was swinging merrily as he strode deeper into the tunnels. Merlin caught up with him and tweaked his cloak. "Please sir, can you carry my mouse more carefully?"

The man laughed. "The Caster wants us to be careful with his familiar. Shall we show him how we usually treat 'em?" He fingered his knife.

Merlin cringed, and Natalie looked round with a frown. She still seemed rather pale but she whispered something to the old magehound. The hound stepped in front of Merlin's tormentor, flipped its ear and growled.

The man took a hasty step backwards and put his knife away. "Don't worry," he told Natalie. "We've orders to look after your little friend and his mouse. Oq likes her Casters undamaged."

They seemed to find this very funny. But when they started off again, the one carrying the cage tucked it under his arm.

"Better?" Merlin whispered.

Phaw! was Redeye's comment. *His armpit smells worse than yours, and you're the scruffiest nestling I've ever seen. I can't understand why that girl didn't leave you behind.*

"I wish she had," Merlin muttered, beginning to regret his impulsive flight from the Lodge. But how was he to know they'd arrive at the Thrallstone just as a Spell Lord was about to open it? And when Natalie had gone blundering through, what was he supposed to do?

You are stupid, aren't you? said Redeye.

"That's not fair. I—"

Before he could defend himself, they rounded a bend in the tunnel and emerged in a large, glowing cavern where several tunnels converged. As Merlin stood and gaped, a faint whistling came from one of the shadowy openings on the far side. Their escort smiled knowingly as a sudden draught whipped Natalie's long hair around her face and blew through the holes in Merlin's jumper, raising goosebumps across his back. In the wake of the warm wind, three shining bubbles the size of small cars whooshed out of the tunnel and stopped in the centre of the cavern, floating a hand's breadth above the floor. A sweet smell lingered in the air, making him think of candyfloss.

This is no time to be thinking of your stomach, Redeye said. *The Spell Lord comes.*

Immediately, Merlin's appetite deserted him. Lord Pveriyan strode into the cavern and crossed to the first bubble. When he touched it, the side peeled open with a sound like plastic tearing. He gave Natalie a mock bow and pointed. The old magehound jumped inside, and after an apprehensive glance back the way they'd come, Natalie followed. The bubble sealed itself. There was a *whoosh*. Then it was gone.

This all happened so fast, Merlin didn't have time to think, let alone act. "Natalie!" He rushed forward, heart banging, and rounded on the Spell Lord. "What have you done with her?"

Lord Pveriyan smiled. "You're worrying about the wrong person, Caster. Get in." He opened the second bubble.

Merlin shuddered. "Not without Redeye," he whispered.

"Do you really think I'm going to let you travel with your familiar? Oq only knows what mischief you two would get up to! In, I said." Merlin shook his head, but two of the cloaked men picked him up by his elbows and thrust him inside. "Hold tight!" Lord Pveriyan called with a chuckle.

There was no time to hold anything. He felt the bubble lift slightly. Then he was hurtling into the tunnel after Natalie, spinning helplessly, rolling forwards, then sideways, then backwards, then head over heels. By the time the bubble floated to a halt and unsealed itself in another cavern far vaster than the one they'd just left, he felt bruised all over. He crawled out, groaning.

Now you know what I feel like, said Redeye, who'd travelled in the third bubble with Lord Pveriyan and his magehound. *Oq's playing with you. Organazoomers aren't normally so uncomfortable.*

"Organa-whats?" Merlin said, forgetting his bruises as he gaped at the sheer size of the cavern. Like shooting stars, more of the shining bubbles whizzed overhead and vanished into the glittering haze.

I wish you'd wash your mind-ears out! Organazoomers. They're how you travel inside a soultree. Don't you know anything?

"We're inside a *soultree*?" Merlin whispered, feeling a bit sick. "I didn't know they were so big." He looked anxiously at Natalie who was clinging to the magehound as if it were the only solid thing in the world.

Lord Pveriyan strode across and nudged him with a toe. "On your feet, Caster. You'll have plenty of time to talk to your mouse when we're up in the trunk."

"Why can't I have Redeye back now?" Merlin asked, scrambling up before the Spell Lord could kick him again. "I'll walk quicker if I can see where I'm going."

The green eyes clouded. "You'll walk as fast as I tell you to."

Merlin's shoulders slumped. But to his surprise, Natalie gave a huge shudder, took a firmer grip on the magehound's ruff and said, "You're no better than his father! That's exactly what he did – took away his familiar. It's cruel."

Merlin stared at her. Did she really understand?

Of course she understands! Redeye said. *She's got a familiar of her own now, hasn't she?*

"But her spider—"

His mouse sighed. *Use my eyes! Look!* Merlin received a clear view of the two magehounds growling at each other again. Suddenly, a lot of things made sense.

"I'm so stupid," he groaned.

You can say that again, said Redeye. *Good job you've got someone who's willing to stand up for you, because you're pretty pathetic about doing it for yourself.*

"He won't do anything if you give him his mouse," Natalie was saying. "It's true what he told you. He can't cast spells. I know, I've seen him try." Merlin might once have protested about that. Now, he kept his mouth shut, grateful she thought he was so useless.

Lord Pveriyan still looked doubtful. But after a moment he sighed and tossed the little carry-cage at Merlin. "I suppose you can't get up to much in the trunk. But the moment you step out of line, young Caster, I'll hang your familiar by his tail from Oq's topmost branches," he warned. "Understand?"

Merlin caught the cage with a sob of relief and tore at the vines. Leaves scattered as he smothered Redeye in kisses, drawing a *Yuk!* from his mouse. Yet his familiar didn't struggle too hard.

"What's this place called?" he whispered, letting Redeye climb on his shoulder where the mouse could peer beneath his ear.

It was Lord Pveriyan who answered. "This is the Central Root Cavern of the soultree Oq," he announced with pride, his voice echoing. "The Council meets in the upper branches at midnight. That just leaves you two time to get cleaned up." He wrinkled his nose pointedly at Merlin.

*

The afternoon passed in a blur. At first, Natalie had difficulty believing they were inside an enormous, intelligent tree called Oq, whose hollow branches and roots formed a labyrinth of passages and tunnels connecting the deepest organazoomer terminals to the highest leafy chambers filled with sunlight and sweet Earthaven air. But by the time they reached a living chamber in the lower branches where rainwater had collected to form an enchanted pool, she'd seen so many strange sights and been told so many strange things by K'tanaqui, she'd hardly have been surprised if the tree had uprooted itself and walked across the clouds. It was as if her store of fear and wonder had been used up, and there was nothing left to be frightened of or amazed by.

Their guide during this time was a young woman who wore orange flowers and berries in her hair. By the green light in her eyes, Natalie guessed she was a Spell Lord even before K'tanaqui informed her of the fact. Her name was Lady Thaypari, and the first thing she said to them was, "Don't worry, we're not all as grumpy as old Pveriyan. You caught him at a bad time, I'm afraid. He's not used to people standing up to him, especially not people a hundredth of his age!" Then she laughed, a warm earthy sound that immediately put Natalie at ease. Even Merlin seemed to relax a bit and his mouse, which had fled under his jumper at the sight of her, wriggled out again to sit beneath his ear.

Lady Thaypari dumped an armful of moss-green clothing beside the pool and smiled at them. "Here's towels and clean clothes," she said. "They belonged to some of the Herder children, so they should fit you all right. Little devils, they're always visiting Oq for a swim and leaving stuff behind, so they won't miss them. When you're done, just ask K'tanaqui to give K'aypari a call and I'll come and dress your hair. Got to look your best when you appear before the Council. Enjoy your swim!"

Finally, they were alone.

Natalie felt her shoulders relax. With a sigh she kicked off her shoes, sat on the edge and dangled her feet in the water. While she and Merlin had been touring the tree, it had grown dark outside. Moonlight shone through Oq's interlaced branches, making silver-green reflections in the pool. The water was pleasantly warm, sliding around her ankles like Earthaven was sliding around her thoughts. She closed her eyes. Then K'tanaqui jumped in, drenching her and drawing a little scream from Merlin.

She shook herself and looked round. "C'mon, silly. It's only water."

"It's magic," Merlin whispered, retreating even further.

Natalie wanted to laugh, only she didn't have the energy. "You're the one who kept going on about spells. I believe you now." She looked fondly at K'tanaqui, doggy-paddling under some vines at the far side of the pool.

Pups swim now, said the magehound in the special place in her head.

She smiled. "In a minute, maybe. That Spell Lady didn't leave us any bathing costumes."

Puzzled amber eyes blinked at her. *Costumes would only get wet.*

She giggled, then became aware of Merlin watching her. He still looked frightened. Was he worried about meeting Lord Pveriyan again? "I won't let the Council hurt you," she promised. "When they hear the truth about your father and everything, they'll understand."

Merlin hugged his mouse. "They hate me," he whispered. "And the tree hates me, too, I can feel it. That old Lord's got it in for me, I know he has. He's only waiting for an excuse."

"He gave you back your mouse, didn't he?"

"He wouldn't have if you hadn't been there."

"Well I am here, aren't I? So cheer up! We'll have a nice swim and maybe something to eat, then we'll talk to this Council of theirs. They'll help us, don't worry. Then they'll let us go home." As soon as the words were out, she mentally kicked herself and added quickly, "You can come home with me, you'll be safe there."

Merlin shook his head, ripples of moonlight playing across his face. "I'll never be safe from Father. He'll be furious I helped you get away. He'll come after me, and then he— he'll—" He choked and clutched his mouse.

Mouse-pup sad, K'tanaqui reported. *Lost motherrr too.*

Natalie frowned, remembering what Merlin had said about Claudia not being his mother. "What happened to your mother, Merlin?" she asked gently.

He came forward a few steps, careful not to get too close to the edge, and stared across the pool. "It was Father's fault. He only meant it as a punishment but something went wrong. She tried to take me away from him, see? I don't really remember that part; I was just a baby. But I know what happened after, all right. She had a sweet little canary for a familiar. It used to sing all the time. Father clipped off one of its toes, just to hurt my mother's foot a bit to teach her a lesson for running off. But the canary died of shock."

His voice broke. Natalie stared at him, wondering if she'd heard right.

He sniffed and went on. "Afterwards, she took a train to the coast and walked off a high cliff. They found her body on the rocks a week later. Father said if I told a soul what had happened, or disobeyed him even a little bit, he'd punish me the same way by hurting Redeye. Only he'd keep me locked in the cellar afterwards so I couldn't escape like she did. That's why I tripped you up in the car park and did all those other things. I *had* to." He dragged his sleeve across his nose.

Natalie sat very still. K'tanaqui jumped out of the pool, shook the water from his coat and laid his head on her shoulder. He whined in sympathy.

"That's awful," she said. "Even worse than what happened to mine. The police said my mother's death was an accident, that she fell in the river because she was blind. Dad told me K'tanaqui had drowned too but there was a flood so they didn't find the dog's body. I believed him." She fondled the magehound's tattered ear. "If only I'd known the truth!"

"Your mother was a Spell Lord, wasn't she? Father said something about her death when we got back to the Lodge with your spider, but I had no idea who she was then."

"The Lady Atanaqui," Natalie said with a surge of pride. "And now I think I know why she died. It was the first day of November when she drowned. The night before, the Boundary would have been open and she'd have been able to see. I think she saw something that night, Merlin! K'tanaqui says they were on their way to Earthaven when it happened but some men came out of nowhere and pushed her into the river. He jumped in and tried to save her but she sent him back to Earthaven to warn the Council. He doesn't know what was so important. I get these flashes of a black bird flying... I thought it was your father's hawk at first, except Hunter's not black all over." She frowned. Along with everything else the magehound had told her since he first spoke to her at the Thrallstone, the truth about her mother's death was almost too much to handle. She needed more time to sort it all out.

Merlin, however, was staring at her. "A raven," he whispered.

"What?"

"When we started the fire in the Lodge, Father said something about a raven in the cellar, didn't he?"

"I'd forgotten that!" She closed her eyes, trying to recall the image K'tanaqui had shown her. "Could it be someone's familiar?"

Merlin shook his head. "No. Hunter ate them all."

"Maybe the Council will know."

The boy crept closer. Hesitantly, he touched her arm. "I'm sorry about your mother."

"And I'm sorry about yours."

There was an embarrassed silence. Then K'tanaqui pushed his wet body between them and flipped his ear. *Pups swim now! K'ayparrri says betterrr hurrry, Council not like to be kept waiting.*

Natalie passed on this message with a smile. She stripped off her two sweatshirts and her jeans and eased herself into the water, careful not to splash her glasses. It was wonderfully warm. She rolled on to her back and kicked lazily. There was a loud splash as the old magehound joined her. She laughed and grabbed his ruff, letting him pull her across the pool beneath the hanging vines at the far side. There seemed to be some kind of fruit over there, like large golden pears hanging temptingly just above the water. "Are they poisonous, K'tanaqui?" she asked.

Soulfrrruit not poison soultrrreee frrriends, the magehound said cryptically.

"Does that mean I can eat them or not?" Their delicious

scent was already making her mouth water. She could imagine the juice spurting between her teeth and sliding down her smoke-sore throat. She trod water and closed a hand around the nearest fruit.

"No, Natalie!"

Merlin didn't even hold his nose but took a running leap that turned into the most painful bellyflop she'd ever seen. She smothered a giggle as he surfaced and started to dog-paddle like K'tanaqui, but not nearly as effectively. He kept sinking, then surfacing again to splutter, "No, don't eat it... Natalie! Help!" His cries became more frantic, his splashing wilder. She frowned, reluctant to leave the soulfruit.

"*Natalie!*" This time, he disappeared under the surface and did not come up again.

"Merlin? Quit fooling around." Heart thumping, she swam across, K'tanaqui paddling after her.

Mouse-pup STUPID, the magehound said.

She was inclined to agree but fear for Merlin kept her from replying. She stared down through the silver-green water and saw his hair floating beneath her feet like red seaweed. Her stomach clenched. "Help him, someone!" she shouted. "He's drowning! Lady Thaypari! Lord Pveriyan! Anyone! Help!" Snatching off her glasses, she threw them towards the edge and prepared to dive.

K'tanaqui caught them gently in his mouth. *Pup so silly. Ask Oq forrr shallow waterrr. Rrrememberrr to say please this time.*

"But—" Then she understood. Grabbing the nearest vine, she yelled, "Shallow! Shallow water, *please* Oq!"

A great wave nearly knocked her over. She clung on to the vine for balance, afraid the tree had decided to take revenge for her calling it stupid when she'd rescued Tim. Then suddenly she was kneeling in water that barely covered her thighs and Merlin lay before her, coughing and spluttering like a landed fish.

K'tanaqui nosed him. *Mouse-pup will live*, he said, sounding pleased with himself.

Natalie stood shakily and addressed the interlaced branches

overhead. "Thank you, Oq."

The leaves rustled.

"How can you *thank* it?" Merlin hugged his bony chest. "It tried to kill me!"

She frowned. "I don't think so."

"It grabbed my leg and pulled me down!"

"I didn't see anything."

"You're bound to say that. Your mother was on the Council."

K'tanaqui growled. *Mouse-pup imagining things. Mouse-pup can't swim.*

"Is that true?" Natalie looked at the shivering boy with new respect. He'd jumped in for her sake.

"Is what true?"

"That you can't swim? Didn't you realize how deep it was?"

His red face told her all she needed to know. She fought a smile.

"Don't laugh at me!" He scrambled out of the pool and retrieved his mouse from the branch where it had taken refuge when he had jumped in. "Everyone laughs at me. I can't do anything right, I'm just a joke, a stupid joke." Tears glittered in his eyes.

"I'm not laughing at you, silly. It's just that no one has ever nearly drowned themselves for me before. I bet you couldn't even see what you were doing after Redeye bailed out. What was it like, watching yourself go under?"

Merlin sniffed, and his lips twitched into a small smile. "Scary."

Natalie couldn't help a giggle as she squeezed the water out of her hair. The swim had made her feel almost normal again. "We'd better get ready, I suppose. I hope this Council doesn't take too long, because the smell of that soulfruit has reminded me how hungry I am. I'm even beginning to regret throwing my spaghetti bolognese over you."

"Yeah, that was stupid," Merlin agreed. "If you didn't want it, you could have given it to me."

11

ϹΗΕ ϹΟUΝϹΙL ΟϜ ΟϘ

Early Friday morning, October 30

The Council of Oq assembled at midnight in the dizzy heights of the soultree canopy. During the long climb from the pool, Lady Thaypari told her two nervous charges that when it wasn't in use, the entire Council chamber could be shrunk to the size of a small hazelnut. She told them that once, long before the Boundary existed, Oq had disagreed with a decision and shrunk the chamber with the Council members still inside. "If you put your ear to the benches on a quiet day, you can still hear the unfortunate Spell Lords crying to be let out," she added in a hushed whisper. "So you've got to be careful what you say or Oq might do it again."

Merlin went white. But K'tanaqui curled his lip in the mage-hound equivalent of a grin, making Natalie giggle in spite of her nerves. "That's not true, is it?" she said.

The Spell Lady smiled. "A pity it isn't, the way the Council members argue sometimes!" Then she noticed Merlin's expression and her tone gentled. "Oh come, young Caster, don't look like that! I was only trying to cheer you up. Natalie's quite right, soultrees don't harm their Council members. And no decision is made unless Oq agrees with it. I thought you'd know that, being of the blood."

"But I'm not a Spell Lord," Merlin sniffed. "Oq might shrink on me."

Lady Thaypari patted his arm. "Not while you're with us, she won't. Now, blow your nose. No, not on your sleeve, use this.… That's better."

While Thaypari handed Merlin a square of mossy material to wipe his nose with, Natalie gave his other hand a small squeeze. "It'll be over before you know it," she whispered, then turned cold. Exactly the words Claudia had used before the goshawk ate Itsy. Might that be what the Council had planned for Redeye?

Magehounds alrrready have full powerrr. Little mouse not worrrth eating, K'tanaqui informed her. Which, far from setting her mind at rest, raised yet more questions. She thrust them firmly aside, adding them to an already long list of things to ask Lady Thaypari as soon as they had another proper chance to talk.

At last, the Spell Lady halted before a thick curtain of ivy. "You wait here until you're called," she told them. "I'll go on in and inform the Council you've arrived." She gave Natalie's hair a final tweak, brushed a leaf off Merlin's tunic, and smiled at them again. "Don't worry, you both look fine."

About the last thing worrying Natalie was how they looked but it did feel good to be clean at last. After they'd swum and changed, Lady Thaypari had woven some small white flowers into Natalie's hair. Their dreamy scent drifted about her as she moved. Thaypari had even managed to make Merlin presentable. With clean hair, decent clothes, and the grubby marks washed from his elbows and knees, he looked almost human.

Mouse-pup less human than daughterrr-pup, K'tanaqui reminded her, making her smile. Then she clutched Merlin's hand as the ivy rustled aside.

A voice boomed, "Enter and kneel before the Council of Oq!"

K'tanaqui went first, claws clicking on the perfectly smooth floor. Natalie took a deep breath and pulled Merlin after the magehound, trying not to think about Lady Thaypari's story of the crushed Spell Lords.

Inside, she got a crick in her neck from staring upwards. The Council chamber was a vast, circular dome ringed by two tiers of glowing greenwood benches. Twelve Spell Lords and Ladies in shimmering Earthaven robes, wearing crowns of leaves and flowers, sat around the upper tier; while their magehounds reclined on the lower bench, bushy silver tails hanging over the edge. A high roof of interlaced branches rose to a central opening through which moonlight poured to form a silver circle on the floor. K'tanaqui padded straight to this circle and sat in the middle of it, his newly washed coat shining. He raised his muzzle and gazed proudly at the twelve magehounds.

Natalie's heart thumped as she knelt beside him and pulled Merlin down beside her. Every Spell Lord, Lady, and magehound in the chamber was looking at her and their intent gazes made her skin prickle. Lady Thaypari flashed her an encouraging smile.

"Welcome, Daughter of Atanaqui," boomed the same voice as before, making her jump. She tried to see who had spoken, but the voice seemed to come from all directions at once. "You may stand."

She breathed a sigh of relief. But scarcely had they scrambled to their feet than Lord Pveriyan leapt from his bench and pointed a gnarled finger at Merlin.

"The Caster is a spy!" he announced. "Sent here by his father, the Spellmage known as Hawk, who we banished across the Boundary fourteen years ago under the terms of the Spellfall Solution. Apparently Hawk has mastered the ancient art of transportation. It's obvious he intends to use this to launch an attack on Oq during this year's Opening, and he's sent his son through the Thrallstone to plant spells at strategic locations within Earthaven. I say the young Caster should be taken at once to the Heart and forcibly drained of all he knows." He sat down.

Natalie's stomach fluttered. She cast an anxious glance at Merlin.

But the Council seemed amused. "The boy doesn't look as if he'd know a strategic location if it hit him in the face," said one of the Lords, raising a few chuckles. "Besides, what would be the point? If Hawk really can transport, he'd simply use a place of power for the destination. Almost anywhere within Oq would work better than a spell. But this is all academic, anyway. No Caster would dare enter a soultree uninvited, particularly during the Opening."

"Hawk has always dared what others do not," returned Pveriyan. "Don't forget he lived on this side of the Boundary for many years. His powers are considerable."

"Even if they transport directly into the Heart, they need a full spellclave to do any real damage." Another Lord.

"They are already twelve. They made a mistake with Natalie, but they could easily find another Caster to make up the number. They might even intend to bond their young one once they get across the Boundary." One of the Ladies.

Merlin paled. Lady Thaypari gave him a sympathetic glance and said firmly, "Then we must make sure they don't. Keep him where they can't reach him until the Opening's over."

"Better to execute his mouse now and make certain they can't use him for anything," Lord Pveriyan muttered darkly.

Natalie squeezed Merlin's hand, wondering if she'd made a mistake bringing him here, but Lady Thaypari was still on their side.

"Don't be silly, Pveriyan," she said, winking at them. "There's no need for that. He'll be safe inside Oq."

Pveriyan scowled round the benches. "I know what you're all thinking. You think because he's small he's no threat. I'm telling you, it's a trick! There's no other reason Hawk would let his son anywhere near a gateway so close to the Opening."

This provoked quite an argument. The Spell Lords' voices grew louder, and some of them stood to shout across the chamber. Magehounds on the lower bench growled. It wasn't clear who was saying what, though Natalie saw Lady Thaypari frown, her fingers twisting one of the orange flowers in her hair.

"Don't say a word," she whispered to Merlin. She tightened her grip on K'tanaqui's ruff and raised her other arm. The argument raged on. She waited a few minutes but still no one noticed her, so she cleared her throat.

The old magehound flipped his ear. *Pup rrrememberrr to be polite!*

"Lords! Ladies!" Natalie called before she could lose her nerve. "There *is* a threat to your soultree, but it's not Merlin!"

That got their attention. Her heart thumped as the chamber went quiet. She faltered under the force of Lord Pveriyan's glare, but raised her chin.

"Merlin's no spy! He helped me escape from his father's spellclave and that's why he was with me when we came through your Thrallstone. It's not his fault he was born a Caster."

"First time I've known a Caster help anyone but themselves," someone muttered, and there were a couple of laughs.

"Shh!" said Thaypari. "Let the girl speak."

Twenty-four pairs of eyes looked expectantly at Natalie. She flashed Lady Thaypari a grateful smile. But before she could sort the images she'd received from K'tanaqui into some sort of order, Lord Pveriyan interrupted.

"It's obvious the boy was instructed to make friends with Atanaqui's daughter so he could tell her all these lies," he said. "The sooner they're separated, the better."

"That's not true!" Merlin blurted out. "Least, I was supposed to make friends with her, yes, but I didn't know who she was then, I swear! Father never tells me anything."

"See?" Lord Pveriyan appealed to the Council. "What did I tell you? Lies."

"He's not lying," Natalie said quickly. "And if you hurt him, I won't help you, no matter who my mother was. I've got a father as well, you know, and I expect he's really worried about me by now." *More likely into his fifth crate of beer,* she thought with a pang, but pushed the thought away. "To say nothing of my stepmother Julie, and poor old Tim! From what I've seen of the way you treat your guests, you're no better than Casters yourselves."

The chamber erupted. Lord Pveriyan leapt to his feet, gesticulating furiously, while K'veriyan put his muzzle in the air and began to howl. Some of the other magehounds joined in, getting to their feet on the lower bench, hackles raised.

K'tanaqui flipped his ear again. *Is pup crrrazy? Big insult to Lorrrds!*

"Now you've done it," Merlin whispered, clutching Redeye and eyeing the ivy across the entrance.

Natalie's mouth dried. But after a few minutes the magehounds settled and the Council quietened. Lord Pveriyan sat down, his face shadowed by thorns.

An old Lord with purple berries in his hair leant forwards and gave her a kindly smile. "Don't be afraid, child. My name's Lord Gerystar, and I'm the Second Member of the Council. What threat are you talking about? Speak up now."

Natalie gripped K'tanaqui's ruff so tightly, the wiry hairs cut her fingers. She closed her eyes. "Before she drowned, my mother saw something. K'tanaqui has shown me flashes in my head, where the words come. There's a black bird and a storm of stars falling from the sky—"

"Not that again!" someone groaned.

"Quiet!" said Lord Gerystar. "Go on, child."

"I don't understand it all, Lord," Natalie admitted. "But when we started the fire in the Lodge, Hawk shouted something about a raven in the cellar, and I saw a tunnel down there. Merlin thinks the spellclave were doing experiments on spells."

"They were always going down there," Merlin put in eagerly. "And they'd stay down hours. Claudia-the-Fish used to be a—"

"No one gave you permission to speak, Caster!" Lord Pveriyan snapped, jumping to his feet again. "If you open your mouth again, I'll be forced to ask Oq to silence you."

"Oh, do sit down, Pveriyan," Lady Thaypari said with a sigh. "We never did get to the bottom of Atanaqui's death, did we? The images our magehounds received from K'tanaqui were very muddled. It makes sense that Natalie's getting clearer ones, so maybe we'll be able to solve the mystery at last. Go on," she said gently. "What did you see in the cellar?"

"Nothing," Natalie admitted, her heart sinking. "But it couldn't have been a real bird, anyway, because Merlin says his father's goshawk ate all the other familiars." She couldn't help a shudder.

"The ancient meaning of Raven is Bringer of Doom," said a dark-skinned Lord. "What if it's a code word of some kind? Or the name of a new human weapon?"

"Then we needn't worry," said one of the Ladies. "Our anti-technology spells will keep us safe. Even if the Casters manage to bring a weapon across the Boundary, it won't work in Earthaven. Oq's safe."

Relief rippled round the chamber.

"Hawk's already tried to harm Oq once," Lord Gerystar pointed out, frowning. "That's why we banished him in the first place, wasn't it? If I remember rightly, he was caught trying to damage one of the outer branches. The storm of stars could mean Spellfall. Hawk's wanted his revenge for years, and he'll be after spells. What if he plans to get both at once? What if he's found a way to kill Oq?"

Shouts of protest greeted this. "Impossible!"… "Nothing's powerful enough to kill a soultree!"…"Oq's still young!" …"Spellfall's centuries away!"

Lord Pveriyan had been listening, eyes narrow. Now he held up a hand. "This merely confirms what I've been trying to tell you all along," he said. "Hawk should have been dealt with properly long ago. Forget this Raven nonsense, it's the man we should be worrying about. He's sent his son here for a reason and the sooner the boy's interrogated, the better."

"Are you sure there's nothing more about this raven, Natalie?" Lady Thaypari asked, ignoring Pveriyan. "Might it be a code?"

Natalie shook her head, suddenly very weary. Even clinging to K'tanaqui's ruff no longer gave her the strength it had.

"K'tanaqui just sees a black bird," she told them in a small voice. "Flying."

"Oq might help sort out the visions if she submits herself to the Heart," one of the Ladies suggested, and sparked off yet another argument.

Natalie closed her eyes, letting their voices wash over her, enjoying the scent of the flowers in her hair. Right now she didn't care what they did to her, as long as they let her sleep soon.

Pup not sleep yet, K'tanaqui said disapprovingly, bumping her thigh with his head. *Thayparrri use too many moonflowerrrs.*

Finally, the chamber became quiet again and the disembodied voice said, "Both young ones will visit the Heart of Oq to be interviewed."

"Yes!" Lord Pveriyan hissed in triumph.

The voice continued, "But before their interviews, both young ones will be permitted to eat and rest. We still have almost two days before the Boundary opens. We should not be seen to panic. The local Herders should be alerted and their unicorns prepared for battle. Messages should also be sent to all other Earthaven tribes warning them of a possible Caster invasion. As a precaution, all entrances to the Root System shall be sealed for the duration of the Opening. Any other business?"

The Spell Lords and their magehounds were stretching and yawning, getting to their feet in preparation to leave the chamber. But Lord Pveriyan raised an imperious hand. "There's the problem of the interrupted cleansing of the human boy. It wasn't completed to Oq's satisfaction."

Natalie looked up, unease penetrating the sweet moonflower haze. *Tim.*

After a short pause the disembodied voice said, "When the Boundary is open, we shall use the Root System to assess his danger to us."

"And finish cleansing him," Lord Pveriyan insisted. "We can't risk a free human knowing our secrets."

Lady Thaypari smiled. "I don't think we need worry too much about that, do you?" she said. "People will laugh if he starts trying to tell them about us. Human scientists think they know everything about their world. No one will take him seriously."

Several Council members nodded agreement but K'veriyan bared his canines in a silent snarl.

"This Council has grown weak in more than numbers!" Lord Pveriyan shouted. "I can remember a time when we used to cleanse humans for merely peering through the hole in the Thrallstone! I can remember when any Caster who dared set foot across the Boundary was hunted the length and breadth of Earthaven and their body displayed in thirteen pieces on the nearest gateway as a warning to all! Now you let the sons of Casters bathe in Oq's pools and dress them in good Herder green. Pah!"

He spat at Merlin but got his own hound on the foot. K'veriyan turned disgusted eyes upon his master, then with great dignity licked the soiled paw clean.

"And the Council remembers it was you who bungled the boy's memory cleansing in the first place," Lord Gerystar said smoothly.

Titters rippled round the chamber.

"The human boy is my responsibility," Pveriyan said through gritted teeth. "And when the Boundary opens, I shall complete his cleansing by any means possible."

With great dignity, he rose to his feet and left the Council chamber, K'veriyan stalking, bristle-furred, at his heels.

With their departure, the air seemed to clear. Natalie swayed on her feet, overcome by another wave of moonflower scent, and felt Merlin grip her arm. "What's wrong?" he whispered.

"Nothing, I'm just tired."

Pup not sleep yet, her magehound said anxiously as Lady Thaypari approached. *Brrreakfast time. K'tanaqui hungrrry!*

12

MEMORIES

Friday afternoon, October 30

Hours after the Council of Oq had decided his fate, Tim woke in Unicorn Wood with a headache to beat all headaches.

He blinked at the overcast sky and dripping trees, stared a moment at the twisted, mossy stone, put a hand to his head and groaned. Had someone hit him? If so, they must have used a boulder. He shouted a few times but no one answered.

Stiffly, he climbed to his feet and began to follow the deep tyre tracks. Last night was a blur. Mr Marlins had brought him up here in the car, there had been an articulated truck and some furtive activity around the stone. What else? An old man with long white hair and green eyes? He shook his head. The rest was like trying to see through smoke. Besides, he had more immediate problems.

The track was uneven and his boots were killing him. They had been made to look good on city streets, not for hiking in muddy woods. To make things worse, it began to rain. He stumbled along, tripping over roots and splashing through puddles, cursing Mr Marlins with all the bad words he knew.

By the time he reached a road, his jacket was so wet and heavy, it was like wearing liquid stone. A few cars passed, spraying him with muddy water, but none stopped when he raised his thumb. Once – crazy – he tried jumping into the path of a four-wheel-drive. The woman driver swerved and mounted the verge to avoid him. "Stop, you stupid cow!" Tim yelled after her. "Can't you see I need help?" Then something broke inside him and he crouched in the middle of the road, hugging his soggy jacket and sobbing as he hadn't done since he was about three years old.

By the time the rain eased to a drizzle, the tears had calmed him. He climbed to his feet, turned up his collar and started walking. To take his mind off his blisters, he planned what he was going to say to Mr Marlins when he got back. How long had he been unconscious? His watch had begun to work again as he left the clearing, but that wasn't much help since he didn't know what time it had been when he woke. The sky was too overcast to see the sun but it felt like late afternoon. His mother would be furious with him.

As he limped up to the front door his steps slowed. He hadn't got his key with him and the last thing he wanted was to have Mr Marlins let him in. He still hadn't perfected a suitable insult.

He was about to sneak round the back in search of a window to climb through when the door opened and Jo Carter came rushing out.

"Did you find…" Her voice trailed off. She stared at Tim in undisguised horror.

Mrs Carter called from the hall, "Who is it, Joanne?"

"What are *you* doing here?" Tim said as the girl continued to stare. "Where's my mother? Is Mr Marlins…" He almost gave himself away but changed the question just in time. "…still in his garage?"

"It's Tim," Jo called back, her tone strange.

Mrs Carter came to the door, took one look at Tim's wet jacket and the mud on his jeans and planted her hands on her hips. "You'll be in trouble when your mother gets back, my boy," she said. "How could you do this to her after what happened to your poor sister? Where have you been for the past two days? She's beside herself. Thought you and your dad had been abducted too—"

"Mr Marlins is *not my father!*" The response was so automatic by now, Tim had pushed past her into the hall before her words registered. Two days?

"Timothy Lockley!" Mrs Carter called behind him. "Come back here this minute! I'm talking to you."

Tim couldn't deal with it. He stumbled upstairs to his bedroom, slammed and locked the door.

He sat on his bed, clamped his teeth into his lower lip, and eased off his boots. Blood crusted his socks. He peeled them off too and stared at his feet, feeling sick. *Two* days?

Someone had come upstairs after him. He got ready to yell something rude. But the voice that followed the knock wasn't Mrs Carter's.

"Tim? You in there?"

Jo.

"Go away."

The handle rattled. "Tim, open up! We have to talk."

He scowled at the door, then struggled off the bed. Hissing with the pain, he limped to the door, dragged Jo through and quickly locked it again. She tripped over his boots, started to tell him what she thought of people who left their stuff all over the floor, then saw his feet.

"What on earth happened to you?" she said.

"Been on a midnight walk in the woods, what do you think? Why's your mother here? Where's mine gone? And where's Mr Marlins?"

"That's what everyone would like to know." Jo plonked herself on the end of his bed and frowned. "Apparently, he took his car out on Wednesday night when your mother was over at our house and he hasn't come back since. You were here. Didn't he say anything to you?"

Tim bit his lip. His head was still swirling with muddled images of the twisted stone, the white-haired man with the green eyes... He shook them away. "When does he ever speak to me? Maybe he's gone off lookin' for Nat?"

Jo gave him a sharp look. "That's what the police said. Your mother's terribly upset, though. Kept going on about him drinking and driving, until the police came. Then she shut up pretty quick. Can't have wanted to get him into trouble. She's down at the station now, giving them some photos of you to go with the ones of Nat. She was convinced you'd been kidnapped too. My mother's phoning to let her know you're home." Her voice changed. "It was my fault, you know, making Nat try those stupid skates. If she'd been able to run away, they mightn't have caught her—" She stared at the window.

Tim followed her gaze. Across the river, Unicorn Wood hung above the roofs of the town like a soggy red and gold blanket whose colours had run in the wash. The top of the hill was wreathed in mist. He shuddered. Wednesday night seemed like a bad dream now that he was safe in his own room. Except he had the blisters and two lost days to prove it.

"It wasn't your fault, silly." Surprising himself, he leant across and touched Jo's arm. "Something very weird is going on in Unicorn Wood. I think it might have something to do with Nat—"

Before he could defend himself, the girl was on top of him, bearing him back across the bed. She grasped his sore ear and twisted hard. "You *bastard!* If you've got anything to do with Nat's kidnapping, I'll— I'll—"

Evidently unable to think of a suitable fate, she settled for giving his ear another wrench.

"Ow!" Tim roared, catching her wrists. "I didn't have nothing to do with it! What do you think I am? Gerroff me! Someone'll hear us."

This got through to her. Blushing, she let go of his ear and scrambled off the bed. She flicked her fringe out of her eyes and gave him a measuring look. "I knew your disappearing like that wasn't a coincidence. All right, tell."

Tim sat up, clutching his ear. Her attack had set his head off again and he'd knocked his blisters on the end of the bed. He couldn't decide which hurt the most. "You won't believe it if I do."

"Tell!"

Reluctantly, he told her all he could remember from the moment Mr Marlins had screeched out of the drive on Wednesday evening to the moment he'd woken in the shadow of the weird, twisted stone. He left nothing out. With every word he expected Jo to laugh and rush out to tell everyone Timothy Lockley had gone totally loopy. But she listened in silence. He could hardly believe it when he looked up and saw her still standing by his window, frowning.

"You don't think I'm crazy?" he said.

She gave him a tight smile. "No more than usual." She began to pace up and down. "It all fits. Nat was convinced something strange happened to her on Saturday at the supermarket and what you've told me isn't any weirder. She saw a man putting what he told her was a spell into a recycling bin. You say Mr Marlins thought the Spell Lord had taken Nat but the Spell Lord claimed the Casters had her and they're some kind of wizards too, right?"

Tim nodded. "I think so."

"So the man in the car park must have been a Caster. And if he was recycling his spells there, he must live nearby. The only question is where?"

"The old lodge," Tim said, startling himself.

"What?"

Tim spoke slowly, dredging the memories from some dark, treacly place in his head. "One of the Spell Lord's men mentioned a spellclave of Casters in some old lodge about half a mile from the Thrallstone."

"That's it, then! That's where she is!" Jo leapt to the door, eyes flashing. "We must tell the mothers, tell the police—"

Tim looked up in alarm. "Uh-uh! D'you really expect me to

tell the police what I just told you? Forget it! They'll think I've flipped. Either that or they'll arrest me for murdering Mr Marlins." He laughed. "I'd like to murder him, actually. When I think of the way he abandoned me up there."

"We've *got* to, Tim!" Jo was already unlocking his door. Her voice hardened. "Whoever those people are, they killed Bilbo. Nobody kills my dog and kidnaps my best friend and gets away with it. It might be a good idea to keep the spells out of it but we have to get someone to search that lodge. If you won't tell them, I will."

"But how do we know it's the same spellclave that took Nat?"

"Must be. How many spellclaves could there be in Millennium Green? Anyway, even if they haven't got her, they might know who has."

"Oh fine, like they'd just tell us." But Tim sighed and crawled off the bed. Once Jo got an idea into her head, she didn't let go. He pushed the door shut before she could rush out and storm the place single-handed. "OK, but we need to get our story straight. If I can't tell the truth, I've got to invent something else."

Jo flashed him a grin. "Shouldn't be too hard, then. You've a reputation for the best excuses in the book."

*

Finally, they agreed on a semi-true story whereby Mr Marlins had taken Tim up to the wood to help search for Nat because he'd received an anonymous phone call that claimed a little girl had been seen wandering alone up there. They'd got separated in the fog and when Tim found the place where they'd parked the car, it had gone. He'd slipped down a gully in the dark and hit his head on a stone. That would account for the strange bruises he'd acquired on his temples. When he came to, he'd had to walk five miles home.

Tim steeled himself for a yelling match. But what happened was much worse. His mother actually hugged him right in front of Jo and Mrs Carter, making his ears burn. Then she wiped her eyes, pulled out a map and demanded Tim show her the exact route Mr Marlins had taken on Wednesday night. He tried his best. But the map seemed to bear no resemblance to the roads they'd raced along in the dark and the fog. In the end, he shook his head in defeat. "It's just not right," he said.

"You *must* remember, Timothy!" she said. "You found your way back, didn't you?"

"Yeah, but I wasn't feeling too good. Maybe I got concussion or something?"

Wrong thing to say. His mother's exasperated expression immediately melted into one of concern. She prodded his bruises, making him wince. "Oh God, I should have thought. Do you feel sick at all? We ought to take you to hospital for a check up."

It was Jo who rescued him. Pointing to the map, she said in a bright tone, "There's a house marked right in the middle of the wood! It looks really isolated. Maybe that's where they're holding Nat? I don't see a standing stone near it, though—"

Tim had to dig her in the ribs, but at least she'd taken his mother's mind off hospitals.

Eagerly, Julie looked at the map. Then her shoulders sagged and she sank into a chair. "We're all overtired," she said. "Timothy, go on upstairs and run yourself a bath. There's some antiseptic cream in the cabinet for your cuts. We'll see how you're feeling later."

"But the lodge!" Jo said. "Aren't you going to tell the police? What if Nat really is up there?"

"It's the first place they looked, Joanne," Mrs Carter said gently. "That old house is boarded up, has been for years. No one lives there and there was no sign of squatters when the police searched it."

"But what if they've taken Nat there since?" Tim said. "And even if she's not there, what if Mr Marlins found the place and fell down some rotten stairs and broke his leg or something?" Catching the expression on his mother's face, he added quickly, "I mean he might have knocked himself out like I did, mightn't he? If no one lives up there, we ought at least go up and see if he needs help."

His mother sighed. "Your stepfather's a grown man, Timothy. You have to understand the police aren't worried about his disappearance, at least not in the same way they're worried about Natalie." She looked at Mrs Carter and an unspoken fear passed between the two women. "I feel a lot better knowing he set out to look for her, though. And that he wasn't drunk at the time. That means a lot to me. Try not to worry too much, love."

Her words were brave but Tim sensed the panic underlying them. "He could've phoned you," he said fiercely. "It's not fair of him to let you worry like this."

Julie looked hard at him for a moment. Then she rested a hand on his hairless scalp. "You're a good boy, Timothy, no matter what your stepfather thinks. When this is all over, things are going to be different, I promise. Sometimes it takes a crisis like this to bring families together."

*

Bring families together? Ha! That was a joke.

Tim ran the water as hot as he could bear it, yelled as it lapped over his raw blisters, then sank back with a sigh and watched the steam slowly thicken near the ceiling. He half hoped his stepfather *was* lying hurt in a ditch somewhere. Except that would upset his mother.

He shook his head. Thralls. Spell Lords. Earthaven. Casters. Spellclaves. What had he got himself into?

He must have drifted off because when a knock at the door roused him the water was cold. He pulled the plug and quickly towelled himself, avoiding his head and feet. "Just a minute!" he called.

There was a giggle outside the door. "Haven't you finished in there yet? You're worse than a girl! Your mother sent me up to help with your feet."

Tim tugged on his jeans in alarm. "I thought you'd gone home! I can manage."

Another giggle. "She doesn't seem to think so." Jo's voice lowered. "But that's not the only reason I'm here. I've got an idea how we can rescue Nat."

Reluctantly, Tim unlocked the door.

Before he knew it, Jo was kneeling on the mat with one of his feet in her lap. "I've got it all worked out," she said as she smothered his blisters in cream. "If no one will believe us we'll just have to search the lodge ourselves and find some evidence that'll convince them. We're going to need help, though. If there are only two of us, we could disappear as easy as Nat. But we'd be safe in a group. I thought of Gaz's gang."

Tim snatched his foot away. "Are you crazy? Gaz'd never help! Maybe you've forgotten what you did to him at school but he hasn't. He's not the forgiving type."

Jo's eyes flashed. "I'm not scared of Gaz!"

"Well, you should be! He's bigger and stronger than he was when you thumped him that day and he's dying for a chance to have his revenge. You stay away from him."

Jo laughed and tugged his foot back into her lap. "Timothy Lockley! I do believe you care!" She slapped on more cream.

"Anyway," Tim said, "we can't just go barging in there on our own. If Nat's kidnappers are in the lodge, we could get into a lot of trouble. And your mother's hardly likely to let you go running around in the woods after what happened to Nat."

This earned him a scathing look. "I thought you liked trouble? You're always in some, aren't you? But I didn't mean we should try to rescue Nat ourselves, stupid. We'll just see if she's there or not. As to letting us go up there, I've already thought of that. You can offer to take me to the Hallowe'en Disco at the rowing club tomorrow night. That way our parents won't worry if we're late home. We can hide our bikes in the old boat shed. I'll borrow my dad's mobile – he never uses it Saturday nights – and we'll call the police as soon as we find anything. We'll be there and back before the disco ends. Promise."

"Hold on!" Tim pulled his foot away again and nearly overbalanced into the bath. "You're not seriously thinking of wandering round Unicorn Wood at *Hallowe'en?*"

Jo grinned. "That's the beauty of my plan. We dare Gaz and the others to enter a haunted house in Unicorn Wood at Hallowe'en. They'll have to do it or lose face." Her eyes sparkled. She was looking forward to this, Tim realized.

He swallowed. "But Nat's kidnappers are some kind of wizards! They'll be up to all sorts of horrible things at Hallowe'en."

"Not scared, are you?"

Yes! Tim wanted to say. Instead, he mumbled, "Ow! Watch what you're doing."

"Think what poor Nat's going through," Jo said then. "We can't just abandon her to her fate. If you won't come with me, I'll go alone."

Tim stared at the thick fringe that had flopped into her eyes again, at the determined set of her jaw. She wasn't bluffing.

He thrust his last encounter with Gaz to the back of his mind and sighed. "The Heads meet by the fountain in the precinct at six-thirty, Saturday nights. We'll dare them to do it then, but only if you promise to let me do the talking. Absolutely no mention of spells or wizards or Earthaven, or they'll laugh in our faces. And if Gaz says no, you come away with me, no arguing, and we forget the whole thing. Agreed?"

"Agreed!" Jo flashed him a smile.

Tim considered her. "I'll have to walk five miles in those boots again some time," he said mischievously.

She coloured and scrambled up from her knees. At the door, she flung the flattened tube of cream at him. "Here, you can finish them yourself! Remember to wear your running shoes tomorrow night, tough guy!"

13

IN THE HEART

Friday night, October 30

It was Friday evening before Lady Thaypari took Natalie to the Heart for her interview. She knew a lot more about the soul-tree by then.

As she'd hoped, Lady Thaypari had proved easy to talk to and it was all so fascinating she'd lost track of the time while they fed their magehounds, explored the fantastic leafy chambers, and met some of the lucky Treemages who lived in Oq's branches and helped care for the tree. They'd breakfasted on an airy, sun-dappled balcony with a view over the entire Earthaven canopy, and though they'd left Merlin waiting below in Lady Thaypari's private chambers (he'd flatly refused to have anything to do with feeding magehounds) Natalie didn't say anything because she wanted to keep the Spell Lady to herself for as long as possible. She did feel a little selfish but at the same time she couldn't help feeling glad the boy wasn't around to ruin her enjoyment of the meal. Soulfruit tasted as good as it looked and, after checking with Lady Thaypari that it was indeed safe to eat, she ate so much of it she became drowsy.

After breakfast, Thaypari told her to lie down and rest if she wanted and, although she didn't mean to, Natalie had dozed off right there on the balcony with the Earthaven breeze playing through her hair. She woke sometime during the afternoon feeling guilty but Lady Thaypari assured her Merlin was resting too and promised she'd be able to see her friend as soon as her interview in the Heart was over.

With complete trust, Natalie followed the Spell Lady through the spiralling passages, deeper and deeper into the tree, with K'tanaqui and K'aypari padding at their heels. As they neared the Heart, however, a heavy green silence folded around them and she began to feel nervous again.

"What's it like?" she whispered, afraid to raise her voice.

Thaypari smiled and spoke equally softly. "It's different for everyone. Don't worry, Oq will be pleased to see you."

"See?" Natalie breathed. "How can a tree *see*? Has she got eyes, then?"

"Just a manner of speaking," Thaypari said with another smile. "You'll be connected directly and might get images in your head like the ones K'tanaqui showed you. Oq will get the same from you. Think of them as human telephone lines, only much better because they don't just carry sound. Hush now, we're here."

She stopped at the entrance to a small chamber filled with emerald light. Natalie peered inside and caught her breath. The walls and floor glowed with layer upon layer of luminous moss. Sweetly scented vines hung in loops from the ceiling. Tiny coloured stars glimmered among their leaves, and a faint music lingered in the air. A stool waited in the centre, half hidden by all the greenery. "Is that where I sit?" she asked.

"That's right. Oq can hear us anywhere, of course, even through her smallest root, and she speaks to us with her public voice in the Council chamber. But this is the only place we can communicate on a personal level. In the Heart you'll hear her private voice and she'll hear yours." She gave Natalie the strangest look, started to say something else, then changed her mind. "You can go in now."

Natalie shivered, suddenly apprehensive. Thaypari gave her a gentle push. "Go on. Oq won't hurt you, I promise."

She had to duck through the entrance and keep her head low as she made her trembling way to the stool. Once she was seated, however, her nerves vanished. Warmth and sweetness welcomed her, and her tense muscles relaxed. K'tanaqui thrust his muzzle anxiously through the opening. *Pup be carrreful. Pup in place of grrreat powerrr.*

Natalie didn't need to be told. An ancient heartbeat throbbed beneath the stool. The tendrils that caressed her hair made her skin tingle. One of them pushed gently under her fringe and attached itself to her temple with a sticky kiss.

She clutched at the stool.

"Don't be afraid, Natalie!" Lady Thaypari called. "Remember I'm out here all the time, and so is K'tanaqui."

She forced herself to sit still as Oq made the remaining connections. There was a peculiar tickle inside her skull. Then words streamed across her head, cool as the wind, very different from K'tanaqui's gruff voice.

WELCOME, DAUGHTER OF ATANAQUI. SOMEONE WANTS TO SPEAK TO YOU.

Natalie slowly unclenched her fingers. "Who?" she whispered.

In answer, stars drifted out of the leaves and formed themselves into a green-eyed woman whose long, silver-gold hair shone like the moon. She wore a robe of green shadows, and her bare feet floated a fraction above the ground. Natalie stared, a thousand different emotions chasing through her. No, they couldn't do this to her.

The woman held out her starry arms and smiled. "Hello Natty," she said. "I'm glad K'tanaqui found you at last."

Natalie's heart lurched. "Mother?" Her voice would hardly work. "But you're— you're—" Her eyes brimmed with tears. The woman looked older than in her photograph and she wasn't wearing her dark glasses, but only one person had ever called her Natty.

She slid off the stool. But before she could launch herself

into those glittering arms a vine coiled about her waist, holding her fast. She struggled wildly, tears spilling out. "Let me go, you stupid tree!" she sobbed. "That's my mother! Let me *go*!" But this time Oq didn't obey her, not even when she thumped the vine, gasping with the pain in her heart.

"Natty," the sparkling figure said softly. "Natty, calm down and listen. Oq restrains you for your own good. It would be highly dangerous for you to touch me in this state. My body is dead. But when a Spell Lord or Lady dies, their spirit returns to the tree they serve, which is how I can appear to you now. Shh, daughter, sit down. We have to talk about some important things and there isn't much time."

Natalie sank on to the stool, her head spinning. "But how—"

"I'll explain in a minute. First, I have to know, are you happy with your stepmother?"

"I..." She closed her eyes, opened them again. "Julie's nice."

"Good. We don't have much power outside Earthaven these days but sometimes it's possible to influence things just a little bit. Were you surprised when your father joined the dating agency?"

Natalie blinked. "*You* made him do that? You made Julie marry him?"

Her mother smiled. "No, I couldn't do that. But sometimes I can still reach your father when the Boundary's open – through dreams and things. Let's say I influenced the odds slightly in her favour. So tell me, how is he?"

"He's fine."

Her expression must have given her away. Or maybe Oq was reading her thoughts and relaying them to her mother? The sparkling figure dimmed slightly. "He loved me very much," she said softly. "It won't have been easy for him. But before I was a wife and mother, I was a Spell Lord, and that's not something you can just give up. He knew that, just as he knew that one day I'd return to Earthaven. It came sooner than either of us expected, that's all."

She drifted closer. "Don't cry, Natty. I know this must all

seem very strange and new to you. I've so much to tell you and I want to hear all your news, but it'll have to wait until this crisis is over. Right now, you must dry your eyes and be brave. There's going to be a Caster invasion this year, isn't there?"

"So the Council say."

Lady Atanaqui sighed. "I knew it would come to this eventually. Human science has advanced faster than any of us expected." She took a deep breath. "Listen, Natty, this is serious. For the past decade, the Caster who calls himself Hawk has been working on a weapon capable of killing a soultree. If he's planning an invasion, that means he's succeeded or thinks he has. He mustn't be allowed to bring that weapon into Earthaven tomorrow night. If he does, Oq could die."

Natalie sat very still. "You mean the Raven, don't you? K'tanaqui showed me a picture of a black bird but he didn't understand what it meant and neither did the Council. One of the Lords thought it might be a new weapon but the Council said Earthaven's anti-technology spell would stop it from working inside the Boundary. They said we'd be safe if we stayed in the tree."

Her mother shook her head sadly. "They're wrong. You have to understand, Natty. The Council have lived so long inside Oq, they think in tree terms now. A century is like the blink of an eye to them. They want to believe nothing has changed. They still think they can live apart here in Earthaven, recycling a few spells now and again to keep the Casters happy. It was only when I left to live with your father that I realized how frustrated the Casters had become. I heard whispers about a weapon that would bring doom to Earthaven, so K'tanaqui and I did some investigating of our own. We discovered Hawk was working on a way to get a weapon past the anti-technology spells but before I could warn the Council, Hawk's spellclave pushed me in the river." The stars around her shivered. "As a spirit, I've certain limitations. I've done my best to warn the Council through their magehounds via K'tanaqui, but I can't communicate with them directly as I'm communicating with you now. It's not the Council's fault they've failed to heed my warnings. They've no idea how rapidly human science has advanced in the past few years."

Natalie thought of what Lord Pveriyan had said about the Raven, and wasn't so sure. But she held her tongue.

"You mustn't blame the Council, Natty," her mother went on, picking up her thought. "Time blindness is a common condition and everyone suffers from it one way or another when they get old. Mothers, for example, like to think their children will stay small forever, then one day they turn around and discover their child has grown up." Something glinted in her eye as she said this. It might have been a star. "Which is why you must tell the Council what I said about the anti-technology spells. Warn them the Raven might well be able to pass them. Persuade them to act before it's too late. It would have been easier if your father had brought you to us when he was supposed to but we've still got time. They can send a force through the Thrallstone to stop Hawk bringing the Raven across the Boundary tomorrow night. It's risky, and might be noticed by the authorities in your world, but this is an emergency. The Raven could be a lot more dangerous than they think."

"I still don't really understand," Natalie said, her stomach doing peculiar things at the thought of her kidnappers attacking the soultree. "Why would Lord Hawk want to kill Oq?"

"You've heard of Spellfall?"

"The Council mentioned it, I think."

"Right. Well, when a soultree dies she creates spells. They're like seeds. Soulfruit doesn't contain any because soultrees live so long and are so huge they can't go producing seeds every year willy-nilly, or Earthhaven would soon be choked with roots. But when a soultree knows she's dying, spells fall from her branches like stars and the one that falls in exactly the right place grows into a new soultree. This takes thousands of years, during which the other spells gradually die of old age unless they're picked up and used by one who has the ancient blood."

"Like Casters, you mean?" Natalie said.

Her mother smiled. "Don't they wish! But yes, when they all lived in Earthaven they could indeed pick up spells like that, which was the whole problem. In the early days, you see, there were plenty of soultrees and plenty of spells to go round. But people breed faster than soultrees and certain Spellmages started hoarding spells to use in their power games with no thought for the future. Naturally, they sought out the most powerful spells that should have been allowed to grow into soultrees; and, although the more responsible Spellmages tried to get other spells to grow by artificially mimicking the conditions of Spellfall, they never succeeded. As the centuries passed, the number of soultrees dwindled, so special Councils were set up to protect those that remained. These soultree Councils drew up a treaty called the Spellfall Solution, decreeing that all new spells should be allowed to lie where they fell. Any Spellmage who refused to keep to its terms was banished across the Boundary."

"The Council said Hawk was banished!" Natalie said.

Lady Atanaqui nodded. "Exactly. But at first, the banished Spellmages weren't allowed spells outside the Boundary, which turned out to be a big mistake. As the number of disgruntled Casters grew, they started to band together in spellclaves and attack the Boundary, destroying gateways and invading Earthaven during the annual Opening, stealing spells whenever they could. They created such havoc, the Councils were forced to amend the Spellfall Solution. In return for the Casters' good behaviour, the Councils agreed to supply them with recycled spells and collect the dead ones for processing in Earthaven. This meant using human agents to collect and distribute the spells outside the Boundary, but it kept the peace... until now. If Hawk succeeds in forcing Oq to Spellfall, he'll have his pick of spells with more power than has been seen in your world since Atlantis lay above the waves. What he'll do with that power, I hate to think. First, he'll probably take revenge on the Council for kicking him out of Earthaven. After that, who knows?"

Natalie shifted uncomfortably on the stool. While Lady Atanaqui had been speaking of spells and soultrees, treaties and revenge, one thing had blazed in her mind brighter than all.

If Oq died, her mother's spirit would be homeless.

"We have to stop him!" she said, already making plans. "The Council will take ages to decide what to do. But K'tanaqui and I could get out through the Thrallstone and tell the police about the Raven—"

"No, Natty!" Atanaqui's figure shimmered in agitation. "Absolutely not! I'm not having you go back into danger like that."

"But you said it yourself! The Council think in tree terms! What if they spend all day and all night discussing it and then it's too late? I don't care about the Council – except maybe Lady Thaypari, she's nice – but if we don't stop Hawk in time, *you'll* die—" She choked. "I couldn't stand that, not again, I just couldn't." More tears threatened. Angrily, she removed her glasses and dashed them away.

Her mother's expression softened. "Shh, Natty. It'll be all right, you'll see. That was a brave thing to offer to do, but the Council will listen to you once they realize how serious this is. Old Pveriyan remembers the Caster Wars and he hates Hawk. He'll make them act."

Natalie took a deep breath. "I'll do my best," she promised, desperately *not* thinking of how she intended to keep that promise, in case Oq relayed her thoughts to her mother.

Lady Atanaqui smiled. "Good girl. We'll get together again when all this is over and have a proper chat. Have you any questions before you go?"

"What sort of weapon is the Raven?" she asked innocently.

"Ah – now, that's the problem. I don't know exactly. All I ever saw were some boxes with a raven symbol on the side, but of course it wouldn't have been built back then. I assume it'll be small enough to carry, though I suppose they might use a horse and cart to transport it."

Natalie stood up and plucked at the tendrils attached to her head. "Can I go now? I'd best hurry."

Atanaqui smiled again. "Yes, you had. Better take those moonflowers out of your hair first, though. Thaypari means well but they dull your senses, and you'll need all your wits about you if you're going to persuade the Council to act in time."

"I *thought* I felt sleepy!" In a fit of rage, Natalie stripped the sweetly scented petals from her hair, threw them down and stamped on them. "She never told me! How could she do this to me? She's as bad as the Casters with their sleeping pills!" She glared at the leaf-concealed entrance.

"Don't be too angry with Thaypari," her mother said gently. "Earthaven has no medicine, and you were in a state of shock when you arrived. Moonflowers are a sedative, and she must have thought they'd help you deal with things. Now, are you sure you can remember everything?"

"Of course!" Natalie crushed the final petal and straightened her shoulders. She felt more alert already, yet a little frightened too. "But what if I— I mean, we're too late?"

Her mother was immediately serious again. "Then, daughter, we'd better pray the Raven doesn't work. Because once human technology gets into Earthaven, there's nothing we can do to stop it taking over."

*

Natalie came out of the Heart trembling. She flung her arms about K'tanaqui's neck and clutched his ruff fiercely.

Pup been crrrying. Her magehound sounded confused. *Why crrry when happy?*

She blinked. Happy? She only had to get out of Oq without the Council's knowledge, find her way back to the Thrallstone, persuade the police to arrest Lord Hawk and confiscate an unknown weapon that might or might not work – and all before midnight tomorrow, or her mother would die for the second time. A huge sob escaped her.

"There, there," Lady Thaypari said. "The Heart can be a bit of an experience your first time, I know. Why don't we go down to my chambers and you can tell me all about it." She fingered a strand of Natalie's hair and frowned. "You've lost your moonflowers, you poor thing. I'll find you some more."

This reminded her she couldn't trust Thaypari. She struggled to her feet and wiped her eyes. She ought to run now before the Spell Lady got too suspicious. But there was Merlin. She couldn't leave him here, tempting though it might be.

"Where's my friend?" she asked. "I want to see him before he goes for his interview."

Lady Thaypari gave a small cough. "The Caster has already been in the Heart."

Natalie stared at her in disbelief. "*What?* But you said—"

"I know, and you mustn't think badly of us but old Pveriyan was quite right. It was vital we found out all we could about the Casters' plans as soon as possible."

"But I promised I'd be there, I *promised!* Poor Merlin, he was so frightened. I should never have left him!"

"Now don't go upsetting yourself," Thaypari said, putting a hand on her shoulder. "He's fine. He's sleeping it off in my chambers even as we speak. Despite what old Pveriyan said in the Council chamber, drainings don't happen these days. He'll get over it, you'll see."

"He won't get over it! You don't know Merlin."

On top of what she'd just learned in the Heart, it was too much. Without thinking to ask what the Council had found out and what they were going to do about it, she broke away from the Spell Lady and ran. Down the spiralling passages, unexpected draughts blowing her hair across her eyes, her breath tight, desperately trying to remember the way back to Lady Thaypari's chamber. Treemages jumped out of her way and shook their heads after her, muttering about crazy youngsters who shouldn't be allowed in the upper branches. K'tanaqui panted behind, telling her exactly what he thought. *Pup crrrazy! Pup slow down beforrre brrreak crrrazy pup-neck!*

Natalie ran faster, grabbing at twigs to catch her balance when she slipped. She supposed she deserved to fall, but Oq must have been looking after her. She reached Thaypari's chambers without injury and fought her way through the entrance vines. Her frantic gaze swept across the table with its bowl of untouched soulfruit, the empty chairs, the mossy cushions. Merlin was curled on one of the couches in the shadows at the back, his arms wrapped tightly around his head.

"Merlin!" She rushed across and dropped to her knees beside the couch. "Oh, I'm so sorry. They tricked me. I didn't realize—"

The boy sat up with a start and rubbed his eyes. For a moment, he looked blank and scared. Then a very sleepy mouse wriggled out of the neck of his tunic and blinked at her, and Merlin broke into a grin.

"Natalie! Where've you *been?* You'll never guess what happened to me in the Heart! It was brilliant, like being in the centre of the world. You should have seen old Pveriyan's face when I came out and he— What's wrong? Why are you crying?"

Natalie clung on to the couch, her legs wobbly. K'tanaqui pushed his way into the chamber, sniffed at her anxiously and began to scold. *Pup stupid! Lorrrds angrrry, fearrr they lose thirrrteenth Council memberrr. K'tanaqui fearrr too. Pup only got two legs, not good forrr balance.*

But she was too busy trying to work out the sudden change in Merlin to laugh at her magehound's comment. The boy seemed to have forgotten his terror of the night before. What was more, he seemed full of energy, happier than she'd ever seen him.

"It's like a huge web," he went on excitedly. "Much better than the Internet! I was plugged right in. All I had to do was think and, *wham*, I was there. I spoke to soultrees all over the world. There's this gnarled old soultree in Romania called Fz and she's got connections under the mountains right through to the other side. Over there, the Boundary is weaker and the locals think magehounds are werewolves. Fz knows some great stories— Hey!"

His excitement ended in a squeak as Natalie grabbed his tunic and pulled him off the couch. "Later, all right? We've got to get back to the Thrallstone as soon as possible. I'll explain on the way. Come *on*!" She dragged the protesting boy out into the passage and checked both ways.

"But we only just got here!"

"Well, we're leaving again. Anyway, I thought you hated Earthaven."

"Not any more. I haven't told you what happens during the Opening yet. It's incredible! Oq's roots go all the way, you know. Right up to the Boundary, and—"

"Tell me later." Natalie's blood was still up after the mad race from the Heart. "We've got to go now, before the Council tries to stop us. Can you remember the way to the Root System?"

Lady Thaypari appeared at the end of the passage, out of breath. "Natalie! Wait. I'm sorry you had a bad experience in the Heart. At least let's talk about it—"

"Go!" Natalie hissed to the still reluctant Merlin, giving him a push.

They left Thaypari shaking her head and hurried down the maze of hollow branches, K'tanaqui bounding in front. He led them unerringly to the vast Central Root Cavern with its floating organazoomers and eerie draughts. Natalie began to lead the way across the floor but Merlin planted himself and folded his arms.

"I'm not going a step further until you tell me why we're running away!" he announced.

She supposed she owed him an explanation. But if she stopped to tell him what her mother had said and her own reasons for not trusting the Council, they'd still be here arguing when the Boundary opened next year, let alone this. "Tell you in the organazoomer," she said, doubling back to grab his sleeve.

Merlin shook his head, his stubborn expression changing to

one of fear. Natalie looked round and her heart missed a beat. Lord Pveriyan was striding towards them, leaving a trail of thorns across the Cavern floor. Merlin backed away, one hand curled about his mouse. K'tanaqui raised his hackles and growled at K'veriyan, who growled back. Behind the Spell Lord, a line of stationary organazoomers sparkled tantalizingly.

"Going somewhere?" the Spell Lord said. "I seem to remember the Council decreed you should both stay inside for your own protection until after the Opening."

Natalie gripped K'tanaqui's ruff tighter. She glanced at Merlin, then at the organazoomers. Lord Pveriyan chuckled and stepped aside. "Go ahead," he said. "Try it."

"It's a trick," Merlin whispered.

Natalie grabbed the boy's hand and dragged him past the Spell Lord. Her skin prickled but Pveriyan made no move to stop them. "Soon as it opens, get in and hold tight," she whispered.

Merlin pulled a face, but didn't say anything.

"Open please, Oq!" she said firmly. "Take us to the Thrallstone."

Nothing happened.

The shadow of failure rippled through her. "K'tanaqui? Why won't they work?" She glared at the Spell Lord. "What have you done to them?"

Oq prrrotects thirrrteeenth Council memberrr, K'tanaqui said, keeping one amber eye on K'veriyan.

While Natalie tried to work out what he meant, Lord Pveriyan strolled towards them, a smile playing on his lips. His magehound padded after him, almost seeming to smile too.

"What can we do?" Natalie hissed to K'tanaqui. "We have to get to the Thrallstone before tomorrow night! We *have* to!"

Orrrganazoomerrrs not only way. Pups follow. Her magehound headed towards one of the tunnels at the far side of the Root Cavern.

Lord Pveriyan frowned after K'tanaqui. "Going outside won't do you any good. It'll take you a week to walk to the Boundary from here. We've no cars in Earthaven, you know.

Believe me, you'll be much safer inside during the Opening. Now be sensible. What's the great hurry, anyway?"

Natalie's heart sank. She hadn't realized it was so far. It looked as if she'd have to trust the Council, after all. She sighed and said, "Lord, when I was in the Heart I spoke to Lady Atanaqui's spirit and she said we must stop Hawk from bringing the Raven across the Boundary. I thought if K'tanaqui and I could get back through the Thrallstone in time, we could get the police to stop him. It's very important. Do you know another way?"

Lord Pveriyan's smile returned. "Stop Hawk? Oh, I think not. Let him come. His Raven will never work but he'll find Earthaven justice isn't quite so lenient this time. I said from the start we should have executed that hawk of his and drained the man completely but no one listened. Maybe they'll listen to me now."

"But Lady Atanaqui said—" One look at Pveriyan's face was enough to convince her that arguing would be useless. She grasped Merlin's hand and tugged him after K'tanaqui.

"Be dark soon," was Lord Pveriyan's parting comment. "All kinds of creatures roam Earthaven in the dark. When you've had enough, just ask Oq to let you in again. I'll be waiting."

Don't look back. Don't.

The tunnel was gloomy and sloped steeply upwards. Cobwebs clung to their clothes and laced K'tanaqui's fur. Then there was a creak ahead, and crimson light poured down the slope. Blinking, they followed the magehound into a vivid Earthaven sunset. The little trunk door creaked shut behind them. Natalie leant against it and gulped air that tasted wild, strange, pure. Beside her, Merlin brushed himself off, shuddering.

She hardly dared ask. "What's Plan B, K'tanaqui?"

Her magehound flipped his ear and gave her a long-suffering look. *Pups rrride unicorrrns, of courrrse.*

14
UNICORNS

Saturday, October 31

They spent all night looking for unicorns, K'tanaqui leading with his nose to the ground, Merlin sulking in the rear. Progress was slow. This close to Oq, the only paths wound between enormous shadowy soultree roots that rose like canyon walls on either side of them, too steep and high for climbing. They had no choice but to follow their twists and turns with much doubling back when K'tanaqui decided he should have taken a different canyon, while far overhead Oq's branches thrust black roads through the stars. Somewhere up there was the Council Chamber and at least two angry Spell Lords. Natalie fretted at the delay but there didn't seem to be much she could do about it and she had enough problems with Merlin.

When she'd told him K'tanaqui's plan, he'd gone pale. "U-unicorns?" he whispered. "But they gore people and eat them! And the other end kicks the bones away."

"All the more reason to get on their backs then."

"You mean *ride* them?" He looked really alarmed, gripped

her arm. "No, Natalie! We can't!"

"Oh, for Oq's sake!" she snapped, shrugging him off. "I should've left you back at the Lodge! You've been no use to anyone so far."

She'd regretted the words as soon as they were out but by then it was too late to say sorry. Merlin had a brief, muttered conversation with his mouse that put him in an even deeper sulk. Since then they'd walked in rigid silence, neither of them willing to admit they were wrong.

Natalie paused to pull a thorn out of her boot, saw the boy's miserable expression, and sighed. Maybe she had been a bit unfair. After all, Hawk was still his father.

"Look," she said. "I don't know how to ride a unicorn either. All I've ever ridden is a donkey on the beach and somehow I don't think that qualifies me for riding a unicorn. But I have to try, otherwise I'll never make it to the Thrallstone in time, your father will kill Oq, and my mother's spirit won't have anywhere to live. You don't have to come with me if you don't want to."

Merlin chewed his lip. He stared along the root canyon back the way they'd come, then ahead to where K'tanaqui waited in the moonlight. He was silent a long while. When he spoke, his voice was small and hard. "Yes I do. I want to be there when they arrest Father, and if that means I have to ride a unicorn, then I'll do it. I'll probably fall off, though."

It was more of a relief than she'd expected to learn she wouldn't have to do this thing alone. "No you won't, not if you hold on to the mane." She gave him a hesitant smile. "I didn't mean what I said earlier, you know. About you being useless."

Merlin gave her a tiny smile in return. "That's OK. It's true, anyway."

After that, they talked to keep themselves awake. Merlin told her more about what had happened to him in the Heart, and she told him about her interview with Lady Atanaqui. He went quiet at this point and she wondered if he was wishing he'd seen his own mother's ghost in the Heart. Where did ordinary Spellmages go when they died? And what about humans? She shook her head, not at all sure she wanted to know.

K'tanaqui found the Herder village just before dawn. They smelt smoke from the cook-fires long before they spotted the lazy coils against the sky. The soultree roots weren't so high here, more like low hills with a valley winding between. Normal-sized trees clung to the ridges and the slopes were thick with moonflowers. Natalie put a hand over her nose but the flowers were already closing, their traitorous scent lost in the cooking smells.

"Breakfast," Merlin whispered, sniffing the air.

She gave him a disgusted look. "Don't you ever stop thinking about your stomach? Where do you think they keep the unicorns?"

"How should I know?" His tone was sulky and she almost snapped at him again. Then she saw the fear in his eyes and bit back the words.

"C'mon," she whispered, taking his cold hand in her sweaty one. "They can't be that hard to ride. They're only horses with horns, aren't they?" All the same, her heart did strange things as K'tanaqui sniffed his way up the ridge, looking back over his shoulder to check they were following.

Horrrses with horrrns beside rrriverrr. He sounded amused. *Pups quiet now. Big herrrd.*

As soon as she saw the unicorns, Natalie realized her mistake. *Horses with horns* didn't even come close. The herd was grazing on the riverbank upwind of the village. A thin mist drifted off the water, curling around their fetlocks. In the half light, their coats glimmered liquid silver. Their tails floated on the air as lightly as dandelion seeds, their manes were clouds, and their horns flashed rainbow haloes around their finely chiselled heads. Long-legged foals rippled among the adults, the tiny horn stubs on their foreheads still covered in silver fur. Natalie tried to count them, but it was impossible to focus on the creatures. As soon as she thought she had an animal fixed in one place, it would *shimmer* – and the next time she looked, it would be grazing on the far side of the herd.

Nothing moves fasterrr than a unicorrrn, K'tanaqui informed her, still sounding amused. *Pups wait herrre. K'tanaqui brrring gentle one.* He was gone before she could protest, wriggling on his belly to get downwind of the herd.

While they waited, Merlin fidgeted. "I don't like this," he whispered. "There's a guard, look."

The guard was asleep in a hollow about halfway up the soul-tree root, a spear across his knees, his forehead resting on the shaft. He didn't react when K'tanaqui slunk past him, and Natalie breathed a little easier. Then her magehound slipped into the edge of the herd and she forgot all about the guard in her concern for K'tanaqui's safety. All those sharp hooves—

With a sudden silver blur, the creatures parted like water around a rock. She pressed her hands to her mouth as one shot out, swerved and galloped up the slope towards them, K'tanaqui panting at its heels.

Pup grrrab horrrn! came his faint voice. *Quick!*

Natalie froze. The unicorn wasn't as big as she'd thought, more pony than horse, but it moved so fast! Its hooves skimmed the ground, making no noise. Its eye, green as a stormy sea, sucked her down.

Merlin's scream brought her to her senses. He started to run, tripped and fell beneath the unicorn's flashing legs. Without thinking, she flung herself into the cloud of mane and made a grab for the horn. A wild almond scent enveloped her, her glasses were knocked askew, she couldn't see for spinning silver. Then her fingers closed about something smooth and warm. She clung on desperately with visions of being dragged. But as soon as she touched the horn, the unicorn lowered its head and stood still, shivering very slightly. Its mane floated around her, tangling with her hair. Wonder banished the last of her fear as she stroked the fine silvery strands. So soft.

Well done. K'tanaqui panted up the ridge. *Now jump on.*

She glanced at Merlin. "K'tanaqui says to jump on. You first."

He shook his head. "Uh-uh."

"Merlin! Quick, before that guard wakes up and sees us. I'll leg you up."

Reluctantly, Merlin approached the creature. It flared its nostrils at him and rolled its eye. He sidled to its shoulder and made a small, ineffectual jump.

The horn jerked out of Natalie's hand as the unicorn reared. It let out a scream that split her head, and lashed the air with its hooves. She flung herself to one side. Merlin was thrown to the other. K'tanaqui growled as the creature plunged back down the slope and *shimmered* into the herd. Heads shot up in an explosion of rainbows. Then the entire herd was galloping upriver, foals in the middle, screaming as they went. The guard leapt to his feet, set a whistle to his teeth and blew a single shrill note.

Natalie flattened herself to the root, heart still pounding from the scare the unicorn had given her. Breathless Herders arrived from the village and held a rapid, arm-waving conversation with the guard. Some began to jog after the herd, while others pointed their spears at the ridge where she and Merlin crouched. She hastily retreated down the other side, K'tanaqui slithering ahead, Merlin sliding behind, one hand cupped about his mouse.

At the bottom, they pushed into the undergrowth and lay panting in the shadows while the Herders ran on past.

"What now?" Natalie said, when their cries had faded. "Can we catch another one?"

Unicorrrns not let mouse-pup rrride, K'tanaqui said. *If daughter-rr-pup want to rrride, must leave Casterrr behind.*

She darted a glance at Merlin. His tunic was ripped and mud smudged one cheek. He was cradling Redeye, whispering to the mouse, promising he wouldn't let the unicorns eat him. "I can't just leave him," she said firmly. "Don't they have normal horses here?"

Horrrses without horrrns not fast enough.

Her spirits sank. Maybe she should have stayed and tried to persuade the Council. She shook the thought away. Too late now.

Then K'tanaqui said, *Therrre might be anotherrr way.*

"What?" Natalie sat up straight.

The magehound blinked his amber eyes. He seemed agitated about something. *Spells burrried nearrr herrre forrr rrrecycling. K'tanaqui smell them. Pups use spells to trrransporrrt to Thrrrallstone.*

Her heart fell again. "I don't know how to use a spell."

Mouse-pup does.

She looked doubtfully at Merlin, who was staring from the hound to her and back again. "What's he saying?" he demanded. "What's all that stuff about spells?"

Natalie hesitated. She didn't know if she could stand a repeat performance of the day they'd escaped from the Lodge, and there was something K'tanaqui wasn't telling. She gazed at the trees, trying to think. The rising sun had transformed the soultree valley into an enchanted glade filled with birdsong and sweet woodland odours. Hardly any of the leaves had turned here, and the air in the shelter of the roots was warm. It felt more like summer than the end of October, but tonight was Hallowe'en. Lord Pveriyan's words mocked her. *It'll take you a week to walk to the Boundary from here.*

She sighed. The herd had gone. The unicorns might have been a moonflower dream, except she had the evidence, soft as mist between her fingers. Curling her hand about the strands of unicorn mane, she told Merlin what K'tanaqui had said.

*

Despite Natalie's claim that there were spells nearby, it took the magehound the rest of the morning to find the cache. As they followed the animal along the shady Earthaven trails, neither of them speaking, Merlin turned over and over in his mind the theory of spell casting. He was determined not to make a mess of it this time but there were so many things that could go wrong, and the longer they walked the more problems he thought of. He was actually quite relieved when K'tanaqui gave a sudden bark, plunged into the trees and began to dig furiously, spraying soil between his hind legs like a common dog after a bone.

Merlin sank on to a nearby boulder and massaged his feet. The soft Herder boots weren't made for walking, and his toes felt as if every stone in Earthaven had bruised them. He guessed Natalie's feet must be hurting, too, because she looked pale. She sat near him and fiddled with her handful of unicorn mane, passing the smoky hairs from hand to hand as she watched the hound dig. He wondered what she was thinking about, then decided he didn't want to know the answer. Ever since she'd come out of the Heart, she'd been acting strange. First, that mad race from the soultree, then the unicorns, and now this.

He watched the hound, his nerves growing along with the hole. What he couldn't understand was why such delicate things as spells, which he'd been brought up to treat as gently as glass, should be buried so casually in the earth.

Redeye soon put him right. *How do you think Spell Lords recycle them, then? Eat 'em and shit 'em out the other end?*

Merlin had never really thought about it before but this made him think of yet another potential problem.

"How long?" he whispered.

Before Redeye could reply, Natalie scowled at him. "K'tanaqui's digging as fast as he can! Maybe you want to help? Go ahead – I know how much you hate being clean."

Merlin's cheeks burned. "That's not fair! Anyway, I meant how long does it take to recycle the spells? 'Cause if the ones your magehound's digging up are still half dead, I'm not going to be transporting anyone anywhere."

She gave him a startled look, then went into the peculiar trance she assumed when talking to her familiar. The mage-hound paused in his digging to flip a long-suffering ear. "K'tanaqui says he wouldn't go to all the trouble of digging up dead spells," she reported with a smile. "He says you should worry about casting them, and let him worry about their power."

Merlin didn't need to be told to worry. He wet his lips. "There's a few things I haven't told you about being transported by a spell," he said. He hadn't planned to tell her but it all came out in a rush. "Remember what happened when I tried to transport Redeye? It only works if there are live spells at the other end. There'd better be at least four of 'em, since there's four of us, and the only ones I know of are in the Lodge cellar."

She stared at him.

"It'll be dark down there," he rushed on. "And it'll probably be locked. We'll need to get out somehow but that's not the only problem. I might, uh, materialize us inside the walls. Then there's the danger of transporting only half of someone. And even if it works, being transported turns you inside-out. You'll probably be sick. I usually am. And then there's the problem of backflash—"

"I don't need to know the details," Natalie said quickly. "You worry about the casting and let me worry about my stomach." She gave him a weak grin and went back to playing with the unicorn mane, her fingers moving faster and faster.

K'tanaqui had now vanished below ground. Just as Merlin began to wonder if the stupid hound hadn't got the wrong place after all, soil stopped spraying out. There was a short pause, then purple and bronze light burst from the hole and lanced into the sky.

Natalie jumped to her feet and ran across. Merlin followed more slowly, clasping Redeye in a suddenly clammy hand. Below them, the magehound sat smugly in the centre of the cache, haloed by the coloured light. Several hundred spells, at least. All alive and rippling with power.

He'd shaded his eyes before he realized. "I can see them!"

Natalie glanced nervously over her shoulder. "Be difficult not to. Quick, let's go down before someone comes. That light must be visible miles away."

"I mean I can *really* see them. I don't need Redeye." Merlin blinked at the trees in sudden hope. But above the pit, every-thing remained monochrome green as before. He sighed.

Get on with it, Redeye said. *We haven't time for sightseeing. I only hope you've remembered your lessons, because I don't fancy ending up with half my tail stuck in some brick.*

Merlin's stomach fluttered. He slithered into the hole and waded through the glimmering spells to join Natalie who had one arm around her magehound's neck and wore a determined expression. "What shall I do?" she whispered.

Merlin took deep breaths to steady his nerves. "I think we'd better both sit down. Uh – hold on to my hand. Keep hold of K'tanaqui."

He made sure Redeye was safe under his tunic, then scooped four of the warm sparkling spells into his free hand and gripped them tightly. No room for error this time. He closed his eyes and thought as hard as he could of the cellar at the Lodge.

Draw the power up your arm, feel its heat fill you—

Before his mind could shy away from the dark, Merlin imagined that heat rushing out of him, out of Earthaven, and across the Boundary. The resulting spellflash left purple ghosts on the other side of his eyelids. Burnt sugar caught in his throat. Beside him, Natalie gasped. Her hand, sweaty, slipped out of his. Merlin collapsed sideways into something soft, his whole body tingling with echoes of power. Redeye squeaked in protest.

Hardly daring to believe it had worked, Merlin picked himself up and blinked to clear his vision of the spellflash... and his heart tumbled into his boots.

Natalie and K'tanaqui had gone all right, leaving two flattened, smoking patches beside him. But he and Redeye were still in the cache. And around the edge of the pit, silhouetted against sun and leaves, eight grim faces glared at him from behind a circle of bristling spears.

*

"Don't move, Caster!" a rough voice called. "Drop the spells and throw your familiar up here!"

Merlin dropped the dead spells. "I can't do anything right," he groaned. "I'm so stupid."

You can say that again, was Redeye's comment. *Fancy getting us captured when you're sitting on enough spells to take the moon out of orbit! Shut up and do as they say or you'll be memory cleansed and I'll be dead. That's the punishment for stealing spells under the revised terms of the Spellfall Solution, in case you didn't know.*

Merlin's stomach gave an uncomfortable turn. He held the mouse close to his chest, reluctant to let the Herders touch a single one of his hairs.

The leader gestured with his spear. "Hand it up here, Caster. Move very slowly."

Merlin swallowed. Live spells lay all around him. Maybe he could grab one and—

The spear pricked his cheek. "*Now*, Caster! I'm not bluffing."

Merlin slowly raised Redeye, groping desperately with his other hand in the shadows at the edge of the pit. There were chuckles when the other Herders caught sight of his mouse. The leader seized Redeye just as Merlin's fingers closed about the waxy heat of a live spell but he couldn't risk trying to cast it under these circumstances. He quickly pushed the spell into his boot and climbed out of the hole, his heart thumping.

The Herders looked down their noses at him. Behind them, shining almost as brightly as the spells, eight unicorns snorted and tossed their cloudy manes. "Don't hurt him," Merlin pleaded, willing Redeye to refrain from biting the leader's hand.

With a grim smile, the Herder leader passed the mouse to one of his men and untied the sash from his waist. He wound the soft material about Merlin's wrists, binding them tightly. Merlin's stomach fluttered again. "You don't have to tie me, I wasn't stealin—"

"Silence!" snapped the leader. "I'll do the talking. How did you get so deep into Earthaven without being spotted by the Boundary patrols? How did you find the spells? Where did you get those clothes? A little squirt like you never dug that hole on your own. Where are the others?"

Merlin bit his lip and thought of Natalie. "I dunno," he said miserably. "I wish I did."

"I see." The leader gave him a disgusted look. "Have it your own way. The Council will soon get it out of you."

He motioned to his men, and they vaulted on to their unicorns. Bridleless, saddleless, the creatures surrounded Merlin,
their horns flashing and their green eyes smouldering. He
cringed, terrified someone might try to lift him on to one of
those shimmering rumps. But the man who'd taken Redeye
simply dropped the mouse on to Merlin's shoulder and backed
off. The leader gave him a prod with his spear. "Walk smartly
now, Caster," he said. "We're in a hurry."

*

With unicorns in front, behind, and on both sides, the journey
back to Oq was even more uncomfortable than the journey out.
But the Herders must have known all the short cuts, because
at least it didn't take them so long. Merlin gathered from
listening to their conversations that they were heading for
a meeting of Earthaven tribes at Oq's trunk and, as the
enormous roots rose around him, he began to feel excitement
at the prospect of another visit to the Heart. His stride lengthened, drawing surprised looks from his escort.

"Told you Casters were crazy," muttered one, which made
the others laugh.

They arrived at the soultree shortly after sunset to find Oq
in a state of frenzied activity. Great arched doorways stood
open all the way round the massive trunk, spilling emerald
light along the root-canyons where the Earthaven tribes had
gathered. The seething mass of excited people and animals
blocked all routes to and from the tree. Some had proper
weapons – long twisted knives, spears, clubs, and axes. Others
were mounted on bears and stags, whose growls and clashing
antlers echoed in the shadows. Still others were armed with
sticks, or heavy metal cooking pots, or ropes with weights
knotted into the ends. Harassed Treemages hurried in and out
of the trunk doors, shouting orders that no one listened to.
Several groups of mounted unicorns, their silver coats lighting
up the dusk, were accorded a respectful distance by the other
tribes.

As Merlin's escort closed around him and began to squeeze

their way through the press of bodies, someone shouted, "It's a Caster prisoner! Kill him!" and there was an angry roar as they all surged forward. It took his escort's combined strength and the threat of their spears to get him safely past the hostile cries. Merlin didn't feel completely safe until they'd passed through one of the doorways and were inside Oq's glowing passages.

Here, the Herders fell silent. The unicorns pranced nervously, flaring their nostrils at the strange draughts and scents. Even Redeye was uncharacteristically quiet, peeping from the neck of Merlin's tunic as they went. "It's all right," Merlin whispered, wishing he could hold the mouse in his hands. "We're safe now."

"Don't count on it, Caster," muttered the Herder leader.

At the first junction he dismounted, prodded Merlin up a short side passage into a chamber where a group of Treemages were gathered, and dutifully handed him over to a harassed Lady Thaypari. "Caught him in a spell cache," he said simply as he freed Merlin's wrists. He shook out the sash and retied it about his waist, bowed his head to the Spell Lady, then hurried to rejoin his men. The Treemages took one look at Thaypari's face and tactfully followed him out.

When they were alone, Lady Thaypari looked Merlin up and down and said, "Where's Natalie?"

"I don't know," Merlin admitted, massaging his wrists.

She gripped his arm and shook him hard. "You little fool! What did you go running off like that for? Haven't you any sense in your head? Have you no idea how serious this is? Oq's lost touch with Natalie and K'tanaqui, and no one's got time to look for them now. You can see what's happening outside. Every resident of Earthaven wants their drop of Caster blood tonight. It's chaos out there! You're lucky they didn't kill you on sight."

Merlin hung his head. "I know. I'm sorry."

"Sorry? Is that all you can say?"

"It was Natalie's idea."

Lady Thaypari gave him a disgusted look. "You didn't have to go along with it!" Then she sighed and released him. "I suppose old Pveriyan didn't help matters. I don't know what he was thinking of, letting you two go outside like that. At least you're back where Hawk can't get at you. Now, tell me exactly how you got separated and then I'm afraid I'm going to have to ask Oq to restrain you in here until after the Opening. It's far too dangerous for you to be running around Earthaven tonight."

Merlin bit his lip. On the whole he was glad to be back inside the soultree but he'd have preferred Natalie to be here with him.

"I transported her," he said in a small voice. "Least, I think I did. K'tanaqui too, only I don't know where. I was trying to get us all to the Lodge."

Lady Thaypari went white beneath her crown of wilting orange flowers. "You little idiot," she whispered. "Did nobody tell you that you can't transport across the Boundary when it's shut?"

There was a sudden flare of gold at the end of the passage as someone outside lit a torch. A ragged cheer went up, the noise level rising as the army prepared to ride out. Merlin didn't have time to wonder how he was suddenly seeing colours again, and the Spell Lady didn't need to speak.

Around them, Oq's leaves rustled anxiously. Merlin's stomach did peculiar things. "Then where— Oh no, what have I done?"

15

SPELLCLAVE

Saturday night, October 31

Tim's stomach did peculiar things as he shrugged into his birthday jacket on Saturday evening. It had set like concrete as it dried out but he wasn't going to wear his old anorak, not tonight. He thought about squeezing his sore feet into his fashion boots, just to show Jo, but his blisters were still too puffy. Anyway, gym shoes would probably be better if they had to run.

He checked his watch. Six o'clock and still no sign of Mr Marlins. He hadn't realized how much he'd been hoping his stepfather would turn up with Nat wrapped in a blanket, or the police would arrest someone, or Mrs Carter would forbid Jo to set foot out of the house, or his own mother would try to stop him going out tonight. But once they'd adjusted to the idea of their offspring going to the Disco together, the two mothers had seemed all for it. They made Tim promise to collect Jo and see her home safely afterwards, then raised their eyebrows at each other and smiled in that mysterious adult way. So here he was, stuck with Jo's crazy plan.

It was a clear, frosty evening, the stars so bright they almost made Tim dizzy. He walked fast to the Carters' house, hands in his pockets, his breath making clouds in the air. Jo was waiting at the door. She hopped from foot to foot, blowing on her hands, as Mrs Carter gave Tim a stern look.

"You look after her, Timothy Lockley, do you hear? If there's any trouble, I'll hold you responsible."

"Yes, Mrs Carter." Tim gave her what he hoped was a reassuring smile, certain their deception must be written in flaming letters across his hot cheeks.

But Mrs Carter must have thought it was embarrassment. She smiled as she kissed Jo goodbye. "Be careful, love," she said. "You two have fun."

They'd hidden their bikes in the boat shed earlier that day, along with torches and other useful equipment. Tim was mildly surprised to find everything was still there. They quickly transferred the supplies to their pockets, checked the torches and cycle lamps, then stared at each other. Jo was the first to break the spell. She pushed her hair under her baseball cap and grinned. "Well?" she said. "What are you waiting for? Let's go!"

Before Tim could stop her, she was off towards town, jumping her bicycle up and down kerbs with a skill he had to admire. He pedalled madly after her, hating to think what might happen if she reached the fountain before him. But he found her waiting at the entrance to the precinct, looking slightly less confident.

Tim didn't blame her. The shopping mall was spooky now all the shops had shut, their metal grilles padlocked in place for the night. A chip wrapper blew against Tim's front wheel. An empty can rattled in the shadows. The echoes made him jump.

"Where are they?" Jo said. "I can't see anyone." She pushed her bike across the paved area to the fountain and sat on the rim, swinging her long legs.

Tim joined her, thankful of the chance to ease his blisters, acutely aware of the arm's length between them. "They'll be here."

He was starting to think this wasn't such a bright idea. The Death Heads' second rule – the one after not talking to the police – was never to bring a girl on a gang outing. But he wasn't exactly bringing Jo, was he? More like her bringing him. He grinned at the thought, and she gave him a sharp look. "Your feet all right?"

"Fine," he said, though blood had been seeping slowly around his left heel since they'd left the boat shed. "Shh! Here they come."

In a raucous burst of jangling bells, five mountain bikes raced towards them, despite the rule about not riding in the precinct. The three older boys raced around the fountain, still ringing their bells, while little Paulie braked a short way off and eyed Jo warily. Finally, Pizzaface turned up puffing, last as usual.

"What we got here, then?" Very deliberately, Gaz kicked Tim's bicycle over, then leant on his handlebars and stared at him, a challenge in his eye. The other Heads ranked themselves behind him, jostling one another. Paulie giggled, which earned him a clout from his brother.

Though his heart pounded, Tim made himself pick up his bicycle and prop it back against the fountain. The spray had been turned off until Monday and the water glittered with ice crystals. Everything seemed twice as sharp as usual, as if he'd been asleep all his life until tonight.

"Where's your earring, then?" Gaz said, when it became obvious Tim wasn't going to rise to the bait. "Mommy make you take it out, did she, diddums?"

Mike and Dave laughed at his sickly tone, though Paulie blushed. Tim got the feeling Paulie wasn't allowed to wear his skull at home.

"Or maybe his *girlfriend* made him," Mike said, leering at Jo.

Jo stiffened, and Tim shot her a warning glance. He said quickly, "We've got a dare for you."

"Not interested. We got stuff planned already for tonight." Gaz reached under his jacket and pulled on a Hallowe'en mask. It had green hair, luminous orange blood, and a bolt through its neck. "Goin' trick or treatin', aren't we?"

"Yeah!" Pizzaface agreed. "Got loads of treats up on the new estate last year."

Tim couldn't help but laugh. "I mean a *real* dare! Not scaring old ladies out of a few measly chocolate bars."

Mike and Dave scowled, but Gaz propped his mask on top of his head and narrowed his eyes. "What dare?"

Tim smiled. He had them. "There's going to be a party tonight, up at the old lodge in Unicorn Wood. I dare you to come up there with us and ask for a treat."

Silence. Litter swirled in a sudden breeze, sending a shiver down his spine. The five Heads glanced at one another. Pizzaface swallowed visibly. Paulie paled. "B-but Unicorn Wood's *haunted*," he whispered.

"Shut up, you little twerp," Dave hissed.

"Of course it's haunted," Tim said, catching Jo's grin. "Otherwise it wouldn't be much of a dare, would it?"

Gaz was starting to look interested. He popped a stick of gum into his mouth and chewed slowly. "Hallowe'en party, eh? How far is it to this lodge, then?"

"Five miles or so."

"You know the way?"

With a flourish, Tim produced the map and spread it on the rim of the fountain. Gaz frowned at it while the others crowded forward, trying to see over his shoulder. Jo sat aloof, kicking her heels against the stone and whistling softly to herself.

Gaz chewed some more. "What d'you reckon, Heads?"

"Take us all night to get up there with Pizzaface and Paulie along," Dave said.

"Hey!" Pizzaface protested. "That's not fair—"

"Shut up," Gaz growled. "I'm thinkin'."

He must have been, too, because he was silent a long time. Then Jo ruined it by saying scornfully, "Told you they'd be too scared, didn't I?"

The mood changed so fast, Tim didn't have time to think.

Gaz spat out his gum, grabbed Jo's ankle and tipped her backwards over the fountain rim. Her cap tumbled into the water and her bicycle crashed over as she lashed out with her feet. One of them caught Mike on the jaw. It was probably an accident but he flung himself on her with a cry of rage, calling for Dave to help.

"No!" Paulie squeaked, "Dad'll kill me if I get into another fight—"

Tim threw his bike at Pizzaface and leapt on to Gaz's back, wrapping his legs around the boy's waist and his arms around his neck. Little Paulie was no threat. He'd already begun to back away from the struggle, darting nervous glances over his shoulder. Gaz went down. Tim momentarily lost sight of Jo while he and the leader wrestled furiously on the ground, though grunts and curses from the other boys suggested Jo was holding her own.

Then there was a splash and a yell. "Get me out of here!" Dave screamed, splashing wildly. "It's freezing!"

While Gaz was distracted, Tim broke free, retrieved his bicycle and dragged Jo round to the other side of the fountain.

"STOP!" he shouted at the top of his lungs.

It was beautiful. Everyone froze – Dave kneeling in the fountain with water dripping from his clothes; Pizzaface holding his eye where Tim's handlebar had caught him; Mike and Gaz looking for someone to hit; Paulie halfway down the precinct.

"Suppose you think you're tough," Tim said. "Attacking defenceless girls?"

Jo opened her mouth. "I'm not a defencele—"

Tim went on quickly. "When I joined you, I thought we stood for something real. I thought we were into doing things. Yes, it might be dangerous up in the wood. And yes, it might be haunted. If you want to know the truth, there isn't a party at the lodge – we think that's where Nat is being kept. If her kidnappers are still there, they might have weapons. They're certainly not stupid. They've already outwitted the police once. But they've got my stepsister. And whether you help or not, Jo and I are going up there to try and get her back." He grabbed the soggy map and stuffed it back under his jacket. "C'mon Jo, we're wasting our time here."

The girl dashed the grit off her jeans and fished her cap out of the fountain. She jammed it back on her head and glared at Gaz. "I thought you'd grown up since I had to brain you that day," she said quietly. "Or we wouldn't have bothered asking."

Tim's stomach clenched. But not one of the Heads moved. They kept glancing at Gaz, who was too busy frowning at Jo to notice. In the end, Mike went to Dave's rescue, Pizzaface picked himself up, and Paulie crept back to his brother's side, sniffing quietly.

"Let's go," Tim hissed, giving Jo a push. *"Now."*

This time she complied. As they raced from the precinct and headed out of town, she gave him a flash of that crazy grin. Tim grinned back and stood on his pedals. His veins sang, the stars fizzed in the sky, and his bike felt as if it had grown wings. Strangely, his feet didn't hurt at all.

*

The euphoria carried them for several miles but quickly wore off once they entered the wood. Here, under the trees, the stars were no longer visible and their cycle lamps seemed very small and feeble. Chill darkness seeped from every side, almost thick enough to touch.

By the time they stopped to consult the map, Tim was having serious second thoughts. As Jo fought the large sheet, trying to persuade it to fold in the right place, a loud screech came from the trees, making them both jump. Jo removed her cap and wiped her forehead with the back of one hand, eyes searching the shadows.

"Fox," she said. "I think."

Tim noticed fresh beads of sweat on her forehead.

He must have walked this route in the opposite direction yesterday, yet nothing seemed familiar. What if the entire wood was under some enchantment? They might wander up here forever and never find their way out again. He guiltily thought of his promise to Mrs Carter.

Jo replaced her cap and gave him a direct stare. "I never thanked you for what you did back at the fountain."

Tim shrugged. "I thought I'd better stop the fight before you hurt someone."

"I'm glad you did. It was pretty brave of you, standing up to the Heads like that. I suppose they'll throw you out now?"

"Doesn't matter." He looked away, embarrassed. "They're not exactly what I expected. I was going to leave anyway."

There was an awkward silence. Then something small and very fast darted across his foot and vanished into the wood, sending shivers right through him. He felt a sudden urge to talk. "Want to know a secret?"

"What?"

"I hate the countryside. Back in London, it was never really dark like this. When it rained, it never got muddy. There was always someplace to go, someplace warm and bright and full of people. When that Spell Lord dragged me through his Thrallstone into Earthaven, I was petrified. I thought I'd never see a streetlamp again."

"Is that why you hate Nat so much?" Jo asked softly.

Tim blinked. It wasn't the response he'd been expecting. He'd thought she might call him a coward, and with good reason. Here he was, acting like a little kid afraid of the dark. "Hate her? I don't hate her."

"She thinks you do."

He said slowly, "I hated leaving all my friends behind. They teased me about moving out into the sticks and I suppose I blamed my mother for that. When she filled in the dating agency form, she never asked me what I wanted, did she? Just went ahead and put *countryside* and *children* and all that rubbish. I could hardly believe it when she went and married Mr Marlins. I mean, even I'd worked out he was a piss-head and I'd only met him twice! But as soon as she heard what had happened to Nat's mother, that was it. Told me we were going to make a fresh start in the country. Said Mr Marlins was a very unhappy man with a confused little girl who needed us." He paused, remembering. "I did resent Nat at first, the way my mother fussed over her as if she was the only person in the world who'd ever lost a parent. But I suppose it wasn't Nat's fault."

Even as he spoke, he knew Jo was right. He had been mean to Nat. Whenever he got frustrated with Millennium Green, she was the one he took it out on. He made a private promise to make it up to her when they got her back.

If they got her back.

"Is your real dad dead, then?" Jo asked, still gently.

Tim shook himself. "No! Ran off with another woman, didn't he? Haven't seen him since. Don't want to neither, the way he treated us. C'mon, we ought to get moving if we're going to make it to this lodge and back before the disco finishes."

Jo didn't move. "And did you leave a girlfriend back in London?"

He blushed furiously, for once glad of the dark because it hid his embarrassment. "Don't be stupid! I was only a kid when we left."

A flash of that white grin. "I'm glad you came to Millennium Green." Before he knew what was coming, she'd pecked him on the cheek, bounced her bike into the woods and was off down the muddy track, her rear lamp winking like a red eye in the night.

Tim stared after it, stunned. He touched his cheek which was tingling strangely. Then his bike fell over on his foot and pain shot up his leg, bringing him to his senses. "Hey!" he called, dragging the machine upright. "Wait for me!"

*

They came across the lodge suddenly. One moment, there were only black trees and silver shadows, unidentified rustles and their flickering cycle lamps. The next, an ancient house loomed behind gates of twisted black iron and an ivy-wreathed wall, lighting up the night.

They dismounted and took cover behind a fallen log. Jo

studied the place in silence while Tim tried to imagine being brought here against his will and imprisoned inside. He shuddered.

There was a lot of activity. The uncurtained windows cast rectangles of yellow light across some of the wildest brambles Tim had ever seen. People clad in dark clothing hurried in and out of the front door carrying spades, sacks, thick gloves, rucksacks, and – more worryingly – business-like bows and quivers stuffed with arrows. They disappeared round the corner of the house, then returned empty handed for another load. He tried to count them but had to give up. Apart from a tall man with feathers in his hair who strode about swinging his stick around as if he owned the entire world and a blonde woman who held her head a little higher than the rest, they could all have been clones. They kept their eyes downcast and flinched whenever the feathered man came near. Tim couldn't see anyone small enough to be Nat.

"Do you think Nat's still in there?" he whispered.

Jo shook herself and rose to her feet. "Poor thing! Keeping her in a place like that! Let's go and see."

Tim grabbed her jacket in alarm and pulled her back down. "Are you crazy? We're not going to get anywhere near the house with all those people around. Looks like they're setting out on an expedition or something. Wonder what they're up to?"

Jo stared at him as if *he* were the crazy one. "What are you talking about? What people?"

"Those people! And keep your voice down. They'll hear you."

"*Who'll* hear me?" Jo's eyes flashed dangerously. "If this is some sort of joke, Timothy Lockley—"

He frowned at her but she seemed serious. Then he remembered the trouble he'd had at the Thrallstone and groaned. "You can't see them, can you?"

She shook her head.

"What *can* you see?"

"Just a dark old house covered in ivy, boarded-up windows, half the roof gone. Looks like it's about to fall down. Creepy." She shivered.

"That sounds like what the police saw." He frowned at the lodge, thinking hard. "Must be some spell on it – that's why they didn't find anyhing when they searched up here. Maybe I can see it because I've been in Earthaven. You haven't, so you can't."

Jo slammed a fist into the leaves. "What do I have to do to see them? They're the people who killed Bilbo. I *want* to see them. What time is it?"

Tim glanced at his watch. "Eleven thirty-three," he reported, turning cold.

"Don't be silly. We can't have been up here that long." Jo switched on her torch and peered at hers. She frowned. "Funny. Mine says the same."

They stared at each other in silence.

"It's just what happened before," said Tim, "when I was waiting for that Spell Lord to finish unloading his truck. Must be something to do with the spells on the Boundary. Careful! They're switching off the lights."

As Jo clicked off the torch the final light went out in the house and the blonde woman emerged from the Lodge. She wore thick gloves and carried a metal cylinder with a handle, like a large vacuum flask. It glinted in the moonlight, revealing a black bird with outstretched wings on its silver surface.

"They're even taking a picnic!" Tim said in an attempt to shake off his nerves. "There goes the coffee."

Jo sighed. "Be serious. Tell me when it's clear and I'll go in and start looking for Nat. You'd better keep an eye on the kidnappers and warn me if they come back."

Tim was reluctant to let her go into the house alone but it made sense. She couldn't exactly keep an eye on people she couldn't see, and if they both went inside they could easily get trapped and find themselves prisoners too. "Maybe you should just ring the police now?" he said. "They're obviously up to something. It'd be safer."

Jo gave him a scornful look. "Great! So how are they going to see the people they're supposed to arrest? We'd end up in custody ourselves for wasting police time." Then she touched his arm and her tone gentled. "I promise I'll phone as soon as I find Nat or if there's any trouble. Whichever comes first." She patted the mobile in the pocket of her ski jacket.

Tim had a horrible feeling he knew which would come first but didn't say anything. The blonde woman had vanished round the corner after the others, leaving the door open. Now all the lights were off an eerie purple glow could be seen flickering behind the house. They waited a few minutes to be certain no one was coming back, then quietly scaled the gates. Jo gave him the thumbs-up, switched on her torch and disappeared into the lodge. Curious in spite of his fear, Tim crept towards that purple glow.

The Casters had assembled on an archery range a short distance from the house. They had set fire to some of their arrows which they were holding aloft like huge sparklers. Tim crouched behind the nearest target and covered his nose. The flames were bright purple like something from a chemistry experiment and even from here the sickly odour of burnt sugar turned his stomach. As he watched, the spellclave formed a circle around the feathered man. Tim's heart gave an uncomfortable lurch as he counted them.

Thirteen.

The feathered man was saying something, his words faint in the purple smoke. Tim worked his way closer, using the targets as cover.

"...priority is digging for roots..."

"...once the Raven's safely at work, we can look for the runaways..."

"...Hunter'll soon find them..."

"...teach that boy a lesson he'll never forget..."

Then the blonde woman said something which sent uneasy mutters round the circle. In answer, the feathered man swung his stick and lashed her across the face. She fell to her knees with a little cry, and her fire-arrow went flying in an arc of purple sparks. The others ducked as it hissed over their heads and plunged into the grass where it started a small blaze.

The feathered man glared around the circle. "If the girl's still with him, we'll deal with her too. She might have opened the Thrallstone but she's not yet come into her full powers, and thanks to Rabbit here our spellclave is complete at last." He pointed his stick at one of the women, who gripped her fire-arrow tighter and gave him a nervous little smile. "Now, I don't want to hear another word about failure. Never underestimate the Power of Thirteen!"

The blonde woman picked herself up and silently lit another arrow. The others pointedly ignored her. "Lord Hawk!" they cried as purple sparks spat into the night. "Long live Lord Hawk!"

*

Neck prickling, Tim retreated along the line of targets until he reached the trees, then hurried back to the Lodge.

"Jo!" he hissed, shining his torch into the shadows. He'd feared a long search but she was crouched behind the stairs, trying to pick a lock with a hair grip. She sprang up, a fierce look in her eyes, a pair of broken rollerblades dangling from her hand. "I found Sarah's skates upstairs! Nat's definitely been here and this door's locked. Looks like some sort of cellar. If they've got her down there—"

"She's not in there," Tim said. "They're hunting her in the woods. Phone the police. *Now!*"

Jo stared at him in horror. "*Hunting* her?"

"She must have escaped. I heard them discussing her. Somehow, she got through the Thrallstone into Earthaven and now they're going after her with bows and fire-arrows. Phone, Jo. Now! We can't do this alone any more." He made a grab for her mobile but she shrugged him off and put it to her ear. She shook her head.

"What's wrong?"

"No signal. I'll go outside."

Tim started to follow but heard footsteps crunch on the gravel outside. A shadow crossed the window of the room to their right. There was a shed on that side of the house he remembered. The path led past it to the front door. Jo was on the step, her back turned, frowning and punching numbers on her dad's phone, shaking it in frustration. He hissed her name and waved frantically to attract her attention but she moved further outside, intent on the phone.

Tim hesitated a fraction of a second, then darted into the room and flung himself at the window. It had an old-fashioned catch which opened with a rusty screech. The figure outside whirled in surprise, a huge hawk flapping for balance on its left wrist. Two sets of yellow eyes glared at Tim as Lord Hawk swung his stick round with a hiss. "Who are you?" he demanded. "What were you doing in there? How come you can see past the illusions?"

Tim looked desperately for Jo. She was out in the open, phone pressed to her ear, staring at him. No telling if she could see the hawk-man but he had to assume not. "*Go!*" he mouthed, then plunged into the brambles and fled for the little gate in the wall at the back of the garden. "Ya, Caster!" he yelled over his shoulder as he ran, sticking out his tongue. "Your stupid spells don't work on me!"

As he'd hoped, the hawk-man came after him.

Tim darted through the gate and into the trees before he risked another look back. His pursuer had stopped just outside the wall, breathing hard, the hawk still on his wrist. "Can't catch me!" Tim called and plunged into the wood, dodging the black trunks, crunching frosty leaves underfoot, biting his tongue every time he stumbled and knocked his blisters. There was no sound of pursuit. He began to worry the hawk-man had gone back to the lodge and caught Jo. Then a prickling sensation at the back of his neck made him glance up.

The hawk was coming straight for him, swift and low, its wings slicing the night like silent blades. Only just in time, Tim threw himself face down in the mud. The bird plummeted into the leaves beside his ear before flapping off, *caaa-ing*, into the night.

Cautiously, his heart still thudding, Tim regained his feet and brushed himself off. Hopefully, Jo would have the sense to get on her bike and pedal like mad. He'd detour until she'd had a chance to get clear, then work his way back. Give her, say, ten minutes.

As he peered at his watch, the moon blurred. For a second, everything glittered as if a veil had been taken from his eyes. He had time to think, *midnight*. Then the most excruciating pain shot up his legs, pierced his spine, and exploded in his head. It took him a moment to realize what was happening. But he'd felt Oq touch his memories before, and the feeling was unmistakeable.

A scream escaped him. He heard a stick thrashing the undergrowth and quickly clamped his teeth into his lower lip. But that scream had already betrayed him. A boot swam into his vision. The stick prodded his cheek.

"Twist your ankle, did you?" Lord Hawk sounded amused. "How unfortunate, but that's the Opening for you. There'll be a lot of accidents tonight. Most humans put it down to the dark or bad weather but some of us know otherwise – don't we?" The stick prodded harder. "Who sent you?"

Tim gritted his teeth. "No one," he hissed, fighting the alien presence in his head. "I came to rescue Nat."

Lord Hawk chuckled. "That's what the Thrall said. Pity I haven't time to question you properly just now but I'm sure you understand I've more important things to do tonight."

He raised his stick against the stars, reversed so its heavy handle hung above his head. Tim made an effort to get up but the agony came again, pouring out of the ground in black waves.

He didn't feel the stick come down.

16

THE OPENING

Midnight, Saturday, October 31

The Opening roused Natalie from a nightmare in which she'd been turned inside-out and transported into the wall of the Lodge cellar, helplessly trapped as slimy creatures that lived between the stones crawled closer and closer.

It took her a moment to realize the wet warm thing sliming her face wasn't some monstrous slug, but K'tanaqui's anxious tongue. She had to push the magehound away so she could be sick. She wiped her mouth on her sleeve, retrieved her glasses and looked around.

Moonlight cast stark shadows through interlaced branches. There was an unnatural silence as if the whole world were holding its breath. Then a sudden inrush of chill air, swirling her hair and spiralling leaves over her legs which were buried in loose soil.

She kicked free with a shudder. "What happened, K'tanaqui? Where's Merlin?" She had a sudden horrible thought. "That wasn't… that wasn't the Raven-weapon going off?"

Her magehound, apparently satisfied she was in one piece, stopped sniffing at her and blinked his amber eyes. *Not Rrraven, but Boundarrry open now. Enemies crrross, see everrrything until dawn. Mouse-pup safe. Much dangerrr to soultrrree.*

Natalie picked herself up and brushed the dirt from her breeches, trying to think. "Merlin blew it again, didn't he? Where are we, K'tanaqui?"

She wasn't really surprised to learn they were still inside Earthaven, half a day's walk from the Boundary. They'd materialized on top of another cache of spells buried for recycling, though not as deep as usual. *Orrr pup would be burrried too,* K'tanaqui added, tongue lolling in his wet magehound laugh.

"That's not funny," Natalie said. "Now we'll never reach the authorities in time to stop Lord Hawk! Merlin's such an idiot. I should've taken that unicorn while I had the chance, I might have known he'd make a mess of things and now Mother's going to die—" She choked and clenched her fists.

Mouse-pup trrried, K'tanaqui said reprovingly, licking her hand. *At least we arrre alive and togetherrr.*

She clutched his ruff and buried her face in his sweet-smelling coat. "You're right," she said, starting to think again. "If we can't stop Hawk bringing the Raven into Earthaven, then we have to stop him using it when he gets here." She took a deep breath. "Can you find the Casters, K'tanaqui?"

He flipped his ear. *Of courrrse. Casterrrs smell verrry strrrong.*

"How close?"

The magehound sniffed the wind. *Maybe an hourrr. Casterrrs come this way, thirrrteen now. Arrrogant hawk comes too.* His lips drew back in a snarl. Then his voice took on a puzzled tone. *Also one human, no powerrr. Most strrrange.*

"Have they used the Raven yet?"

Not yet.

Natalie straightened her shoulders and pushed her hair behind her ears. She drew a deep breath. "Take me to them."

K'tanaqui gave her a steady look. *Pup brrrave, like motherrr.*

She flushed. "I'm not brave, I just haven't any choice. Oq's sealed the root system. We're closest."

Always choice. Pup make brrrave one.

K'tanaqui led the way at a good pace, his silver form threading silently between the dark trunks. Natalie followed, feeling very small and alone. She didn't have the first idea what she was going to do when she found the spellclave. The very thought of seeing her kidnappers again turned her cold all over, so she blanked her mind and pushed herself to keep up. She didn't allow herself to feel the chill of the night, nor the bruises on her feet, nor the dreadful danger, pretending instead that she was taking her dog for a walk through Unicorn Wood with nothing more to worry about than whether Julie had cooked chips for tea.

This worked so well that when K'tanaqui suddenly halted and growled softly, she almost tripped over him.

Pup bewarrre, he said. *Casterrrs ahead with spellfirrre.*

Natalie blinked at the purple glow flickering through the dark branches. Then she smelt it too. The same horrible smell that had filled the cellar when the goshawk ate Itsy.

Her heart started to race. "What are they doing?" she whispered.

Digging, her magehound replied, full of scorn. *Casterrrs not verrry good at it.*

"Digging? What for? Are they looking for spells?" She crept as close as she dared and parted the leaves.

Hawk's back was turned, his attention on the activity in the clearing, but at the sight of him her skin tightened. She fought an overpowering urge to leap up and flee. The spellclave had assembled around a colony of moonflowers, flaming arrows held aloft. The spell smoke tainted the flowers' scent, neutralizing its effect. As Natalie watched, Lord Hawk stepped forward and prodded the white petals with his stick. He nodded. Black-bearded Ferret and another man picked up spades and started to dig. Soon, two large mounds of soil devastated the moonflower colony. Ferret scraped with his spade, then reached quickly into the trench and gave a triumphant shout.

The Casters crowded forward for a closer look, but fell back again as Hawk strode to the edge. Almost invisible in the branches of a nearby oak, the spellclave's goshawk screeched.

Natalie backed further under the bush, heart hammering. K'tanaqui joined her, his belly fur dragging in the mud. "I don't see anything that could be the Raven," she whispered. There were several rucksacks, though, piled with the Casters' bows and arrows at the far side of the clearing. She eyed the spellclave. They seemed fascinated by whatever they'd unearthed. Hawk had joined the diggers in the bottom of the trench.

Keeping one eye on the goshawk's perch, every nerve taut, Natalie started to work her way towards the rucksacks. K'tanaqui followed, still wriggling on his belly. He was trying to tell her something but she needed all her concentration for the Raven. What would she do if it was there? She hesitated, turned to ask K'tanaqui if he had any ideas, and stared in dismay.

Gone.

"K'tanaqui!" she hissed, her heart pounding uneasily. "Come back! This is no time to go off chasing rabbits—"

From the thicket came a little scream.

K'tanaqui find human. Her magehound sounded smug. *Pup not worrry, though. Human frrriendly.*

He wriggled out of the bushes and a tall girl wearing jeans and a black-and-green ski jacket crawled out after him. Natalie gaped, open-mouthed, as the girl flicked her thick chestnut fringe out of her eyes and grinned. "About time," she whispered. "If I'd had to follow this lot much further, my feet would've dropped off!"

"Jo!" Natalie squeaked, finally finding her voice. "What are you doing here?" Her whole being filled with a warm golden glow. They fell into each other's arms and hugged tightly.

"It's a long story," Jo said, pushing her back so she could examine her from head to toe. "Oh, Nat, we've been so worried about you. You wouldn't believe what's been happening at home."

"Yes I would. But you won't believe what's happened to me!"

The two friends retreated into the trees and exchanged stories in excited whispers, while K'tanaqui kept an eye on the spellclave.

"...illusion spells..."

"...wonderful tree..."

For Natalie, the most unbelievable part of Jo's story was that *Tim* had come up to Unicorn Wood to look for her. But Jo wouldn't lie about a thing like that. Apparently, they'd got separated while searching the Lodge. They still hadn't found each other when Jo had stumbled across the spellclave. Her voice tightened. "I hung on as long as I could but I was afraid I'd lose them if I waited for him any longer, and I didn't dare take my eyes off them in case they vanished again. I couldn't see them at first. Tim thought it had something to do with the spells."

"Illusions," Natalie said. "They don't work during the Opening."

Her friend pulled a face. "Tim saw through them straight-away. When he lost me, he must've thought I'd gone back to town to fetch the police. I was supposed to phone but my mobile wasn't working. Maybe he didn't notice my bicycle was still there in the dark." She smiled. "Tim's not the idiot everyone thinks he is, you know. I expect he did the sensible thing and went for help but all I could think of was the spellclave hunting you with their bows and fire-arrows. So when they set off into the wood, I followed."

"They're hunting *me?*" Natalie shivered, not sure she'd have had the nerve to do what Jo had done.

"That's what Tim said, though I must say it's the strangest hunt I've ever seen. They keep stopping to dig up those white flowers. They've been at it for hours." She glanced at her watch, then shook her wrist and grinned sheepishly. "Stupid thing stopped at midnight, I keep forgetting."

K'tanaqui, who had been growing more and more agitated as they talked, came back and blinked his amber eyes. *Casterrrs dig up soultrrree rrroot. Pups stay. K'tanaqui fetch help.*

Before Natalie could protest, he'd slipped into the trees and vanished into the night. She fought a crazy impulse to race after him. With an effort, she turned her attention back to the spellclave.

Lord Hawk climbed out of the trench. He planted his stick in one of the soil mounds, wrapped his scarf around his nose and pulled on a pair of thick gloves. Carefully, he opened one of the rucksacks and extracted a metal canister which reflected the spellfire. All the Casters stepped back. Cold prickles worked their way up and down Natalie's spine as she saw the symbol on the side.

"What do you think it is?" Jo whispered. "A bomb?"

Natalie's heart clenched. "They're going to blow up Oq!" She fought her way out of the bush and would have raced into the middle of the spellclave there and then, had Jo not grabbed her ankle and pulled her down.

"Are you crazy?" her friend hissed.

"But we have to stop them! You don't understand!" Never taking her eyes from the Raven, she explained.

Jo's eyes narrowed. "All right... suppose it is a bomb? They won't set it to go off immediately, will they? Not unless they want to blow themselves up too. Wait until they've gone, then maybe we can defuse it or something. Getting yourself caught isn't going to help anyone."

Natalie sighed and dropped into the leaves. Part of her knew Jo was right. Yet, what if they waited and then it was too late? They certainly didn't know enough to defuse a bomb on their own.

"Anyway," Jo whispered, wriggling forward on elbows and knees and craning her neck to see into the trench. "I don't think it is a bomb. He's unscrewing the end. Looks like there's something inside."

Natalie joined her friend. There wasn't much cover but the Casters were all watching Hawk. Hardly daring to breathe, she raised her head until she could see.

The root the spellclave had dug up was only about as thick

as her leg, nothing like the impressive tunnels she and Merlin had whizzed along in the organazoomers. But it glowed as brightly as the rest of Oq. And it was struggling. Legs braced and sweat streaming down their faces, four men wearing gloves like Lord Hawk's dragged the writhing tendrils out of the earth and stretched the root between them while Lord Hawk used his stick to scrape off a patch of Oq's protective fur. He carefully dripped black liquid from the canister on to the exposed soultree flesh. Steam hissed out of the trench, along with the sickly smell of rotting fruit. The root convulsed in the men's hands then went slack, its glow fading. The watching Casters cheered.

Natalie grabbed Jo's arm in dismay. "We've got to do something! They're hurting Oq! Oh, I wish K'tanaqui would come back." She looked round in anguish and Jo's warm hand squeezed hers.

"Shh. This is the first one they've found. Destroying a single root's hardly going to kill the whole tree, is it? Especially not if it's as big as you say it is. They could chop that little root off entirely and the tree would just grow another one."

She bit her lip. What Jo said sounded sensible, except the bad, cold feeling remained in her gut.

While she watched the spellclave suspiciously, the goshawk flapped out of its oak and glided over the clearing, wings black against the stars. She and Jo retreated into the bushes and flattened themselves to the ground. The Casters shot nervous glances up at the sky. Some retrieved their bows, nocked their arrows and knelt, watching the trees with alert eyes. The hawk dwindled to a speck against the moon, then wheeled and came back, *caaa-ing* loudly.

Natalie's heart thumped. "K'tanaqui?" she whispered in hope. "That you?"

Help coming, answered her magehound, faint but clear. *Pups stay. Wait for unicorrrns.*

Natalie dug her fingers into the earth and tried not to think about that struggling root. Jo's right, she told herself fiercely.

Killing a single root won't harm the tree. It *can't*.

*

Oq's smallest twigs and leaves began to tremble first, as if stirred by a summer breeze. Then small branches began to shake, followed by the larger branches, until the soultree's fear and pain rippled through the trunk like the first shocks of an approaching earthquake.

Merlin hugged himself tighter and stared nervously at the tightly-woven vines across the entrance of the chamber where Lady Thaypari had left him with strict instructions to stay out of trouble. With Redeye's sharp teeth to help, he might have been able to force his way through the vines. Or he might have tried to cast the spell which was still warm in his boot. But outside were unicorns and bears and men who wanted to kill him. At least in here he was safe. Or so he'd thought.

He brushed a leaf out of his hair and stared at the petals littering the floor. "What's happening, Redeye?"

In answer, his mouse squeaked and fled beneath his tunic. Since it was the Opening, Merlin no longer needed his familiar's eyes to see but he reached into his sleeve and dragged the mouse out. "Don't be so silly!" he hissed. "If the tree falls on me, it'll crush you in there just as easy—" He broke off as the entrance vines unlaced themselves with a crackle, revealing the source of Redeye's fear.

Lord Pveriyan strode into the chamber, closely followed by Lady Thaypari, Lord Gerystar and the other nine Council members and their magehounds, all darting nervous glances at the roof.

Before Merlin could move, Lord Pveriyan seized his arm and shook him until his teeth rattled. "What do you know about this, Caster?" he demanded.

"N-nothing—"

"Don't give me that! You've done something to Oq, haven't you? I don't know how but you've smuggled something in here. What was it? You'd better answer me, Caster, or I'll—" He broke off, scowling.

Behind him, Lady Thaypari coughed. "We should get him to the Heart as soon as possible, Pveriyan."

Merlin stared at them, excitement battling with terror.

But Pveriyan whirled on Thaypari. "That's the last place this boy is going! Have you any idea of the damage he could do in the Heart, if he can do this much out here?"

"I didn't—" Merlin began, but Lady Thaypari silenced him with a raised finger.

"Don't be silly, Pveriyan," she said. "Of course it isn't him doing this. Oq would never have allowed the boy back inside if he was a threat to her. It's obvious the Casters have deployed this Raven of theirs. None of us know enough about it but Merlin's from over the Boundary. Oq thinks he might be able to help her. We have to let him try."

"Try what?" Merlin asked.

Shh! Redeye said.

"I'm telling you we can't trust a Caster in the Heart!"

Thaypari gave Lord Pveriyan a weary smile. "That wasn't what you said last time. I seem to remember you were only too eager to drag the poor boy in there." There were a few chuckles.

"This is no laughing matter!" Pveriyan snapped. "Are you all blind? I don't know how he managed it but the boy obviously tricked Oq the last time he was in the Heart, and now you're going to let him finish the job! We shouldn't be wasting our time arguing in here. It's the Opening, for Oq's sake! We have a Caster invasion on our hands. We've units of bears and stags that need transporting to the battle site. We should be out there with our people. Fighting Casters!"

His magehound's hackles went up, and there were several mutters of agreement. Merlin looked from face to face and swallowed. Then Oq gave a fresh shudder, and above them a branch broke with a noise like a thunderclap. Everyone glanced up in alarm as the chamber roof creaked and more leaves came spiralling down, settling like green snow in the Spell Lords' hair.

"Thaypari's right," said Lord Gerystar, reassuring his nervous hound. "And so is Pveriyan. We've no time to waste arguing. Has anyone thought to ask the boy if he's willing to help us?"

Merlin shuffled his feet uncomfortably as every eye turned to him. Lady Thaypari smiled. "Well?" she said softly. "Will you?"

"Will I what?"

"Will you help Oq fight the Raven?"

Merlin licked his lips. "But I don't know how."

"See?" Lord Pveriyan said. "Let's seal the Caster back up, leave one of our magehounds to make sure he doesn't get into any mischief while we're gone, and get out there where we're needed." He jabbed a finger at the shivering entrance vines.

Lady Thaypari ignored him and went down on one knee. She took Merlin's spell-singed hand in her soft, clean ones and looked him in the eye. "All we're asking is that you try. Oq thinks your knowledge of human technology will help her fight the Raven, but no one's going to blame you if it doesn't. Please, Merlin. We don't know the right things. You do."

Merlin had never been so embarrassed in all his life. But if they let him in the Heart, he might be able to find Natalie. "All right," he mumbled, cheeks burning. "I'll do my best. Please get up, Lady, you're making your skirt all dirty."

Lord Gerystar spluttered, then arranged his features into something more appropriate for a Spell Lord and said solemnly, "Thank you, Caster. We won't forget this."

Lord Pveriyan snorted. "I can't believe you're going through with this! Trust a Caster in the Heart during the Opening, of all times! What is the world coming to?"

"The world is changing," Thaypari said calmly, brushing leaves and petals off her robe. "And we have to change with it. In future, we'll need to study this Raven-technology so we can set more effective spells on the Boundary to keep it out, but tonight it appears Merlin's the only one who can help us. We should be thankful he's agreed to, after the shameful way some of us treated him last time he was here." She glanced at Pveriyan, her look saying more than her words. "I'll stay outside the Heart and monitor the boy while you—"

"*I'll* monitor him," Pveriyan said, scowling at Merlin.

"...while you catch up with the army and coordinate its transportation," Thaypari continued smoothly, taking Merlin's elbow and guiding him out of the chamber. "The Unicorn Herders, in particular, need a firm hand. Oq already reports an Eight has broken away from the main force and gone off alone. If they find the enemy first they'll be outnumbered. You're needed at the front, Pveriyan. None of us have your experience of fighting Casters."

Lord Pveriyan's glower became a small, hard smile. "True enough," he said. "But I'm going to check the boy is properly installed before I go. I still don't trust him."

They hurried along passages that trembled under their feet, through flying twigs and spiralling leaves. Merlin couldn't help thinking of his last journey to the Heart, when he'd been separated from Natalie, terrified and alone. But tonight, things couldn't have been more different. The Spell Lords and their magehounds followed at a respectful distance, an escort to a prince rather than a prisoner, and crowded inside to watch him being connected. The tremors that shook the rest of the tree weren't so noticeable in the Heart but the glittering air crackled with tension. The twelve magehounds watched him intently – a disconcerting ring of amber eyes.

Ignore 'em, Redeye advised.

Ignore twelve magehounds who were regarding him as if he were their next meal? Merlin didn't think it possible. But as soon as he felt the squirts of warm, sticky sap at the contact points on his temples he relaxed.

Lord Pveriyan crouched in front of him, checking the connections. "Don't get above yourself, Caster," the Spell Lord whispered softly so the others couldn't hear. "I have influence on this Council. I've already had the human boy cleansed. He passed out with the pain. You harm a single one of Oq's twigs, and I swear I'll do the same to you, only I won't stop at memories of Earthhaven. I'll cleanse every thought in your head until you're an empty husk."

"Stop fussing, Pveriyan!" Lady Thaypari called. "I'm sure Oq won't have made a mistake with the installation."

"You can be sure of nothing!" Pveriyan snapped, giving one of the tendrils attached to Merlin's temples a hard jerk. "The Raven might strike here first, precisely to stop us trying this."

Stars whirled behind Merlin's eyes. Redeye fled into his boot. The watching Spell Lords shuffled their feet and gave uneasy coughs.

"If the Raven's attacked the Heart already, then we're all in trouble," Thaypari said firmly. "Come on out of there, Pveriyan. Give the boy some peace to do whatever he has to do."

With a final glare at Merlin, Lord Pveriyan swept his robes around him and strode out of the Heart with his magehound trotting at his heels. One by one, the other Spell Lords followed, some of them whispering "Good luck" as they went. Soon, only Thaypari remained, her hound peering anxiously at Merlin from behind her skirts.

"Are you all right in there?" she asked. "Do you need anything?"

Merlin gripped the stool. "Food," he whispered. Then he took a deep breath, closed his eyes and forgot about his stomach as Oq whirled him away.

It was even better than before. A great rushing river of images from every corner of Earthaven and beyond. Now the Boundary was open, Oq's roots connected with the roots of other trees, stretching across two worlds. Carried at incredible speed by the awesome power of the soultree, Merlin whirled past silver Eights of unicorns, lumbering brown bears and leaping stags, their riders grimly clutching weapons. He sensed the vivid spellflares as relays of Treemages transported the slower units of the army from cache to cache. He poured himself into the maze of roots and branches, detoured along creepers and vines, searching, searching, until in one of the outer roots—

Pain.

*

Out of the soultree's reach, Tim came to in complete darkness with a headache and a strange sense of déjà vu. He groaned and touched his skull. His hand came away sticky.

Carefully, he eased himself into a sitting position. He was lying on stone – damp, cold and very hard. Every millimetre of him was stiff. He had bruises in places he didn't remember belonged to him.

What had happened?

For a few seconds there was a frightening blank, as black as his surroundings. Then glimpses came, like flashes of light in the darkness. A man with yellow eyes and feathers in his hair... A large hawk diving at him, screeching... A tall girl trying to raise a signal on a mobile phone...

"Jo!" he called. His voice echoed but there was no reply.

He fumbled in his pockets, remembering more every second. He and Jo had come up to Unicorn Wood looking for something important. They'd brought equipment for emergencies such as this. Torch, torch... yes, here it was. He clicked the switch, half afraid it wouldn't work. A dim orange glow flickered across brick archways, revealing whitewash streaked with slime. He shook the torch until the bulb brightened, then swung the beam around. A silent generator, smelling of diesel. Benches. Empty, soiled cages, a fish tank containing water but no fish, an overturned stool... Was that a rabbit's foot beneath it? Tim recoiled. His torch picked out a flight of stone steps leading up to a door. He crawled up. He was shivering so hard his teeth chattered. Reaction from being hit, he supposed.

The door was locked. He hammered his fists on the unyielding wood. "Oy!" he yelled. "Let me out of here!" But he was too weak to keep it up for long. He sank on the top step, dropped his head into his hands and closed his eyes. Think, Tim, think.

He must be in the Lodge he decided. It was the only building in the area likely to have a cellar – the only building in the area, period. Also, he vaguely remembered the hawk-man saying he didn't have much time. Time before what? He made his way back down the steps and began a half-hearted search for the key, shining his torch into dark corners. He'd hardly started looking when something moaned in the shadows.

Tim froze, the back of his neck prickling. *Ghost.*

"Don't be silly," he muttered. "Ghosts and witches are just stories to frighten kids." But a niggly itch inside his head said, *Are you sure?*

The moaning started up again. He crept towards the sound, the torch held before him like a weapon, his breath coming faster. A tunnel had been dug into the back wall of the cellar. The moaning was coming from down there. Tim crouched at the entrance and cautiously aimed his torch beam inside.

A monster heaved towards him, making strange muffled cries. Its shadow writhed around the tunnel walls as Tim scrambled backwards, heart thumping. The moaning started up again, more frantic now. Whatever was in there couldn't get out.

Encouraged, he peered into the tunnel again. This time, he saw the "monster" was a man. Tape tightly bound his arms and legs and covered his mouth. Tim's stomach lurched as he recognized the prisoner. "Mr Marlins!" he whispered. "What are *you* doing here?"

Relief flooded through him, mingled with a hot tight fury he couldn't understand. He shook the anger away. This was no time for stupid feuds. It took him less than a minute to slice through the tape with his penknife and free his stepfather. Mr Marlins was soon sitting against one of the arches, rubbing his wrists and the stubble about his mouth. Tim winced at the sight of coarse black hairs stuck to the gag.

Mr Marlins gave him a long measuring look, then staggered to his feet. "Come on, we have to get out of here."

"Door's locked," Tim muttered. Of all the people to be locked in a cellar with, he thought.

His stepfather swayed and caught himself against the wall. His eyes burned from dark hollows. His lips were cracked. He seemed to be looking for something. After a moment, he staggered across to the fish tank, cupped his hands and actually drank the foul green water. Tim's stomach churned. "How long have you been down here?" he whispered.

Mr Marlins splashed a second handful of the filthy water on to his face and sighed. "Ever since I delivered you to the Thrallstone. Came up here to rescue Nat and got myself caught, didn't I? My own stupid fault."

"The Thrallstone," Tim repeated, the itch starting up again. "Nat—" As if a curtain across his head had been ripped in half, memories blazed. *"Earthaven!"* he breathed, the fury returning. He took a step away from Mr Marlins. "You left me there! You knew what that Spell Lord would do to me and you just drove away!"

His stepfather coughed. "Uh... Tim... I'm really sorry. Honestly. I was out of my mind with worry over Nat but that's no excuse. I should never have done that to you. I might have known they wouldn't take you as a Thrall against your will. Apparently the memory cleansing isn't pleasant if you fight it and I assume from the marks on your head that you did." He frowned. "But you can still remember, can't you? I wonder what went wrong."

"You tell me," Tim said. He was still furious but Mr Marlins looked so pale and defeated, he couldn't keep it up. Besides, they had more important things to think about right now. Like getting out of this cellar before the hawk-man came back.

"Look," he said, rummaging through his pockets until he found a rather squashed chocolate bar. "Are you hungry? Jo and I brought supplies in case Nat was starving when we found her. I know it ain't beer but it's better than nothing." He held out the chocolate.

Mr Marlins shook his head. "You keep it," he said quietly. "We might be down here a while."

Tim set his jaw and forced the chocolate bar into his stepfather's hand. "Take it! I'm not being soft. I just won't know what to do if you faint on me, and... I don't want to go through this alone." Until he'd said it, he didn't realize how true it was. He smiled wryly, thinking of his mother's words. *Sometimes it takes a crisis like this to bring families together.* He hadn't thought there was a crisis big enough in the world to bring him and Mr Marlins together.

The chocolate bar disappeared in two sticky bites. Mr Marlins licked the wrapper and sighed. "Seems I misjudged you, Tim," he said gruffly. "Thank you, that was much better than beer."

Tim shrugged, embarrassed. "There's plenty of bottles back at the house, no one else has drunk 'em."

A hard glint came to his stepfather's eyes. "I mean it. I've had my last hangover. Being tied up in the dark gives a man time to think. When Atanaqui died, I convinced myself that finding a replacement mother for Nat would be enough. After you and Julie came to live with us, I thought I could retreat into my own misery and leave you all to get on with your lives. I see now how wrong that was. I've failed Nat and I've failed you, to say nothing of your poor mother. She didn't just move here for Nat's sake, did she? She needed me as much as I needed her, only I was too selfish to see it. She must be desperate by now with both of us missing."

"She was pretty worried when I saw her last." Tim fiddled with his jacket zips. "And if I don't find Jo and get back before dawn she'll go spare and so will Mrs Carter. They think we've gone to the Hallowe'en Disco."

Mr Marlins sucked in his breath. "Hallowe'en? Already? I should have guessed. No wonder the Casters were in such a rush when they tossed me down here! What time is it?"

"Dunno. My watch stopped at midnight."

"The Opening." Mr Marlins closed his eyes, then looked thoughtfully at the tunnel. "There's something I think we should investigate. Bring your torch."

Reluctantly, Tim followed his stepfather into the tunnel. It twisted around several turns until it reached a metal door that looked as if it would withstand a tank attack. The door had a combination lock.

"Looks like someone doesn't trust their own spells," Mr

Marlins said, peeling a bronze glimmer off one of the hinges.

Tim shone the torch at his hand, curious. "Is that a spell?"

"Yes." Mr Marlins knocked the torch away. "Keep the light on the door." He fiddled with the combination, then slammed a hand against the metal in frustration.

"What do you think is in there?" Tim asked.

"Live spells, probably. Casters value them above everything else. But there was a lot of coming and going down here before they left, and Lord Pveriyan said the Council were expecting trouble this year. I don't know if even a Caster would go to all the trouble of constructing an underground vault just to store spells."

"We saw them take a lot of stuff out of the Lodge." Tim searched his memory. "Bows and arrows, rucksacks, spades, stuff like that."

"Bows and arrows? Yes, that figures. Technology poisons their powers, and there's an anti-technology spell on the Boundary so anything more hi-tech won't work inside Earthaven. But they've got an archery range out in the wood, so the arrows are no secret. It's my guess they were building something else down here, something they took in with them. Come to think of it, we're probably in the safest place right now. Maybe we shouldn't try too hard to get out."

Tim stared at his stepfather. Had he just made a joke? Then Mr Marlins closed a hand over the torch beam. "Shh! I think I heard something."

All Tim could hear was the sound of their own breathing, loud in the enclosed space. Then it came again – a faint scraping. Keeping the torch covered, they crept to the end of the tunnel and cautiously peered out. The scraping was coming from the other side of the cellar door.

Mr Marlins put a finger to his lips. Quietly, he lifted one of the empty animal cages and began to creep up the steps. Tim's opinion of his stepfather, which had changed considerably in the past half hour or so, soared. Not to be outdone, he crept after him, gripping the torch in a sweaty hand. It was probably heavy enough to knock someone out if he hit them in the right place. Give them a nasty bruise, at least.

From outside came muffled voices, a cut-off laugh, then the rattle of a key in the lock. The door swung open to reveal five faceless figures, black against the moonlight that poured down the passage. Mr Marlins leapt at them, the cage glinting above his head. Tim swung the torch beam into the startled eyes glittering through holes in their masks, and laughed in relief as he recognized their skull earrings. "No!" he yelled, catching his stepfather's arm just in time. "They're friends!"

The Death Heads recognized Tim just in time to save face and halt their screaming flight back along the passage.

His Hallowe'en mask glowing luminous orange in the torchlight, Gaz pushed to the front of the group and grinned cheekily at Mr Marlins.

"Trick or treat?" he said.

17

THE RAVEN

Midnight to dawn, Sunday, November 1

As soon as they were out of the cellar, Mr Marlins took charge.
He sent Gaz and Dave, as the two fittest cyclists with the most
serviceable bikes, back to Millennium Green with a hastily
scribbled note and orders to hand it straight in at the police
station. Neither boy argued. It seemed that finding the prisoners in the cellar had tapped some previously unsuspected vein
of responsibility; or maybe Gaz and Dave were just glad of an
excuse to get out of Unicorn Wood. They skidded off into the
wood, leaves and mud spraying from their wheels. Mr Marlins
organized Tim and the remaining Heads to do a thorough
search of the Lodge. They were looking for spells, he explained
matter-of-factly, and showed them the one he'd peeled off the
vault door. If they glittered, they were alive and needed cau-
tious handling. If they didn't glitter, they were dead. "What
you're looking for are the ones creating the illusion on the
Lodge," he told the wide-eyed boys. "It's the Opening, so you
should be able to see them all right, but be careful. They can
give you a bad burn, maybe worse."

The younger Heads' eyes lit up at this promise of danger
and they were soon crawling under tables and inside cupboards, shining their bicycle lamps behind heavy items of furniture and into the attics, making ghostly noises and leaping
out of dark corners with blood-curdling yells. Meanwhile, Mr
Marlins disappeared back into the cellar to see if he could get
the generator working.

Tim pulled his jacket closer and went outside, needing air.
Jo's little speech must have really got to Gaz, he thought with
a smile. The gang's appetite for excitement had done the rest.
Apparently, they'd found the key to the cellar door hanging on
a large hook on the wall of the passage. "Even stupider than
hiding their front door key under the mat!" was Mike's comment, until he heard about illusion spells. Then he went quiet.
There had been a live spell wrapped around the cellar key.
Pizzaface had burnt his fingers on it when, hearing noises in
the cellar, the Heads had dared one another to open the door.
They'd all thought Pizzaface was making excuses so he wouldn't
have to complete the dare. Strange how things worked out.

Tim looked at the trees. Their branches still had that unnatural shine as they creaked in the night breeze. Nat and Jo were
out there somewhere. He hoped they were OK.

By the time the convoy of flashing blue lights and wailing
sirens arrived at the gate he had found three live spells. One
flattened beneath the doormat, the second caught on a bramble that overgrew the path, the third tucked inside the padlock
on the gate itself. He extracted the final spell with the tweezers
in his penknife and slipped it into his pocket just as the first
mud-spattered squad car drew up. A uniformed officer armed
with a large pair of wire cutters made short work of the chain
on the gate, then helped Tim drag the gates wide to let the convoy through. The hinges complained with a noise like a giant's
fingernails scraping down a blackboard, and shed clouds of
rust.

Mr Marlins emerged from the Lodge and exchanged a few
words with the officer in charge while the others unloaded

some interesting looking equipment from the back of a van and disappeared inside. Tim hurried after them before anyone thought to keep him out. Gaz and Dave, eyes sparkling with excitement, climbed out of one of the cars, dodged the man who'd taken up position at the door, and ducked inside too.

They found the other three Heads at the top of the cellar steps, hopping up and down trying to see what was going on. A large uniformed policeman barred their way with folded arms. "You lads had best stay up here for the time being," he said. "They might have to blow the door."

"Cool!" Gaz said. "Are they using dynamite?"

Tim thought of the spells. "Isn't that dangerous?"

The Heads gave him scathing looks but the policeman smiled. "Don't worry, lad, your father's explained. The boys are very experienced in these matters. They'll take every precaution."

Tim let the *father* bit go. More important things were happening here. But the explosion when it came was disappointing. Barely a pop, followed by a small puff of dust from the tunnel.

"Can we go down yet?" Gaz said, craning his neck to see over the big man's shoulder.

"Not yet."

"But my stepfather's down there," Tim said.

"I'm sorry lad, you'll have to wait until the boys have checked it over."

"But—"

The policeman tightened his lips and refolded his arms. Tim sighed. This was obviously one of those times when it would be useless to argue with authority. The Heads backed off and sat against the passage wall, exchanging stories while Tim shared out the rest of his chocolate. Predictably, Pizzaface ate most of it. Meanwhile, radios crackled and official looking men and women rushed in and out, clattering up and down the stairs, cursing equipment that evidently wasn't working quite as well as it should. Then two figures clad from head to toe in crackling silver came through the front door, one of them lugging what looked like a picnic coolbox covered with bright yellow hazardous-substance stickers. They disappeared into the cellar and emerged a few minutes later carrying the cool-box carefully between them.

Tim stood. "Can we go down now?"

The man guarding the cellar door still looked doubtful but after a moment Mr Marlins came to the bottom of the steps. "It's safe enough now, isn't it?" he called back up the tunnel and someone mumbled an affirmative. Mr Marlins smiled. "Tim? You can come down as long as you don't touch anything. Want to see what the Casters were up to?"

After seeing the silver suits, Tim wasn't so sure he did. But aware of the Heads' envious eyes, he descended the steps. Someone had strung temporary lights along the tunnel which fizzed and flickered as he followed Mr Marlins through the settling dust. As they stepped carefully over the thick metal door, which had been taken off its hinges by the explosion, Tim let out a whistle.

It was like the science lab at school, only bigger and better equipped. Everywhere he looked, glass tubes and bottles and flasks glittered in the beams of powerful torches. He recognized a centrifuge but much of the equipment looked hi-tech and expensive. Boxes stored under the benches had flying black birds stamped on their sides. Tim's eye was drawn to a rack of test tubes that contained rolled-up spells in different coloured liquids, some glimmering, others dull.

He looked at Mr Marlins. "What were they doing with the spells?"

"Shh!"

His stepfather nodded to a prowling plainclothes man making a report into a hand-held tape recorder. "Herbicide... systemic... heterocyclic... genome..." The recorder kept switching itself off. The man shook it, looking annoyed.

Science wasn't Tim's strong point. He latched on to the only word he recognized. "Herbicide?" he said. "That's like a weed killer, isn't it?"

Mr Marlins nodded. "That man's from the Ministry of Agriculture. He's pretty worried. He thinks they've been manufacturing an unauthorized biochemical down here." He lowered his voice. "It's clever. Earthaven's defences keep out technology but something like this might well confuse them. The Casters have been tinkering with genes and things. My guess is they've been analysing spells to mimic the enchantment-gene, and fixed their poison to attack the soul-tree. All they have to do is apply it to a small branch, or maybe a root, and soon the whole tree will be infected in exactly the same way our bodies get infected by a virus."

Tim's head began to throb again. "What's a soultree?"

Mr Marlins smiled. "I keep forgetting, you're not one of us. I'll explain later. Shh, now."

The Ministry man had given up on his tape recorder and was heading their way. He frowned at Tim. "I understand you were watching when these people left the Lodge? It'll help if we know how much of the substance they took with them. Did you see anything that might have contained a dangerous liquid? A can or a drum, for example?"

Tim started to shake his head. "Only bows and arrows and stuff, though they had some rucksacks—" Then he remembered. "The coffee!"

"I'm sorry?"

"They had a metal flask – about so big – and it had one of those black birds on the side!"

A heavy sigh. "More than enough to do damage." The Ministry man turned to Mr Marlins. "We've a helicopter on the way with an infrared camera, and the police are going in with the dogs. We'll soon find these people if they're out there. I only hope your daughter and her friend have the sense to stay away from that flask. We can't be sure until we've analysed it, of course, but such cocktails are often highly poisonous to humans as well as plant life." He gave them a distracted glance, then left the lab.

Tim looked at Mr Marlins in alarm.

His stepfather was staring at the flattened door, the strangest expression on his face. "Oh, they're out there," he said softly. "But I'm not sure you're going to find them."

*

With their ears pressed to the earth of another world, the two girls heard the unicorns coming long before they saw them – a wild rushing sound, like surf across pebbles. They shifted closer together and gripped hands as leaves spiralled out of the stars. The goshawk gave a warning screech, and the Casters drew back their bowstrings as yelling Herders mounted on blurs of silver light burst from the wood.

Lord Hawk sprang out of the trench, shouting orders. Unicorn hooves *shimmered* over the wilting moonflowers, spears glittered, horns trailed rainbows through the night. Then the first rush was past, and the Casters loosed their arrows. Spellfire arced overhead, trailing purple sparks, missing their targets by miles.

Nothing moves fasterrr than a unicorrrn, said K'tanaqui, bounding out of the trees, his tongue lolling in a magehound laugh.

Natalie flung her arms around his neck and hugged him hard. "Clever K'tanaqui! But they've already done something to Oq."

Jo gaped at the unicorns, wide-eyed. "Are those what I think they are?" she breathed. "Oh, they're *beautiful!*"

Casterrrs have hands full now, K'tanaqui said smugly. *Not hurrrt Oq again.*

Natalie watched a unicorn charge the black-bearded Ferret. Its rider, a woman with a long golden braid coiled about her head, crouched over the luminous neck and levelled her spear. Ferret let fly an arrow which missed; and reached over his shoulder for another. But there was no time to reload. He flung down his bow and sprinted for the trees. The unicorn caught him before he was halfway there, dug its horn into the centre of his back and flung his body high into the wood. It thudded against a tree trunk and disappeared in a flurry of snapping twigs and whirling leaves. The unicorn reared, the tip of its beautiful horn dripping blood.

Natalie pressed a hand to her mouth in horror. She had thought Merlin was just being pathetic when he'd said unicorns gored people and ate them.

Horrrrns useful weapons, K'tanaqui informed her. *But unicorrrns vegeterrrrians.*

"But he's dead, isn't he? That unicorn killed him!" An hysterical giggle escaped her. Jo hugged her close, looking shocked too.

Now the initial surprise was over, the surviving Casters closed ranks. They used their trench for cover, shooting deadly fire-arrows over the edge, then quickly ducking back down before a Herder could throw a spear. The unicorns pulled up out of bow range, snorting frosty breath into the night. Natalie made a quick count. She'd thought there were hundreds but there were only eight. Bearing their proud riders without bridles or saddles, they *shimmered* between one patch of burning grass and the next, untouchable.

"We'll smoke you out like rabbits from a burrow!" shouted the woman whose mount had gored Ferret.

"Trample you into the earth!"

"You made a mistake coming here, Casters!"

The spellclave was quiet, huddled in their trench with their heads down. Natalie frowned. "They're up to something," she whispered. Even as she spoke, there was an unearthly screech as Hunter dived at the golden-haired woman, his powerful wings beating her face, talons clawing at her eyes. Her mount reared, causing the others to shy. At the same moment, Lord Hawk gave a shout and the Casters let fly another volley of fire-arrows.

The woman Herder got her mount under control but a lucky shot struck it on the rump. The arrowhead caught fast and the unicorn screamed as spellfire licked its silver hide. She immediately beat the flames with her cloak but to no avail. With another scream, the wounded unicorn took off through the trees, its tail streaming purple sparks, the woman clinging valiantly to the mane. Hunter gave chase, *caaa-ing* in triumph.

"I feel sick," Jo said. "That was horrible. Did you see its tail burning?"

Natalie forced her mind from the unicorn's pain and pushed Jo's arms away. "You can be sick later. We've got to get that canister off Lord Hawk before he has a chance to use it again. Quick, while they're distracted."

Jo gave her a startled look. "You've changed, Nat, you know that?" She reversed her cap and set her jaw. "I'm ready."

They began to work their way round to the rucksacks, keeping to the undergrowth as much as possible. The Casters were busy watching the remaining seven unicorns, and the goshawk had yet to return, so the approach wasn't as difficult as Natalie had feared. K'tanaqui wriggled anxiously on his belly behind them, his coat gathering yet more leaves and mud.

Pups be carrreful. Neverrr underrrestimate Casterrrs.

The spellclave and the Herders appeared to be at a stand-off. While the unicorns remained beyond bow range, the Casters couldn't harm them. But neither could the Casters risk climbing out of the trench, in case a unicorn charged and gored them.

The rucksack that had contained the Raven was empty. Mouth dry, Natalie crept to the edge and peered down. Lord Hawk and Claudia were crouched over a pile of arrows, Claudia unwrapping the live spells from their heads, while Lord Hawk twisted them around his stick. The canister lay in the soil behind him, apparently forgotten. Natalie frowned. Then she understood. "They're going to transport out!" she hissed. "If they do, we'll never find them again! We've got to get the Raven. Right now!"

Before she had time to think about it too much, she slithered into the trench and grabbed the canister. The Casters swung their bows round in alarm. Claudia's eyes went wide, betraying astonishment and then fear. Hawk whirled, his stick unravelling spells. Natalie made a leap for the edge but the sides were too steep and high to climb without hands, and the canister too heavy to tuck under her arm. Also, the cap wasn't properly screwed on. As she scrabbled desperately at the loose soil, black liquid leaked out and splashed her hand.

Burning.

She cried out as a hand grabbed her ankle and pulled. Still clutching the canister, she sprawled at Lord Hawk's feet. Her glasses flew off, and there was a crunch as Hawk deliberately stamped on them. She rolled clear, fixed the cap and raised her burning hand to her mouth.

"No, Natalie!" Claudia shouted. "Don't lick it! It's poison!"

Her heart fluttered. She squinted at the edge of the trench, trying to focus, and made out Jo jumping up and down clapping her hands. "Throw it up here!" her friend shouted.

Natalie checked the cap and took careful aim. Before she could throw, Lord Hawk's stick smashed across her shoulders. All the wind whooshed out of her, and she sprawled on top of the shrivelled soultree root. A Caster aimed an arrow at Jo, who danced out of range. Then there was a furious snarl as a silver blur launched itself at Lord Hawk.

"K'tanaqui!" Natalie gasped in relief that turned to alarm as she remembered what had happened to Bilbo. "Be careful!"

Pup crrrazy! Pup rrrun! Quick!

Lord Hawk fended off the magehound with his spell-wrapped stick and laughed. "If it isn't my little Spider! Found yourself a familiar with teeth, I see. You're too late. Your precious tree's dying."

"That's not true!" But her stomach clenched. The root was cold and black.

"What did you do with my son?" Lord Hawk went on. "Did your hound eat him? Or is he hiding like the little coward he is?"

Natalie's blood rose. "Merlin's not a coward! He—"

She didn't have a chance to explain. One of the spellclave shouted, "Look out! They're charging again!"

The Herders must have seen her jump into the trench and decided to take advantage of the distraction. As the Casters hurriedly scrambled back to their positions, a unicorn reared at the edge of the trench and a spear hissed over Natalie's head straight for Lord Hawk. She caught her breath but he casually deflected the spear with his spell-wrapped stick.

"Do I have to do everything myself?" he said. With an equally casual flick of his wrist he cast one of his spells at the unicorn. Purple lightning cracked across the night. The Casters covered their eyes. The air filled with the smell of burnt sugar. When the smoke cleared, the unicorn and its rider had vanished.

K'tanaqui growled, snarling and snapping at any Caster who came too close to Natalie. *Spell strrrong to trrransporrt unicorrrn. Pup rrrun now!*

Natalie backed to the side of the trench, hugging the canister to her chest. Her hand was on fire. She could barely keep her grip, let alone throw.

Hawk's yellow gaze followed her. "Make a spellrope, Claudia," he said. "We'll take Spider here with us. Bind her hound – that'll keep her quiet."

Something flickered across Claudia's face but she raised a hand to the weal on her cheek and her eyes went blank. Slowly, she unwrapped two spells from her supply of arrows and twisted them together. She chanted under her breath and the spells began to glow. Between her dancing fingers, they slowly lengthened into a rope of bronze and green light that writhed in the night with a life of its own. As Natalie watched in horror, the spellrope formed a noose and floated towards K'tanaqui.

Spell rrrope verrry bad… As the noose tightened around his neck, the magehound's voice faded and he pressed himself against Natalie's feet, whining. Her own legs turned weak.

"Nat!" Jo screamed, jerking her back to her senses.

With the last of her strength, she threw the canister as hard and as high as she could. Everyone ducked as it whizzed above their heads, even Lord Hawk. This gave Jo the few seconds she needed to leap into the air, catch the canister and run. She wasn't centre forward on the school netball team for nothing.

Lord Hawk gave a cry of anger. "After her!" he roared.

Several Casters scrambled out of the hole, more afraid of their leader than they were of the unicorns.

Natalie flung herself on the spellrope, tearing at the horrid noose with her nails while her poor magehound shivered and sweated. "Hold on, K'tanaqui!" she sobbed. "I'll get you free."

From a long way off, Jo was screaming for her to run but how could she leave poor K'tanaqui like this? Above them, the remaining unicorns were locked in furious battle with the Casters who had gone after Jo. Arrows hissed, screams and bitter purple smoke filled the night – no, night no longer. With a shiver, she realized the sky was paling.

Lord Hawk smiled down at her. "I've won, you know. Your friend won't reach the Boundary before it closes; nor will she be able to get through the Thrallstone without help. We'll pick her up later. My Raven is already killing your soultree and nothing anyone can do will stop it now." He bent to stroke the captive magehound who trembled under his touch. "Soon the entire Council will crawl at my feet like this. I think they're going to be very sorry they banished me, don't you? Now then, Spider, are you going to be sensible or do I have to waste spells on you too?"

She clenched her fists, tears coming. "I'll never join your horrible spellclave!"

Even as Hawk's yellow eyes glittered with anger, K'tanaqui gave a whimper and said very faintly, *Spells die soon. Then K'tanaqui be frrree. Find pup.*

Natalie shuddered. With an effort she unclenched her fists. *Play along.* "I'll be sensible," she whispered, hanging her head. She peeped through her hair to see if she'd succeeded.

Hawk's smile broadened. "See how easy it can be when you try? Now then, I think it's time we left these unicorns to their own devices, don't you?" He called the Casters and started to wrap two extra spells around his stick. Very slowly, Natalie backed away. Claudia's blue eyes followed her but she didn't say a word. Quietly, Natalie pulled herself out of the trench, biting her lip against the pain in her hand.

She was almost clear when Hawk noticed her. He looked startled for a moment, then his brows lowered. "Where do you think you're going, young Spell Lady? I've got your mage-hound, remember?"

Heart thumping, Natalie kicked loose soil into his eyes and scrambled free. The goshawk *caaa-ed*, making her neck prickle. Without her glasses, the wood was a confused blur and for a horrible moment she didn't know which way to run. Then Jo shouted, "Over here!"

She raced towards the voice, her breath coming in gasps. The trees swayed around her, making her feel ill. She thought she saw Jo mounted on a unicorn. Then light and shadow flashed and another unicorn trotted out of the wood. Natalie slithered to a stop, not at all sure it would count her as a friend after last time. But it lowered its proud head and huffed at her as its rider smiled and reached down a hand.

Pups rrride, came K'tanaqui's voice, so faint Natalie could barely hear it. *Rrride like the wind.*

As the Herder caught her round the waist and swung her up in front of him, Natalie cast a final anguished glance at the trench. "Hold on, K'tanaqui," she whispered, her words lost in an ocean of almond-scented mane. "I'll come back for you, I promise. Soon. Soon as I can..."

18

POWER OF THIRTEEN

Sunday morning, November 1

The six unicorns raced through spinning leaves and snapping twigs beneath pale stars, their hooves trailing mist, their legs a silver blur. Riding them was marvellous and exciting and terrifying, all at once.

Nothing moves faster than a unicorn. As the creature's powerful muscles rippled under her, Natalie hoped this was true. Its warm almond scent made her dizzy and trees blurred at the edges of her vision as they leapt ditches, sprang up ridges and plunged recklessly down the other side. She buried her hands in the soft mane and glanced at the brightening sky.

"Faster!" she whispered.

Did the Boundary shut at first light or at sunrise? How long would it take for the spells that bound K'tanaqui to die? Could she open the Thrallstone without his help? She wanted to ask so many things but the terrible speed pushed the questions back down her throat.

Then the ground rippled under them like the sea, causing their mount to stumble. Natalie's heart leapt into her mouth but the Herder merely tightened his arms about her and laughed as he urged the creature to go faster. She heard Jo laughing, too, and in spite of everything couldn't help a smile. Her friend would talk about nothing else for weeks.

She was still smiling when they galloped into cold air and everything around them blurred. Her ears popped, the trees darkened, and the ground shook a second time. "Moons and stars!" exclaimed the Herder as their mount skidded to a sudden, lurching stop with its muzzle almost touching the Thrallstone.

Natalie was thrown forwards, banged her nose on the unicorn's neck and tasted blood in her mouth. Shakily, she pushed herself upright. A short way off, the other five had skidded to an equally abrupt halt. Jo was lying flat on her back in the grass, the canister still clasped to her chest.

"Jo!" she shrieked in alarm.

"Don't panic, I'm not hurt. That was *amazing*!" Her friend sprang to her feet, laughing, then raised a tentative hand to her face. She blinked a few times and her laughter died. "My eyes—"

Natalie breathed easier. "It's all right, Jo, there's nothing wrong with them. It's the Boundary closing, that's all. I'll have to open the Thrallstone."

She slipped to the ground and stumbled to the stone on wobbly legs, closed her eyes and thrust her arms inside the hole. The unicorns snorted nervously at the diesel smells that wafted through. Natalie's left hand began to hurt again where the Raven had splashed her. She thrust the pain to the back of her mind and sighed in relief as she felt the edges of the hole begin to melt.

Jo, clinging to the back of her tunic, caught her breath. "Who are all those people? What are they doing? There's a helicopter!"

Natalie opened her eyes. It might have been only a few days since she'd seen cars, yet already they seemed alien. On the other side of the Thrallstone, blue and amber lights flashed in a grey November dawn. Uniformed men and women ran back and forth shouting into radios, and a monstrous machine hovered over the trees, blades chopping noisily. As the hole opened further, some of the people turned, calling and pointing excitedly. "Hold it!" came a voice over a loud hailer. "Identify yourselves!"

Natalie stepped aside. "You first," she said, giving Jo a little push. Her friend hesitated. "Go on! I have to hold the gateway open. I'll be right behind you."

It wasn't quite a lie. She kept the hole open long enough for Jo to duck through, long enough to hear a voice call, "It's one of the girls, sir!" Then a unicorn snorted behind her and one of the policemen stared straight at the creature and breathed, "My God! What's *that*?" and she quickly withdrew her arms.

"Natalieeee!" came Jo's anguished cry from the other side.

"Tell Dad and Tim and Julie I love them!" she called as indistinct figures surrounded her friend. Then the lights and noise receded as if down a long tunnel and she staggered backwards.

Straight into the arms of Lord Hawk.

At her scream, the Herders wheeled their unicorns and levelled their spears. Hawk laid his stick across Natalie's throat, cutting off her breath. "Don't be stupid," he said. "This child belongs to your soultree Council. I can kill her long before you kill me."

The Herders stared at Natalie in dismay. "He must've transported," they muttered as the goshawk flapped across and landed on top of the Thrallstone.

Its master chuckled. "But of course! Did you really think I'd risk getting trapped in Earthaven? We planted a few spells near the Thrallstone, just in case. You seem to have deprived me of the Raven, but even a single infected root is enough. Your precious soultree is dying as we speak."

"No!" Natalie squirmed in his grip, choking on the words. "That's not true!"

Another chuckle. "Oh, but I'm afraid it is and we'll all wait nice and quietly just here until the Raven finishes its work. I knew you'd be back, Spider. You'll be my insurance. In the meantime, let's see if we can't finish what we began last week."

He glanced at the goshawk which beat its wings and *caa-ed* loudly. One by one, the spellclave stepped out of the trees. Last of all came Claudia, dragging the shivering, sweating K'tanaqui at the end of that cruel spellrope. At the sight of him, Natalie's struggles died. The exhausted K'tanaqui flopped to the grass in the shadow of the stone, flanks heaving, and gazed at her with dull amber eyes. Taking advantage of the Herders' hesitation, the rest of the spellclave joined their leader and formed a defensive ring around the Thrallstone, bows drawn, spell-wrapped arrows aimed at the unicorns.

"Muzzle the beast and tether its feet, Claudia," Hawk ordered. "Someone bind the girl too. She's done enough damage for one day."

A black-bearded Caster stepped out of the ring. Natalie stared in horror. It was Ferret who'd been gored in the battle for the Raven and flung into the trees. He should have been dead. A unicorn's horn had opened his back and three broken ribs showed through the glistening blood, yet he was still walking. Only his eyes betrayed his condition, chillingly blank. While she trembled, he took a rope from one of the packs and lashed her wrists together, propped her against the Thrallstone and secured the end of the rope about its base. Natalie tugged at her bonds and burst into tears. Why didn't the Herders do anything? Why didn't they *help* her?

Lord Hawk crouched before her and fingered a strand of her hair. "Watch and learn, little Spider," he said. "You see Ferret?" He indicated the gored Caster. "A mere scratch from a unicorn's horn is lethal, let alone a wound like that. But Hunter consumed Ferret's familiar, so he can't die. He's bound to obey me until I decide to release him – which I shall do just as soon as you've replaced him."

He chuckled at Natalie's shudder and pointed his stick at Claudia, who was hugging herself and shaking her head, muttering, "You can't do this, no one's ever done this, it'll destroy us."

"You see my cold-eyed Fish? She fights me, oh how she fights! But she can't win, not while Hunter lives."

Now, the end of the stick touched Natalie's cheek. "You're an intelligent girl. I'm sure you can see that the more you resist, the harder this'll be for you. Try to relax and let Hunter do his work. It'll be painful while he feasts, I know, but afterwards you can rest as long as you need to. There's no hurry now."

He took the stick away and wiped her tears with a surprisingly gentle finger. Then he stepped back and motioned to his familiar. The last of Natalie's strength flowed from her as she realized what he intended.

The goshawk glided down from the stone, perched on the helpless magehound's shoulder and tore a chunk out of K'tanaqui's flank with its cruel beak. It was too much. The sun, which had started to rise out of the unicorn-mist, vanished in a great roaring darkness. From a long way off, someone began to scream.

*

In the Heart of Oq, Merlin was screaming too.

Pain rushed along the infected root, destroying everything it touched, a black river of poison surging towards the Central Root Cavern.

"It burns!" he shrieked. In panic, he leapt off the stool and tugged at the tendrils attached to his head. Only when Lady Thaypari started towards him and hesitated, held back by her magehound's teeth in the hem of her skirt, did he belatedly remember his promise.

"I'm sorry!" he gasped, still wrestling with the tendrils. "I can't do it. Get me out of here. Please! It's too much. I don't know how—"

The burning came again and for a dreadful dark moment flooded Merlin's whole body. Then Redeye's voice cut through the pain, scathing as ever.

You do know how, you brainless nestling. It's like that silly computer of yours, isn't it? Don't think I didn't know what you were up to while

I was surviving on mouldy fruit in the cellar. Oq's better than the Internet... Pah! Not soon she won't be, not if that Raven thing gets much further.

As if to reinforce his words, stars spiralled wildly around the Heart.

Merlin sat down again, something clicking in his head. "Like my computer? Infected! Oh no, poor Oq! If it's like a virus, it'll be multiplying every second."

He gritted his teeth and forced his attention back to the infected root. His father had done this. But for the first time in his life, Merlin knew how to fight back. He had the ancient might of a soultree of Earthaven on his side. Plus, on the ground, a vast army of unicorns, stags and bears, all converging on the Thrallstone where his father's spellclave had assembled. "You won't win this time, Father," he hissed through gritted teeth as Oq took the information from his head, digested it in milliseconds, and began to modify some of her own cells to fight the Raven. The Heart shook like a building during an earthquake, and Merlin had to grip the stool to stop himself falling off. But he didn't care. He wasn't afraid any more.

He caught the look of alarm on Lady Thaypari's face and grinned. "It's all right, Lady!" he called with a glow of pride. "I'm doing it, I'm really doing it!" Closing his eyes, he added in a fierce whisper, "Hold on, Natalie, wherever you are. I'll come and find you soon, I promise."

*

When Natalie next became aware of her surroundings, she and K'tanaqui were in the middle of a battle. The hawk had abandoned its feast – she could hear it screeching somewhere overhead. K'tanaqui was bleeding but still very much alive. With a great cry of, "Kill the Casters!" and a rush of hooves, unicorns charged the spellclave.

Her heart leapt in hope. This time there *were* hundreds of the creatures. This time the Casters had no trench to hide in. They were kneeling in a circle with their backs to Natalie and the Thrallstone, firing volleys of spellfire arrows into the oncoming silver tide, while the goshawk directed their aim from above.

It was a stirring sight. The unicorns haloed in crimson, a huge Earthaven sun rising out of the mist behind them, purple smoke drifting across the battlefield. After the unicorns, lumbered huge brown bears each one bearing several riders armed with axes and clubs. Behind the bears came stags, who lowered their antlers and pawed the ground. And behind the stags, shadowy foot soldiers waving their makeshift weapons and brushing dead spells out of their hair. Last of all came the Treemages who had transported the army to the Thrallstone, their shoulders drooping wearily but a glint of triumph in their eyes. Natalie crawled as close to K'tanaqui as the rope allowed and pressed her cheek to his bleeding flank. "Hold on, my poor darling, just a little longer." She almost felt sorry for the Casters.

The first charge was over and the unicorns wheeled round to regroup. Caster arrows had felled several of the Herders who rolled on the ground trying to quench the flames. The others seemed reluctant to charge again while their wounded comrades were in the way. A bear, however, lumbered through. With a defiant yell, one of its riders threw an axe that fell just short of Claudia's knees. She calmly picked it out of the earth and placed it at her side. Then she fitted another flaming arrow to her bow, took careful aim, and hit the axe-thrower in the chest. The bear reared up on to its hind legs and all three of its riders fell off backwards, the wounded one screaming.

Natalie closed her eyes as the unicorns charged again. This time they must break the Caster ring. They *must*. But again they were driven back and when she opened her eyes she saw why. Two of the spellclave had been fatally wounded in the charge. One had a spear sticking out of his lung, while the other – a woman she didn't remember seeing at the Lodge – had taken a unicorn horn in the stomach. But both were still upright, firing arrows as if nothing had happened. Like the man called Ferret, unable to die.

She turned cold all over and, beneath her, K'tanaqui trembled. *Powerrr of Thirrrteen*, he said weakly. *Hawk-man verrry strrrong now. Pup must be strrrong too. Crrry laterrr.*

Natalie drew a deep breath and wiped her face with her bound hands. He was right, she was wasting an opportunity here. The Casters were paying her no attention, maybe believing her spirit broken. With numb fingers, she tugged at the spellrope that bound her magehound but it was as impossible to loosen as before. She turned her attention to the Thrallstone. If she could drag K'tanaqui to the stone, somehow work her tether up as far as the hole and open it—

But even as she struggled to grip the magehound's ruff with her numb fingers there was a commotion at the rear of the Earthaven army. The ranks parted to allow three Spell Lords in formal Council robes to step through. She turned to watch, her heart beating faster.

Lord Pveriyan led, his white hair prickling with fresh thorns and thistles. Lord Gerystar, crowned with purple berries, strode at his right shoulder, while a Lady she didn't know strode at his left, golden flowers glimmering in her dark hair. Behind the Council members padded their magehounds, hackles up, growling loudly. A wary escort of Treemages surrounded them, live spells glimmering in their cupped hands.

"Casters!" Lord Pveriyan called in a terrible voice. "You are surrounded and outnumbered! Surrender, and you'll be given the choice of being returned across the Boundary to face your own world's justice, or receiving an Earthaven memory cleansing and execution of your familiar under the terms of the Spellfall Solution. Resist, and we'll leave you to the mercy of the unicorns."

"And bears!" someone shouted.

"And stags!"

"And our knives!"

As the cries fell silent, Lord Hawk scrambled on top of the Thrallstone and stood facing the sun, legs spread, feathered braids fluttering down his back. The goshawk screeched as it circled above the army. A Herder threw a spear at it but the bird was too high.

Lord Hawk laughed and pointed his stick at Natalie. "Have you forgotten I hold your thirteenth Council member? Attack us again, and I'll kill her *and* the magehound. Leave, and I'll let one of them live."

Natalie's blood chilled.

But Lord Pveriyan wasn't standing for any nonsense. "You harm her or the hound, and we'll have no mercy. Your deaths will be as painful and prolonged as Oq can make them. And since you can't see so well now the Boundary's shut, I'd better warn you Oq is as healthy as ever and itching for revenge. Your pathetic attempt to poison her failed."

A frown crossed Hawk's face. Then he laughed again. "I can see quite well enough. I used to live here, remember? And I'd say from all the litter around us that Oq is far from healthy. Besides, you can't kill us, can you? Not while I hold the Power of Thirteen!"

It was a challenge. By exposing himself on the stone like that, Hawk both mocked the Spell Lords' power and invited attack. Natalie shaded her eyes and squinted up at him, uneasy.

"It's a trick," she whispered.

K'tanaqui blinked his dull eyes. *Pup may be rrright. Take carrre.*

The three Spell Lords held a muttered conference. Around them, bears fidgeted, stags rattled their antlers, and unicorns dug up the earth. The Earthaven tribes fingered their weapons, eager for Caster blood. The spellclave waited, tense and wary, arrows nocked, spellfire bathing their faces in purple light. The smoke made Natalie cough. She crouched by K'tanaqui, afraid to move as everyone else seemed afraid, even Lord Pveriyan. The air crackled with hatred and unbearable tension. Then, with a cry of anger, a lone Herder galloped his unicorn right up to the kneeling Casters and hurled his spear at Lord Hawk's heart.

It happened so fast, the Spell Lords had no time to react, the spellclave had no time to aim their arrows, the goshawk had no time to dive, and Lord Hawk's stick, glimmering with a single live spell, was only half raised by the time that spear was sailing over the Casters' heads. Before it reached its target, however, the air above the Thrallstone *shimmered* and Lord Hawk vanished in a purple flash. Bitter spell smoke drifted down, and the spear rattled harmlessly against stone before falling to the ground.

*

For a full thirty seconds, no one moved. Casters and Earthaven army alike stared at the Thrallstone in stunned disbelief. Then the ranks surged forwards, muttering angrily.

"Where did he go?"

"Rush 'em now before he comes back!"

"What are we waiting for? There's only twelve of them now!"

And, inevitably, "Kill the Casters!"

"NO!" Lord Pveriyan shouted, pushing his way through to the front. "It's Hawk we want." K'veriyan raced along the front line, snapping and snarling at the unicorns and bears until they retreated out of bow range again.

The spellclave backed closer together. Hunter wheeled higher into the clouds, eyeing the army and the spellclave with equal suspicion. Natalie pressed herself against K'tanaqui's sweaty coat, keeping as far from the Casters as possible. Three of them should be dead, she thought. It's horrible.

Lord Pveriyan called, "Casters! Your leader has abandoned you. Throw down your weapons and spells!"

The muttering of the army abated. The Casters glanced at each other. "They won't dare touch us while we've got the girl," Ferret growled, seizing Natalie's elbow and dragging her away from K'tanaqui. He'd chosen her left arm which had gone numb all the way to her shoulder.

"No," she sobbed, kicking his shins.

The dead-alive Caster didn't seem to feel her. She turned desperately to Claudia but the woman was already scrambling up the Thrallstone, using the hole as a foothold, to stand where Lord Hawk had stood only minutes before. She pulled a spell-wrapped arrow from her quiver and unslung her bow.

"Lift the girl up here so they can see her," she ordered.

Natalie struggled wildly but the Casters were many and

strong and she was weak with K'tanaqui's pain and whatever was wrong with her arm where the Raven had splashed her. Between them, they lifted her on to the stone where she knelt in frozen disbelief as Claudia aimed the arrow at her heart.

"Do you trust me?" Claudia whispered.

Natalie blinked at the unexpected question. "Why should I?" she sniffed. "You stuck that needle in my neck! You helped make the Raven that's killing Oq. You were there when Lord Hawk drowned Bilbo. You put sleeping pills in my food! And you put a spellrope on K'tanaqui—" She choked, unable to go on.

Claudia nodded, her eyes sad. "I did all that, yes. And now I'm going to make amends. *Please*, Natalie, do what I say. We haven't much time."

Natalie glanced down at her magehound. The height made her dizzy. For the first time, she was aware of the silent army staring up at her – a blurred sea of silver unicorns, shadowy bears, foot soldiers and Treemages, their spears, blades and live spells all glinting and flashing and glimmering in the sunrise. Waiting. Even as Claudia was waiting for her answer.

"K'tanaqui?" she whispered. "What do I do?"

The magehound sighed. *Sometimes pup must decide forrr self.*

She took a deep breath, not daring to look down again. It would be so easy to throw herself off the stone, maybe knock Claudia off with her. Give the army a chance to move in and overpower the Casters. But Claudia had been kind to her in the Lodge and Lord Hawk had said she fought him – but couldn't win. "What do you want me to do?" she heard herself say.

The Caster woman smiled. "Good girl. Stand between me and the Spell Lords. Be ready for my signal."

As Natalie moved cautiously around the edge of the stone, Claudia chanted a soft word and the spell wrapped around the arrow burst into flame. Natalie couldn't help a flinch as that purple fire followed her.

"Stay back!" Claudia called in a clear voice. "This child is the last of your blood. Before any of your spears can reach me, I'll have put spellfire in her throat. Now, you do exactly what I say.

I'm going to send our hawk down so our familiars can negoti-
ate in the ancient manner. Don't anyone move except your
leader's magehound. And don't even think about trying to
harm the hawk… or the child dies."

Natalie's chest tightened. How could she have been so
stupid? She'd played right into Claudia's hands.

There was a short pause. Then, at a signal from his Lord,
K'veriyan padded out of the ranks into the dangerous territory
between the army and the spellclave, within range of enemy
arrows. Claudia looked up. After a moment, the goshawk
dropped out of the clouds and glided towards the magehound,
within range of the Earthaven army's weapons. Claudia held
her bow steady, the arrow aimed at Natalie's throat, until the
two familiars were perhaps an arm's length apart, Hunter back-
winging in preparation to land. Then she whispered, "Now,
Natalie, duck!" and she released the arrow.

Sparks hissed through Natalie's hair as she flattened herself
to the stone. She twisted her head and watched that arrow trail
death across the Earthaven sky. It seemed to move in slow
motion, blurring with distance until she couldn't see the
intended target.

There was a single surprised *caaa—*, cut off and followed by
a soft thud. Absolute silence reigned for the space of three
heartbeats. Then the three wounded members of the spellclave
screamed and crumpled to the ground. Claudia staggered as if
she herself had been hit, and the spellrope disappeared, taking
K'tanaqui with it.

As she squinted round to see where her magehound had
gone, Natalie made out a bundle of smoking feathers in
K'veriyan's jaws, the shaft of Claudia's arrow buried deep. The
other two magehounds bounded forwards and lost no time
tearing the hawk apart, snarling and snapping at one another
amidst a storm of smouldering feathers and bright drops of
unnatural yellow blood.

19

SACRIFICE

Sunday, November 1

After the death of their hawk, the spellclave surrendered without fuss. Willing hands helped Natalie down from the Thrallstone and dragged Claudia – rather more roughly – to the ground beside her. Under Lord Gerystar's direction, foot soldiers seized the Casters' bows and snapped the arrows across their knees, laying the spells in a neat pile for collection. Meanwhile, Herders rounded up the surviving Casters and held them at spear-point. The wounded three were lifted and carried away – the new woman moaning, the other two already dead.

"Why?" Natalie whispered.

"For all of us," Claudia said. "We're all free now." But the blue spark had gone from her eye, replaced by a dull look that reminded Natalie of Ferret.

She shuddered and hoped fiercely that Lord Hawk, wherever he had transported himself, was suffering a similar fate.

The Herders started to escort Claudia across to the others but Lord Pveriyan stopped them. Lips tight with rage, he glared at the Caster woman. "Where is he?" he snapped.

"I don't know—"

Pveriyan slapped her across the face. "Don't lie to me!"

Natalie's heart clenched. One of the Treemages had cut her bonds with his knife and was helping her away from the Casters, murmuring sympathetically. She broke free, fought a sudden wave of dizziness and tugged Lord Pveriyan's robe. "Don't hurt her, please don't! She helped me."

The Spell Lord scowled down at her. "Stay out of this, Daughter of Atanaqui." He turned back to Claudia. "I'll ask you once more. *Where is he?*"

Claudia shook her head. "I wish I knew. He transported when he realized the soultree wasn't dying as it should, that's all I know. But you needn't worry, he's powerless without his familiar."

This reminded Natalie of her own loss. "What about K'tanaqui?" she said. "Ask her what happened to my magehound..." Another dizzy wave struck. She staggered and would have fallen had Pveriyan not caught her.

Immediately, Claudia was on her knees, fingers probing the blistered flesh of her arm. "I was afraid of this," she said, resting a hand on Natalie's forehead. "Do you feel sick? Dizzy? Are you having any trouble breathing?"

"Yes," Natalie admitted to all three. "But I'll feel better when K'tanaqui comes back."

Claudia glanced at Pveriyan. "The girl's very sick. I'm afraid the Raven splashed her. There isn't time to explain properly, but we manufactured the Raven to attack the enchantment-gene so it would not only kill Oq but also poison the soulfruit and Spellfall and everyone of the ancient blood who ate the fruit or tried to use the spells. Hawk was willing to sacrifice his own power to see Earthaven die – and he did like his little jokes. Hence the Raven being a liquid, his very own Spellfall solution."

No one laughed. Pveriyan was staring at Claudia. Natalie felt worse.

"I'm glad your soultree has managed to fight off the Raven," Claudia went on. "But Natalie needs help. She has to get to a hospital immediately. I'll go with her and—"

"You will do nothing of the sort!" Pveriyan snapped. "Think I'm stupid, do you? Trying to blind me with your human science? There was never any threat from your Raven, I knew that from the start. If the child's sick, Oq will soon heal her. In the meantime, I want to know where Hawk is, and you're going to tell me." He snapped his fingers at the hovering Treemages. "Connect her to the soultree. We'll get it out of her the hard way."

Natalie watched uneasily as two men took Claudia's arms and dragged her across to the trees. Lord Pveriyan and his magehound followed. Without her glasses she couldn't see what they were doing. But when Claudia's scream cut the Earthaven sunrise, she staggered after them, the ground swaying beneath her. "Don't hurt her! Oh, please don't! Claudia!"

Sweetly scented arms caught her and the Spell Lady with the golden flowers in her hair guided her back to the Thrallstone. "Shh, silly," she said. "Sit down, that's right. I'm Lady Fayhilia, Third Member of the Council." She hitched up her long robes and sat on the grass beside Natalie. "Now then, what's all this fuss? You've had a terrible experience, I know, but it's over now. Pveriyan's experienced in these matters, he'll get results. Then we'll find your magehound and we'll cleanse this Caster who calls himself Lord Hawk along with the rest of his spellclave. It'll be a complete draining, every thought, every memory. He won't hurt you again, don't worry."

Natalie stared at her. "But Lord Pveriyan said they'd have a choice!"

"They'll choose cleansing. You'll see."

"But... why? They won't have their memories taken away in my world. They might go to prison, I suppose, but—" A second scream from Claudia drove the rest of what she'd been going to say from her head. "Please stop him," she begged. "If she knew anything, she'd have told us."

Lady Fayhilia smiled. "Maybe, maybe not. But this is the best way for everyone. If she really doesn't know, then Oq will tell Pveriyan she doesn't, and he'll stop trying to get it out of her. Cover your ears if it disturbs you. It shouldn't take too much longer."

*

Confusing data was coming from one of Oq's outer branches. It was a long way from the original poisoned root but Merlin shifted uncomfortably on his stool. What if he'd missed a Raven cell and it had sneaked into a healthy branch while his attention had been on the root and was even now multiplying for another attack? Then he realized. The data was coming from the vicinity of the Thrallstone where people were clearing up after the battle.

Merlin didn't bother investigating. His head was spinning, his stomach growling with hunger, and he was stiff from sitting in one place so long. Besides, the excitement was over now. He'd missed his father's defeat but it had been worth it. He smiled. Oq would probably lose the infected root all the way to the fifth junction. But a single root was nothing compared to the damage the Raven would have inflicted had the poisoned cells been allowed to rampage through her entire system.

He stretched the kinks out of his shoulders and was just about to initiate a search for Natalie when the air in the Heart *shimmered* and something smashed into the delicate tendrils attached to his head. They came loose with a wrench of pain. The world jerked. Merlin found himself on his knees, clutching at his temples. A sticky mixture of blood and sap oozed through his fingers.

"What did you do that for?" he said. "We just won!" He struggled to his feet, certain the tall figure standing over him was Lord Pveriyan. "I didn't do anything to hurt your precious tree! Ask her yourself—"

The stick crashed across his back, sending him to his knees again, knocking all the breath out of him. This time Merlin stayed down, dismay surging through him. He knew the feel of that stick. It had bruised him often enough in the past.

He raised his head and looked for Lady Thaypari, fearing the worst. But she was still at the entrance, staring open-mouthed at Hawk. "What do you think you're doing?" she cried, recovering from her shock. "Stop that at once! How did you get in here?"

Her magehound growled at the intruder and gathered itself to spring. But Hawk pointed his stick at the Spell Lady and laughed – a terrible, cracked sound, worse than anything Merlin had heard his father utter before. "Go on, try it! I am Hawk, Lord of Thirteen! I have the power to send your hound to the fire in the bowels of the earth and you after him!"

Merlin risked a peep at his father's face. The yellow eyes glittered. But there was something wrong with them. He wasn't looking at Thaypari, rather staring at a point past her shoulder.

Heart thudding, Merlin slithered out of range of the stick. He willed Lady Thaypari to do the sensible thing and fetch help. But she drew herself up straight and tall and folded her orange-flowered hair around her like a cloak.

"How dare you threaten a member of the Council in the Heart of her own soultree?" she said quietly. "K'aypari! Get his familiar."

Lord Hawk threw back his head and let out that terrible laugh again. "Oh, you don't think I'd be stupid enough to transport Hunter in here with me, do you? I must admit the last person I expected to find here was my pathetic son. I suppose you're letting your soultree drain him now you think you've neutralized the Raven? You should have remained connected, my proud Lady. Oq might have helped you. Now you die." He opened his hand and tossed a crumpled bronze spell at Thaypari.

"No!" Merlin surged to his feet and grabbed his father's arm. He hung his whole weight on it. The spell, only half cast, missed its target and fluttered harmlessly to the floor. Lord Hawk grunted and threw Merlin against the Heart wall. Stray orange petals swirled to the floor as Thaypari and her magehound fled.

Cursing, Lord Hawk turned. His mouth twisted as he peered down at Merlin with those fever-bright, unfocused eyes. The sight of his son cowering on the floor seemed to amuse him. "Not quite drained yet, I see. Maybe I should have looked more carefully to see who it was before I smashed those tendrils. Then again, you never did have much between those grubby ears of yours. I don't suppose it would have made a lot of difference."

Merlin clenched his fists. "*I* destroyed the Raven," he said.

"You?" His father laughed. "Don't be silly! You wouldn't have the first idea."

"Wouldn't I?" Merlin sat up a bit straighter. "What do you think I was doing all the time you and Claudia-the-Fish were down in that cellar? Zapping aliens on my computer? I soon got bored with that! I read every word of those magazines – forwards, backwards, and inside-out. I know more about viruses in systems than you think, and Oq is a system too. She might be huge and alive but she works the same way. It wasn't hard."

Bighead, Redeye muttered from inside his boot. *I was the one who pointed you in the right direction, remember? Your foot stinks, by the way.*

Hawk paced around the Heart, prodding the soft glowing flesh with his stick and whacking any tendril that moved. Oq sparkled in anger. Merlin shifted his foot where Redeye was wriggling like mad, tickling his toes. "Stop that," he hissed. "I've got enough to worry about." Then he had a sudden thought. "Can Father see?"

About as well as a bat, Redeye said scornfully. *The hawk's dead. Good riddance, if you ask me.*

"Dead?" Merlin whispered, a chill going through him. "No wonder he's acting so crazy! We have to get out of here." He crawled towards the entrance, only to find his father's stick blocking the way.

"Going somewhere, little mouse?" Hawk hissed, the insane glitter back in his eyes. "You think you're so superior, don't

you, with your clever computer-talk? Little traitor, that's what
you are. You and that pathetic familiar of yours. Take off your
boot!"

"Lady Thaypari will be back soon," Merlin said, trying to
sound more confident than he felt. "She'll bring Herders with
spears! They hate Casters."

His father smiled. "No she won't. They're all far too busy at
the Thrallstone. We're alone in here and I think some punishment is due for all the trouble you've caused me, don't you?
Remember your mother's sweet little canary?"

Merlin felt ill. He darted a glance at the entrance. Still no
sign of Lady Thaypari. As slowly as he could he began to ease
off his right boot.

The stick crashed into his ankle. "Not that one! The one
with your mouse in it. Stop delaying! No one's going to help
you now."

Which might be true now their tree was safe. Merlin took a
deep breath. "Run, Redeye!" he shouted, whipping off his left
boot and turning it upside-down, at the same time making a
dash for the entrance.

Several things happened at once.

Hawk made a grab for the mouse but missed. Redeye
scurried up Merlin's leg, dragging a rather creased spell that
nevertheless glittered and flashed with power. A pack of silver
magehounds poured into the Heart and sprang at the intruder,
snarling and snapping. Lady Thaypari shouted to Merlin to get
out of there. Lord Hawk swung his stick – and froze, his gaze
fixed on Merlin's hand.

Cast it, you fool! Redeye said.

"No," his father whispered, his eyes showing the first flicker
of sanity since he'd appeared in the Heart. "Don't—"

Merlin set his jaw. "Couldn't transport a flea if it hopped half
the distance itself, huh Father?" Twelve years of frustration and
pain streamed down his arm and into the spell. The heat and
power of the casting knocked him backwards. The resulting
spellflash stained the Heart purple, blinding Merlin, Redeye,

magehounds and Spell Lords alike. He smelt burnt sugar mingled with singed hair and flesh. When he could see again, his father had gone.

He stood very still while the magehounds sniffed around the Heart, whimpering in confusion. The Spell Lords wafted smoke away from their faces. Then Lady Thaypari gathered him into her soft, warm arms. "It's all right, young Caster," she said, holding him tightly. "You're safe now. It's over."

*

The questioning at the Thrallstone was soon over. After only a few minutes, Lord Pveriyan came striding back, dragging Claudia by the wrist. Lady Fayhilia stood and brushed grass off her robe, one eyebrow raised in query. Natalie looked up, afraid of what she might see. But apart from two small bruises on her temples, Claudia appeared to be unharmed.

Pveriyan flung the Caster to her knees in the shadow of the Thrallstone and regarded her in disgust. "She hasn't a clue!" he said. "She doesn't even know where K'tanaqui went, let alone Hawk. All she keeps saying is she has to take Atanaqui's daughter through the gateway to this place called Hospital so she can be properly treated. Pah!"

"Then maybe it's true," Lady Fayhilia said quietly.

Pveriyan scowled. "She's lying to save her skin. The Caster poison must have damaged Oq, and—"

"Changed your tune rather, haven't you Pveriyan?" said an amused voice behind them. "I seem to remember you saying the Raven was no threat to us."

Everyone swung round. Pveriyan's scowl deepened, but Natalie saw Fayhilia's lips twitch up at the corners. The voice belonged to Lady Thaypari, who had brought the rest of the Council with her. Their magehounds chased one another around the Thrallstone, getting under the unicorns' hooves, tails waving. They greeted Fayhilia's hound and Lord Gerystar's with playful bites. Only K'veriyan remained stiff and unfriendly, his hackles raised and a growl beginning in his throat.

Natalie's spirits lifted at the sight of the small, grubby figure jogging behind the newcomers. The boy's Herder clothing was virtually unrecognizable, being torn and covered in mud, but his grin was undiminished. A white mouse peered from under one ear. "Merlin!" she said. "How did you get here?"

The boy crouched beside her. "Used the Root System, of course. Lady Thaypari thought we'd better see if the organa-zoomers still worked. They do! Better than before, actually. Not so many bruises."

"But the Raven?"

"Gone. Just like Father."

Natalie's stomach clenched. "Lord Hawk, you mean? Did you see him? He was here, but then he transported—"

"Into the Heart. I know, I was there. But I soon transported him out again."

"Where to?"

Merlin smiled. "As far as possible."

"Merlin!" Natalie clutched at her arm. She couldn't cope with this now.

Immediately, his grin faded. "Are you all right? You look terrible. What's wrong with your arm? Did you get wounded in the battle? Did Father do it? I hope I hurt him, I hope I *killed* him."

The Council were discussing Lord Hawk too. Lord Pveriyan seemed furious that the spellclave leader had vanished again but Lady Thaypari said soothingly, "Even if he survived the transportation, he's trapped in Earthaven until the next Opening. We can deal with him later. He's powerless now you've destroyed his familiar."

Lord Pveriyan grunted. "We didn't have to destroy it. Seems there was a rebel in the spellclave." He pointed to Claudia. "*She* shot the goshawk."

Everyone stared at Claudia. Thaypari helped the Caster woman to her feet, touched the bruises on her temples and frowned at Pveriyan. While the other Spell Lords gathered round, murmuring excitedly, Thaypari extracted some orange berries from her hair, mashed them between her palms, and smeared the juice on Claudia's wounds.

The Caster woman smiled. "Thank you, Lady," she said quietly. "But I'm afraid your Earthaven remedies won't work for Natalie. Her world made the Raven and only her world can heal her now. We really do have to hurry."

Lord Pveriyan's lips twisted. "Sure you wouldn't prefer a nice quick cleansing, Caster? If you go back, they'll lock you up for a long time. Sure you can stand it without your hawk? The others couldn't."

He pointed to the far side of the clearing, where glowing creepers curled out of the clouds to weave thick cocoons about a line of struggling bodies. Natalie squinted at them and was suddenly glad she'd lost her glasses. No wonder the army was cheering so loudly.

Merlin paled. "They're *torturing* them," he whispered.

Lady Thaypari shook her head. "The pain won't last long. When it's done, they'll be put to work in Earthaven – simple tasks that don't require them to think. Sometimes it's a blessing not to remember."

Claudia winced, as if she didn't need to be reminded. She grasped Natalie's hand. "The doctors will need to know the exact formula of the Raven," she said firmly. "I think I can keep my sanity long enough to tell them that. Come on, Natalie. Are you strong enough to open the gateway, or shall I ask one of the Spell Lords to let us through?"

Natalie hung back. "What about Merlin? I'm not leaving unless you let him go too."

The boy grinned. "It's all right, I'm going to stay and teach the Council about viruses and stuff and how to access other soultrees so they can communicate with each other, maybe even set up a world-wide Root System. Soultree roots go right under the oceans, you know. It'll be brilliant, Natalie! Imagine taking an organazoomer anywhere you want – *whoosh*, and you're there!"

She stared at him. "But I thought you hated organazoomers?"

"That was before. Besides, now Oq's opened my Earthaven eyes, I'll probably need Redeye to see in your world, and I've had quite enough of that— Ow!"

In spite of her sickness and the worry over K'tanaqui, Natalie giggled. The mouse had nipped his ear. Then her legs gave way and she sagged against Claudia.

"We have to go," the Caster woman said. "Now!"

Lady Thaypari nodded and opened the gateway herself. "Don't forget us, Natalie, will you?" she said. "There's still a vacant seat on the Council. I hope you'll fill it some day."

Lord Pveriyan stepped in front of them, his jaw working. Natalie stiffened. But he said gruffly, "Hurry up and get well, Daughter of Atanaqui. And while you're in this Hospital of yours, remember to ask if their wonder technology can find K'tanaqui, because Oq certainly can't."

Natalie was saved from making a reply as Claudia pulled her through the stone. There was a green flare. Her ears popped, she tasted diesel fumes, felt chill air on her burning cheeks. Then a lot of people were running towards them, all shouting at once.

Just before the gateway closed, Natalie looked back. The Spell Lords and their magehounds were watching silently, flanked by exhausted Treemages. Behind them, unicorns with rainbow horns, huge bears each carrying three or four riders, and stags with proud antlers, all blurred into the secret Earthaven shadows. The last thing she saw was Redeye creep from Merlin's shoulder, steal a berry from Thaypari's hair and eat it.

Her chest tightened and she made a feeble effort to go back. But everything was spinning. Rough hands dragged her and Claudia apart and slammed the Caster woman against the stone. Someone wrapped a blanket around Natalie and led her away while handcuffs were snapped on Claudia's wrists. She tried to tell them not to hurt her, that Claudia had helped her, but the effort was too much. Before she'd taken two steps from the Thrallstone, darkness claimed her.

*

Sirens wailing, they took Nat away in the ambulance that had been waiting ominously at the edge of the clearing since the official search adopted the Thrallstone as their base. An unmarked car followed, skidding along the churned-up track. Handcuffed in the back was the woman kidnapper who'd brought Nat out of the woods. Two patrol cars went along as escort, blue lights flashing. Mr Marlins had gone in the back of the ambulance to hold Nat's hand. Julie, who had been phoned by the police as soon as Nat appeared, would meet them at the hospital. The Ministry men had already taken the Raven canister away at breakneck speed in their black van. The remaining police officers and their dogs were now conducting a search of the area around the Thrallstone, apparently still hopeful of finding Claudia's accomplices. Which left Tim, Jo, and the Death Heads ignored at the edge of the clearing, desperately trying to keep their eyes open now the excitement was over.

Tim stared after the convoy until he could no longer hear the sirens. He pulled his birthday jacket closer about his shoulders and shivered. Day might have come but it was a damp grey November day and the cold had worked itself into his bones. "I hope Nat's going to be OK," he said, voicing all their fears.

No one spoke for half a minute. Then Gaz said, "I'm sure she will be, Tim. You don't get rid of kid sisters that easy."

The younger Heads giggled but soon went quiet again.

"It must be really frightening being kidnapped," Paulie said after a pause.

"Oh, I dunno," Pizzaface said. "I bet it was pretty exciting. Now she can sell her story to the newspapers and get loads of pocket money for sweets."

The others gave him disgusted looks.

"Best fun we've ever had!" Gaz declared, breaking the tension. "I think we should come up here every Hallowe'en. What d'you say, Heads?"

There were cries of, "No way!" as the gang leapt on their

leader, rolling him in the leaves. They laughed as they stuffed slimy handfuls down one another's backs.

Jo had been given one of the ambulance's blankets which she clutched about her like a cloak. Her cap had gone and her fringe straggled into her eyes. "Nat was so brave in Earthaven, grabbing that leaky canister like she did," she said quietly.

Tim cast an anxious glance at the Heads. But they were too busy rolling in the mud to notice her slip. "You went after the Casters," he pointed out. "*That* was brave. All I did was find a few measly illusion spells."

He'd been a bit worried what Gaz and the others might get up to with the live spells they'd found in the Lodge. But as soon as the Boundary shut, they'd frowned at the glimmering things in their hands, screwed them up and tossed them away – only to scramble after them again when Mr Marlins shouted at them not to drop litter. Now, all the spells were safe in a black plastic dustbin liner hidden in the shed back at the Lodge. Mr Marlins had promised Tim that as soon as everything calmed down, he'd collect them and take them to the Thrallstone, make his peace with Lord Pveriyan and assure the Council Tim didn't remember a thing. "That way they'll leave you alone," he'd told Tim with an awkward smile. "Only you've got to promise me you'll be responsible. No silly business, using spells to play tricks on your friends or anything like that."

"Course not!" Tim had replied, hurt. But Mr Marlins' words had given him a few ideas.

He smiled at Jo. "At least I can still remember everything. Who knows? Maybe I'll even volunteer my services as a Thrall one of these days. Beats stacking shelves at the supermarket."

There was a short, awkward silence. Then Jo said, "Your head's bleeding again. You should have let them take you to hospital."

"Don't fuss. You're starting to sound like my mother."

"Well, someone has to. You're such an idiot, Timothy Lockley! Next time you try taking on a spellclave single-handed, remember to duck."

Tim grinned. He still hadn't heard all of Jo's story, and she didn't know all the details of his. But he had a feeling they were going to enjoy putting the pieces together later.

"You're lucky they didn't drag *you* off to be tested for contamination," he shot back. "If those Ministry people had got you in that black van of theirs, you'd never have been heard of again."

Jo gave him a withering look. "You watch too much TV."

"That's what my mother says, too."

They weren't the only ones talking about the night's strange happenings. Groups of weary officers stood around stamping their feet and drinking coffee from paper cups while they discussed the night's work. Their equally weary dogs waited nearby, tails drooping. Overhead, the police helicopter could still be heard, clattering low over the trees, circling the area around the Thrallstone.

"Looks like the woman was telling the truth," said one of the officers. "No sign of anyone else creeping around in there – though I kept seeing ghosts all night, only to find there was no scent when I put my dog on it."

"You think *you've* been seeing things?" said another. "Larry here swears he saw a unicorn!"

"I seen three," Larry mumbled but the others were too busy laughing at him to hear.

Tim and Jo exchanged a glance.

"And what about the riot that was supposed to be going on right under our noses, then?" said another. "Hundreds of bodies? Ha! Pull the other one."

"Bet it was them government people, jamming the signals."

"Yeah, mighty secretive about what they had in that van of theirs, weren't they?"

"Shh!"

The men fell silent as an Inspector approached. He pointed to the Thrallstone, and the men groaned. But they whistled for their dogs and went to investigate, obediently tapping the stone with their sticks and poking the undergrowth around its base. One shone his torch into the hole. The helicopter hovered overhead.

Jo drew a sharp breath. "What are they doing? You don't think they can see Earthaven, do you?"

Tim stared at her. A chill rippled down his back at the thought of having to go through all that again.

But after a few minutes, the searchers returned shaking their heads. "That fancy infrared camera of theirs is up the creek, if you ask me," one muttered. "You wouldn't believe some of the wild goose chases they sent me on last night. Someone hiding in the stone, indeed! Have you seen the size of that hole? Couldn't even fit my little finger in. They'll be asking us to believe in magic swords next." Which set them all off laughing again.

One of them noticed Tim and Jo were listening, and quickly straightened his face. "Hey, isn't someone supposed to be taking these kids home? The poor mites look all done in to me."

20

REUNION

Saturday, November 7

It was almost a week before Natalie was allowed home from hospital. The doctors said she'd made a "miraculous recovery", but wanted to keep her in a few extra days for observation.

They were the worst days of Natalie's life, worse even than her imprisonment in the Lodge. She wanted to scream that she wouldn't get sick again and they had to let her out but they wouldn't have understood why, and screaming in hospital only brought another needle.

During this time, her magehound was a flickering, fuzzy presence at the edge of her thoughts. All night she lay awake whispering, *"K'tanaqui, K'tanaqui, K'tanaqui,"* under her breath in the hope he'd reply. But wherever he was, he couldn't hear her. She thought about climbing out of the window while everyone else was asleep and going to look for him, but the memory of what her family had already been through kept her lying meekly in bed. Besides, she didn't have any outdoor clothes, and running around scantily clad in the November fog would only have put her straight back in hospital again.

Dad and Julie visited every day. They told her Claudia would go to prison but she'd have the minimum sentence because of her cooperation with the doctors and the Ministry people. This cheered Natalie up a bit. The Caster woman had been punished enough by the loss of her familiar. It didn't seem fair that she should be locked away too.

When the doctors eventually let her out on Friday afternoon, all Natalie could think of was starting the search for K'tanaqui. But Julie, Mr Marlins and Tim watched her every second, as if she might slip between the floorboards the moment they took their eyes off her. Then Jo came round to say Mrs Carter was taking her and Sarah to the kennels tomorrow to choose a new puppy, and would Nat like to come? Julie looked doubtful but to Natalie's surprise Mr Marlins said he thought it was an excellent idea and offered to drive them. At which Julie said she certainly wasn't going to be left behind, Jo said Mr Carter was going too, and Tim said, hey, what about him?

In the end, the kennel visit turned into a real family outing. The Carters led the way, while Mr Marlins followed with Julie, Tim and Natalie in his sleek black car. This was a first for the Marlins family, but Natalie was too busy trying to hear K'tanaqui to appreciate this. As they drove, she stared hopefully out of the window, fingering the handful of unicorn mane that had replaced Itsy's box in her anorak pocket. She didn't notice the little smile on Julie's face, nor the way Tim and Mr Marlins kept glancing at each other, and then at her, as if planning a surprise.

The kennels were at a farm about ten minutes' drive from Millennium Green. The outbuildings had been converted into pens, and as soon as they opened their car doors, the excited yapping and whining and scrabbling claws of hundreds of dogs greeted them. Jo tugged her cap further over her eyes and stared at the dogs, a strange expression on her face, while Sarah immediately rushed to a pen full of squirming Labrador puppies and pushed her hand through the netting so they could lick her fingers.

Natalie barely noticed the puppies. She wiped a few drops of
rain from her new glasses and made a quick search of the pens.
But no white wolf-like mongrel flipped its tattered ear, no
amber eyes blinked at her, no voice spoke in her head. She
sighed. It had been too much to hope for.

"I want this one!" Sarah announced. "His eyes are exactly
like Bilbo's used to be – look!"

Mrs Carter glanced at Jo. "It's your sister's dog too, Sarah,"
she said gently.

Jo shook herself. "It's OK, let Sarah choose. I think I'll go
take a look round. Coming, Nat?" She walked quickly down
the rows of pens, her shoulders stiff, face averted from her family.
Natalie hurried after her, concern for her friend momentarily
dislodging K'tanaqui from her thoughts. Tim came too.

They caught up with Jo in a long barn where older dogs and
those recovering from illnesses were being kept warm. The girl
was staring at a scruffy brown mongrel lying on its side in
some straw. Natalie hesitated. Tim whispered, "She took it
pretty hard. You should've seen her just after it happened."

Jo heard them and looked round with a little smile. "It's all
right," she said. "I'm not going to burst into tears or anything
like that. I wanted to get you away from the mothers, that's all."
She glanced round the barn to check they were alone and gave
Tim a hesitant look. "Do you still remember?"

"Course I do! Nobody wipes Timothy Lockley's memories!"

"Right." Jo took a deep breath. "Then I think I know what
happened to Hawk."

"What?" said Natalie and Tim together.

"I've been thinking about what happened up at the
Thrallstone, with the infrared camera? What if it *was* working
properly? After all, the Boundary had shut by then and my
watch was working again."

"Don't be silly." Tim said, frowning. "They detected a body
inside the stone, didn't they? A *living* body."

"Exactly."

They both stared at her.

"It was probably one of the Spell Lords checking to see the gateway was closed properly," Natalie said. But her stomach was doing strange things.

"If that's so, then why doesn't our technology detect people in Earthaven the rest of the time? No, listen, it all makes sense. You said transporting was risky, didn't you Nat? And that no one can transport across the Boundary once it's shut? If this Caster kid Merlin really did transport his father as far from the Heart as possible, mightn't he have ended up inside the stone? It's big enough, isn't it?"

Tim started to grin, then shook his head. "Na, even I know that's impossible. People can't breathe inside stones. Worse luck, 'cause that hawk-man deserves it if anyone does." He grimaced and rubbed the back of his neck.

"How do we know?" Jo insisted. "The Thrallstone's a place of power. It's not like normal stone. Nat? What do you think? You know more about Earthaven than we do— Hey, what's wrong?"

Natalie was growing colder by the second. Most of the dogs were standing up at the fronts of their cages now, panting and whining for attention; but she saw only a silver wolf with curling yellow fur, hurt and trapped, crying for her to rescue him.

"K'tanaqui," she whispered, hugging herself. "What if it was *K'tanaqui* the camera detected inside the Thrallstone? That would explain why he's so fuzzy and I can't hear him any more."

The other two glanced at each other. Tim mouthed, *"Now, see what you've done?"*

"I'm sure it's not K'tanaqui," Jo said quickly. "Tim's right. The camera must have been malfunctioning, that's all."

"No," Natalie said, trying to think. "You're right about the Boundary shutting. Their equipment would have been working again, and maybe their camera could sort of see inside it. I've got to get up there! Oh poor K'tanaqui, I'm so stupid, I should have thought."

She was already running, out into the November drizzle,

across the yard, past the astonished group of adults clustered around the puppy pen.

"Nat, wait!" Jo shouted, coming after her. She saw Tim pull Mr Marlins away from the others and whisper something in his ear. Julie hurried after them, demanding to know what was going on. There was just one building between Natalie and the wood now. She ran faster, not stopping to think how far it might be to the Thrallstone from the kennels, nor what might happen if she collapsed in the wood on her own.

She was almost past the building when emerald stars burst behind her eyes, forcing her to stop and clutch her head. When the stars cleared, she found herself staring at a notice on the door.

Jo panted up behind her. "You're acting crazy, Nat! If you're not careful, they'll put you straight back in hospital again. At least let your dad drive you up there, instead of trying to finish yourself off like this."

Then she saw what Natalie was looking at, and her eyes brightened with sudden understanding. "Veterinary Section? You don't think—"

Slowly, her head itching inside, Natalie opened the door. They found themselves in a well-lit corridor that smelt of antiseptic. At the far end was another door, this one with a small square window near the top. People wearing green aprons and masks could be glimpsed moving about inside. Without hesitation, Natalie reached for the handle.

"Wait!" a uniformed woman said, hurrying up behind them. "You can't go in there!" But Natalie had already ducked through the door, leaving Jo to explain.

The metallic smell of blood hit her, bringing memories of the battle. Her stomach clenched but she forced herself to stillness. A large silver dog was having an operation, stretched out under a green plastic sheet beneath bright lights. A tube ran from a bottle of anaesthetic into its muzzle, and a tattered ear flopped over the edge of the table. The vet and his assistants glanced round in surprise as Natalie burst in. One of the women frowned and came towards her, pulling off her mask and blood-spattered gloves.

Natalie stared at the table, relief surging from her toes, up her wobbly legs and into her heart. Her head blazed with a bright amber light. She didn't know whether to laugh or cry, and ended up doing both at once. "That's my dog," she told the veterinary nurse. "He'll be all right, won't he?"

The nurse's initial anger melted to sympathy. She put an arm around Natalie's shoulders and drew her gently to the door. "He'll be fine, don't worry. He was in a bad way when we found him, but we've operated and he's got a strong heart. We thought he was a stray. What happened? Did he get hit by a car?"

"I lost him."

The nurse steered her out of the operating theatre. "A handsome animal like that deserves a good home. To tell you the truth, the vet wasn't very enthusiastic when we brought him in, him not being a young dog, but I had a strange feeling about that one from the start. He has such intelligent eyes, you'd almost think he was trying to talk. You can watch from out here, all right? I'm sure you understand we have to keep the operating theatre as sterile as possible."

By now everyone was clustered in the corridor, all asking questions at once. Jo was trying her best to explain without giving anything away. Tim kept quiet, fingers hooked in his jacket pockets, though Natalie saw him fighting a smile. Julie raised an eyebrow at the sight of the magehound and murmured, "I was thinking more of a puppy."

But Mr Marlins took one look through the window, linked an arm through Julie's and smiled at the nurse. "Yes, that's him all right. We'll take him home as soon as he recovers from the anaesthetic – if that's all right with you, Nat?"

Natalie could only nod dumbly. As her father led the others back outside, she pressed her nose and palms against the window of the operating theatre and smiled through her tears.

"I know you can't hear me, K'tanaqui," she whispered. "But

I promise we'll visit Earthaven soon. We'll go to see Lady Atanaqui in the Heart and tell her everything, maybe take Dad along too. I might even let Merlin show us what he's done with the Root System. You concentrate on getting better, and I'll take you for walks in the river meadows to get your strength back. You might have to put up with Jo's new puppy, and you'll have to pretend to be an ordinary dog for a while, but I'm sure you've done that before."

Why pup crrry when happy? came a faint tickle in her head, making her breath catch. *Does pup think K'tanaqui not hearrr? Ourrr bond strrrong. Pup nothing to fearrr now Hawk-man trrrapped between worrrlds.*

Natalie wiped a stray hair out of her eyes and stared at the bleary-eyed magehound, hardly daring to believe. "K'tanaqui! I can hear you!" Then she realized what he had said. "Lord Hawk trapped? Then Jo was right! Oh, wait till I tell everyone!"

Heart singing, she rushed out into the cold to spread the good news.

GUIDE TO EARTHAVEN

Boundary Invisible barrier between our world and Earthaven, protected by spells that disrupt human technology.

Caster Derogatory term applied to a Spellmage who lives outside Earthaven (having been banished or born to banished parents).

Earthaven An enchanted realm, parallel to our own world. A sanctuary for creatures whose existence is threatened by modern technology, Earthaven is protected by anti-technology spells and accessed through gateways that only a Spell Lord can open. Most residents of Earthaven are virtually blind in our world, just as we would be virtually blind in Earthaven. However, Spellmages who cross the Boundary can see through the eyes of their familiar.

familiar Spellmage's best friend and ally, usually an animal.

magehound White wolf, a familiar belonging to a member of a soul-tree Council. Earthaven Spellmages can voluntarily sacrifice their familiars to a magehound, after which they become Treemages (a position of great status) and are allowed to live in the soultree.

moonflower Small, white Earthaven flower that opens in moon-light. Moonflowers live in colonies wherever soultree roots are close to the surface. They have soporific qualities.

Opening The time when Earthaven merges with our world. The Opening occurs once a year, between midnight and dawn on October 31, when it allows free access across the Boundary (not just at the gateways). We call this night Hallowe'en. During the Opening, Earthaven becomes visible and illusion spells fail.

organazoomers Specially adapted cells that transport people at high speed along the large, hollow roots of a soultree. They are controlled by the Spell Lords but powered by the tree.

Power of Thirteen Power possessed by a complete spellclave of thirteen Spellmages but wielded by the leader, whose familiar must first consume the familiars of the other twelve Spellmages.

soulfruit Fruit of the soultree, rather like a pear, very nourishing. It has magical properties such as the power to ensure human loyalty.

soultree Huge, sentient tree whose root system permeates Earthaven with magic. When a soultree dies it produces live spells (see **Spellfall**) which if allowed to grow will eventually develop into a new soultree. Otherwise, a soultree does not produce seed, nor drop its leaves.

soultree Council Special council of thirteen Spell Lords and Ladies of equal power who are sworn to protect the soultree they live in. All Council members have magehounds as familiars, and each individual member possesses the Power of Thirteen, making the Council more powerful than any normal spellclave.

spell A seed produced by a dying soultree. It looks like a large coloured leaf and is often mistaken as litter in our world. Colour varies between bronze, green and purple, depending on the soultree that produced it. A spell can only be *cast* once, although spells can be recycled by burial in Earthaven. Warm and glimmering when *live*, they are extremely cold and dull when *dead*.

Some Uses of Spells

— **illusion** Temporary image created to hide from ordinary human eyes the real nature of an Earthaven object or person. An illusion remains in place until the spell dies or until it is removed. They are much weaker during the Opening when some humans see things they should not. They are the easiest type of spell to cast.

— **spellrope** Once tied, a knot in a spellrope cannot be undone by anyone but the Spellmage who tied it or until the spells that were used to make the rope die.

— **spellfire** Purple fire produced as a side effect of burning live spells. Cannot be extinguished until the spell dies.

— **transport** To move objects or people from one place to another instantly. Normally, a live spell is required at each end but it is possible to use a *place of power*, such as the Thrallstone, instead of one of the spells.

spellclave A spellclave is made up of a Spell Lord, or Lady, and their twelve *bonded* Spellmages.

Spell Lord or Lady A Spellmage whose familiar has successfully consumed twelve other familiars, thereby releasing the Power of Thirteen.

Spellfall Fall of live spells from a dying soultree. Very rare since soultrees live so long.

Spellfall Solution Treaty drawn up between the soultree Councils and the Casters, forbidding the use of new spells fresh from Spellfall, and committing the Councils to recycling old spells for Caster use.

Spellmage Someone who has the power to cast spells. Every Spellmage is bonded to a familiar.

Thrall A human agent bound to serve a soultree Council after eating soulfruit from their tree to ensure loyalty.

Thrallstone One of the gateways to Earthaven, situated in Unicorn Wood. A standing stone with a hole in it which is supposed to be large enough for a small child to crawl through. Earthaven can sometimes be glimpsed through this hole.

Treemage Spellmage who has voluntarily sacrificed his or her familiar to a magehound in return for being allowed to live in the soultree and serve the Council. Duties include caring for the soultree.

unicorn Silver horse with luminous rainbow horn, the fastest living creature in the world. They are very proud and will not allow an enemy on their back.

(unicorn) Herder Person sworn to protect the unicorns and manage the herds.

SPELLFALL